D1134200

THE VICAR OF WAKEFIELD

OLIVER GOLDSMITH.
(Drawing from the Portrait by a pupil of Sir Joshua Reynolds.)

THE
VICAR OF WAKEFIELD
A TALE

BY

OLIVER GOLDSMITH

WITH ILLUSTRATIONS BY

WILLIAM MULREADY, R.A.
JOHN ABSOLON
AND GEORGE THOMAS

1933
DAILY EXPRESS PUBLICATIONS
LONDON

OLIVER GOLDSMITH—THE MAN AND HIS BOOK

OLIVER played the flute for boon companions of his youth, when—as a student at Trinity College, Dublin—he had to eke out his means by pawning his books and by writing street-ballads at five shillings apiece. Next, at the age of 26, when he made his vagabond tour on the Continent (1754–6), he sometimes paid for a night's hospitality by tunes on his flute. Then, while earning a scanty livelihood as an usher at a Peckham school, a year or so later, he played good-natured tricks on the boys and servants, told entertaining stories, and "amused everybody with his flute." And when, in his early days as a writer, he settled in a squalid lodging in Green Arbour Court (which was near Old Bailey), he would charm its swarm of noisy children into silence by playing his flute. That flute is the symbol of Goldsmith's career. He fluted his way through a short and chequered life. And the melody of the reed seems to come down to us in the limpid prose and the idyllic spell of his only novel—*The Vicar of Wakefield*.

The story of Goldsmith's literary life mirrors his epoch. He was born in a remote village in county Longford, Ireland, in 1728; and two years later his father became rector of Kilkenny West in county Westmeath. Oliver's student days were not very successful; but he early gave an example of that spirit and quickness of repartee which characterised him subsequently. He had been very much marked by smallpox; and an unfriendly acquaintance observed with a sneer: "Why, Noll, you are become a fright! When do you mean to get handsome again?" Quick came the boy's retort to the ill-natured man: "I mean to get better, sir, when you do!"

But he provided a much better example when, years afterwards, he became the close friend of Dr. Johnson. He was discussing the art of writing fables; arguing, for example, that in the one about little fishes, who envied birds their power to fly, they should be made to *talk* like little fishes. Observing the master of sonorous prose shaking his sides with laughter, Goldsmith proceeded: "Why, Dr. Johnson, this is not so easy as you seem to think; for if *you* were to make little fishes talk, they would talk like whales."

Oliver was intended for the church; but he either would not or could not take orders. His father having died in Oliver's teens, he was helped time and again by a fairy-tale-like good uncle; who once gave him £50 with which to go to London, and begin training for the law. Within a few hours the money was lost in a Dublin gaming-house. Another start enabled young Goldsmith to study medicine in Edinburgh; but he was soon away on that continental tour, during which, despite his flute, he often found himself with only one shirt.

His return to London was followed by experiences of destitution and genuine efforts to establish himself in various occupations. But even at this time, as throughout his life, he gave of his scanty means to anyone who appeared to be worse off. Becoming an ill-paid reviewer and hack-writer, he wrote and published his *Enquiry into . . . Polite Learning* while "in a garret, writing for bread, and expecting to be dunned for a milk-score." However, the quality of his writing attracted to him men like Smollett and Dr. Johnson, who befriended him as well as lay in their power. It was a bad age for the profession of letters: and these two geniuses were themselves often struggling with poverty.

When Johnson paid his first visit to Goldsmith, he departed from his usual custom and wore a new suit of clothes and a new wig nicely powdered—explaining the transformation to Bishop Percy thus: "Why, Sir, I hear that Goldsmith, who is a very great sloven, justifies his disregard of cleanliness and decency by quoting my practice; and I am desirous this night to show him a better example." Forster, the biographer of Goldsmith, says that the example was not lost on the younger author. But it seems more likely that Johnson was pulling the bishop's leg. Whatever whim prompted such a sartorial revolution on the part of the great lexicographer, it is hardly likely that Goldsmith was a sloven: he was too fond of fine clothes, however ill he could afford them.

It was Dr. Johnson who, as Boswell relates, was one morning sent for by Goldsmith; whose landlady had arrested him for debt. Johnson sent a guinea by the messenger; and, following, found the distressed author consuming a bottle of Madeira, to buy which he had changed the guinea. Goldsmith said he had a novel ready for the press; Johnson straightway took it to a publisher; who advanced sufficient money to release the author. This was the genesis of the publication of *The Vicar of Wakefield*; which, although it eventually went into countless editions, only brought its creator some 60 guineas.

The charm and sentiment of Goldsmith's novel, as well as the beauties of his poems *The Traveller* and *The Deserted Village*, and the comedy of his plays, brought the poor author a splendid renown, and money to indulge his foible for finery. But it did not bring freedom from embarrassment of debts. He died at the age of 45; and, at the news of his passing, Burke burst into tears; Reynolds laid down his palette, too distressed to paint any more that day; and Johnson mourned over "a very worthy man" and "a plant that flowered late."

There are passages in *The Vicar of Wakefield* that are clearly autobiographical. Sometimes Goldsmith appears in the portrait of the Vicar; and sometimes he puts his experiences into the mouth of Dr. Primrose's son—as when he played merry tunes for French peasants. There is also something of Goldsmith's father and of his brother the Rev. Henry Goldsmith in the sketch of the Vicar. The combination of models perhaps explains the queer mixture of innocence and shrewdness, unselfishness and pride, in the Vicar's character. He had such a natural antipathy to the face-washes which his daughters were concocting that he says, "I approached my chair by slow degrees to the fire, and grasping the poker, as if it wanted mending, seemingly

by accident overturned the whole composition"—yet he was a willing ally to his wife's worldly schemes for their daughters. But notwithstanding his naïvely-revealed weaknesses, there remain his faith in the triumph of good over evil, his patience in suffering— recorded with that humour and grace which make the tale (for all its faults) a classic of unfailing delight.

WILFRED PARTINGTON.

OLIVER GOLDSMITH: Born 1728—Died 1774

LIST OF ILLUSTRATIONS

LIST OF ILLUSTRATIONS—*continued*

ADVERTISEMENT

THERE are a hundred faults in this Thing, and a hundred things might be said to prove them beauties. But it is needless. A book may be amusing with numerous errors, or it may be very dull without a single absurdity. The hero of this piece unites in himself the three greatest characters upon earth : he is a priest, a husbandman, and the father of a family. He is drawn as ready to teach, and ready to obey ; as simple in affluence, and majestic in adversity. In this age of opulence and refinement, whom can such a character please ? Such as are fond of high life, will turn with disdain from the simplicity of his country fireside. Such as mistake ribaldry for humour, will find no wit in his harmless conversation ; and such as have been taught to deride religion, will laugh at one whose chief stores of comfort are drawn from futurity.

OLIVER GOLDSMITH.

THE VICAR OF WAKEFIELD

CHAPTER I

THE DESCRIPTION OF THE FAMILY OF WAKEFIELD, IN WHICH A KINDRED LIKENESS PREVAILS, AS WELL OF MINDS AS OF PERSONS

I WAS ever of opinion, that the honest man who married and brought up a large family, did more service than he who continued single and only talked of population. From this motive, I had scarce taken orders a year, before I began to think seriously of matrimony, and chose my wife, as she did her wedding-gown, not for a fine glossy surface, but such qualities as would wear well. To do her justice, she was a good-natured, notable woman; and as for breeding, there were few country ladies who could show more. She could read any English book without much spelling; but for pickling, preserving, and cookery, none could excel her. She prided herself also upon being an excellent contriver in housekeeping; though I could never find that we grew richer with all her contrivances.

However, we loved each other tenderly, and our fondness increased as we grew old. There was, in fact, nothing that could make us angry with the world or each other. We had an elegant house, situated in a fine country, and a good neighbourhood. The year was spent in a moral or rural amusement; in visiting our rich neighbours, and relieving such as were poor. We had no revolutions to fear, nor fatigues to undergo; all our adventures were by the fireside, and all our migrations from the blue bed to the brown.

As we lived near the road, we often had the traveller or stranger visit us to taste our gooseberry-wine, for which we had great reputation; and I profess, with the veracity of an historian, that I never knew one of them find fault with it. Our cousins, too, even to the fortieth remove, all remembered their affinity, without any help from the herald's office, and came very frequently to see us. Some of them did us no great honour by these claims of kindred, as we had the blind, the maimed, and the halt amongst the number. However, my wife always insisted that, as they were the same *flesh and blood,* they should sit with us at the same table. So that, if we had not very rich, we generally had very happy friends about us; for this remark will hold good through life, that the poorer the guest, the better pleased he ever is with being treated; and as some men gaze with admiration at the colours of a tulip or the wing of a butterfly, so I was, by nature, an admirer of happy human faces. However, when any one of our relations was found to be a person of very bad character, a troublesome guest, or one we desired to get rid of, upon his leaving my house I ever took care to lend him a riding-coat

"I . . . CHOSE MY WIFE, AS SHE DID HER WEDDING-GOWN."

or a pair of boots, or sometimes an horse of small value, and I always had the satisfaction of finding he never came back to return them. By this the house was cleared of such as we did not like ; but never was the family of Wakefield known to turn the traveller or the poor dependant out of doors.

Thus we lived several years in a state of much happiness, not but that we sometimes had those little rubs which Providence sends to enhance the value of its favours. My orchard was often robbed by schoolboys, and my wife's custards plundered by the cats or the children. The 'Squire would sometimes fall asleep in the most pathetic parts of my sermon, or his lady return my wife's civilities at church with a mutilated curtsey. But we soon got over the uneasiness caused by such accidents, and usually in three or four days began to wonder how they vexed us.

My children, the offspring of temperance, as they were educated without softness, so they were at once well formed and healthy ; my sons hardy and active, my daughters beautiful and blooming. When I stood in the midst of the little circle, which promised to be the supports of my declining age, I could not avoid repeating the famous story of Count Abensberg, who, in Henry the Second's progress through Germany, while other courtiers came with their treasures, brought his thirty-two children, and presented them to his sovereign as the most valuable offering he had to bestow. In this manner, though I had but six, I considered them as a very valuable present made to my country, and consequently looked upon it as my debtor. Our eldest son was named George, after his uncle, who left us ten thousand pounds. Our second child, a girl, I intended to call after her aunt Grissel; but my wife, who during her pregnancy had been reading romances, insisted on her being called Olivia. In less than another year we had another daughter, and now I was determined that Grissel should be her name; but a rich relation taking a fancy to stand godmother, the girl was, by her directions, called Sophia; so that we had two romantic names in the family; but I solemnly protest I had no hand in it. Moses was our next, and after an interval of twelve years, we had two sons more.

It would be fruitless to deny my exultation when I saw my little ones about me; but the vanity and the satisfaction of my wife were even greater than mine. When our visitors would say, "Well, upon my word, Mrs. Primrose, you have the finest children in the whole country."—"Ay, neighbour," she would answer, "they are as heaven made them—handsome enough, if they be good enough; for handsome is that handsome does." And then she would bid the girls hold up their heads, who, to conceal nothing, were certainly very handsome. Mere outside is so very trifling a circumstance with me, that I should scarce have remembered to mention it had it not been a general topic of conversation in the country. Olivia, now about eighteen, had that luxuriancy of beauty with which painters generally drew Hebe; open, sprightly, and commanding. Sophia's features were not so striking at first, but often did more certain execution; for they were soft, modest, and alluring. The one vanquished by a single blow, the other by efforts successfully repeated.

The temper of a woman is generally formed from the turn of her features; at least it was so with my daughters. Olivia wished for many lovers; Sophia to secure one. Olivia was often affected, from too great a desire to please; Sophia even repressed excellence, from her fears to offend. The one entertained me with her vivacity when I was gay; the other with her sense when I was serious. But these qualities were never carried to excess in either, and I have often seen them exchange characters for a whole day together. A suit of mourning has transformed my coquette into a prude, and a new set of ribbons has given her younger sister more than natural vivacity. My eldest son George was bred at Oxford, as I intended him for one of the learned professions. My second boy, Moses, whom I designed for business, received a sort of miscellaneous education at home. But it is needless to attempt describing the particular characters of young people that had seen but very little of the world. In short, a family likeness prevailed through all, and properly speaking, they had but one character—that of being all equally generous, credulous, simple, and inoffensive.

CHAPTER II

FAMILY MISFORTUNES—THE LOSS OF FORTUNE
ONLY SERVES TO INCREASE THE PRIDE OF THE
WORTHY

THE temporal concerns of our family were chiefly
committed to my wife's management; as to the
spiritual, I took them entirely under my own
direction. The profits of my living, which
amounted to but thirty-five pounds a year, I
made over to the orphans and widows of the
clergy of our diocese; for, having a fortune of my
own, I was careless of temporalities, and felt a
secret pleasure in doing my duty without reward.
I also set a resolution of keeping no curate, and
of being acquainted with every man in the parish,
exhorting the married men to temperance, and
the bachelors to matrimony; so that in a few years
it was a common saying that there were three
strange wants at Wakefield—a parson wanting
pride, young men wanting wives, and ale-houses
wanting customers.

Matrimony was always one of my favourite
topics, and I wrote several sermons to prove its
happiness: but there was a peculiar tenet which I
made a point of supporting; for I maintained with
Whiston, that it was unlawful for a priest of the
Church of England, after the death of his first
wife, to take a second; or, to express it in one

word, I valued myself upon being a strict monogamist.

I was early initiated into this important dispute, on which so many laborious volumes have been written. I published some tracts upon the subject myself, which, as they never sold, I have the consolation of thinking were read only by the happy *Few*. Some of my friends called this my weak side; but, alas! they had not, like me, made it the subject of long contemplation. The more I reflected upon it, the more important it appeared. I even went a step beyond Whiston in displaying my principles; as he had engraven upon his wife's tomb that she was the *only* wife of William Whiston, so I wrote a similar epitaph for my wife, though still living, in which I extolled her prudence, economy, and obedience till death; and having got it copied fair, with an elegant frame, it was placed over the chimney-piece, where it answered several very useful purposes. It admonished my wife of her duty to me, and my fidelity to her; it inspired her with a passion for fame, and constantly put her in mind of her end.

It was thus, perhaps, from hearing marriage so often recommended, that my eldest son, just upon leaving college, fixed his affections upon the daughter of a neighbouring clergyman, who was a dignitary in the church, and in circumstances to give her a large fortune. But fortune was her smallest accomplishment. Miss Arabella Wilmot was allowed by all (except my two daughters) to be completely pretty. Her youth, health, and innocence were still heightened by a complexion so transparent, and such an happy sensibility of look, as even age could not gaze on with indifference. As Mr. Wilmot knew that I could make a very handsome settlement on my son, he was not averse to the match; so both families lived together in all that harmony which generally precedes an expected alliance. Being convinced, by experience, that the days of courtship are the most happy of our lives, I was willing enough to lengthen the period; and the various amusements which the young couple every day shared in each other's company seemed to increase their passion. We were generally awaked in the morning by music, and on fine days rode a-hunting. The hours between breakfast and dinner the ladies devoted to dress and study; they usually read a page, and then gazed at themselves in the glass, which, even philosophers might own, often presented the page of greatest beauty. At dinner my wife took the lead; for, as she always insisted upon carving everything herself, it being her mother's way, she gave us upon these occasions the history of every dish. When we had dined, to prevent the ladies leaving us, I generally ordered the table to be removed; and sometimes, with the music-master's assistance, the girls would give us a very agreeable concert. Walking out, drinking tea, country dances, and forfeits shortened the rest of the day, without the assistance of cards, as I hated all manner of gaming, except backgammon, at which my old friend and I some-times took a twopenny hit. Nor can I here pass over an ominous circumstance that happened the last time we played together. I only wanted to fling a quatre, and yet I threw deuce ace five times running.

Some months were elapsed in this manner, till at last it was thought convenient to fix a day for the nuptials of the young couple, who seemed earnestly to desire it. During the preparations for the wedding, I need not describe the busy impor-tance of my wife, nor the sly looks of my daughter; in fact my attention was fixed on another object—the completing a tract, which I intended shortly to publish, in defence of my favourite principle. As I looked upon this as a masterpiece, both for argument and style, I could not, in the pride of my heart, avoid showing it to my old friend Mr. Wilmot, as I made no doubt of receiving his approbation: but not till too late I discovered that he was most violently attached to the contrary opinion, and with good reason; for he was at that time actually courting a fourth wife. This, as may be expected, produced a dis-pute, attended with some acrimony, which threatened to interrupt our intended alliance; but on the day before that appointed for the cere-mony, we agreed to discuss the subject at large.

It was managed with proper spirit on both sides. He asserted that I was heterodox: I retorted the charge; he replied, and I rejoined. In the

"I COULD NOT, IN THE PRIDE OF MY HEART, AVOID SHOWING IT
TO MY OLD FRIEND."

meantime, while the controversy was hottest, I
was called out by one of my relations, who, with
a face of concern, advised me to give up the
dispute, at least till my son's wedding was over.
"How," cried I, "relinquish the cause of truth,
and let him be a husband, already driven to the
very verge of absurdity? You might as well advise
me to give up my fortune as my argument."—
"Your fortune," returned my friend, "I am now
sorry to inform you, is almost nothing. The merchant in town, in whose hands your money was
lodged, has gone off, to avoid a statute of bank-
ruptcy, and is thought not to have left a shilling
in the pound. I was unwilling to shock you or the
family with the account till after the wedding;
but now it may serve to moderate your warmth
in the argument; for, I suppose, your own prudence will enforce the necessity of dissembling,
at least till your son has the young lady's fortune
secure."—"Well," returned I, "if what you tell
me be true, and if I am to be a beggar, it shall
never make me a rascal, or induce me to disavow
my principles. I'll go this moment and inform
the company of my circumstances; and as for the
argument, I even here retract my former con-
cessions in the old gentleman's favour, nor will
allow him now to be an husband in any sense of
the expression."

It would be endless to describe the different
sensations of both families when I divulged the
news of our misfortune; but what others felt was
slight to what the lovers appeared to endure. Mr.

Wilmot, who seemed before sufficiently inclined to break off the match, was by this blow soon determined: one virtue he had in perfection, which was prudence, too often the only one that is left us at seventy-two.

CHAPTER III

THE only hope of our family now was, that the
report of our misfortune might be malicious or
premature; but a letter from my agent in town
soon came, with a confirmation of every particular. The loss of fortune to myself alone would
have been trifling; the only uneasiness I felt was
for my family, who were to be humble without
an education to render them callous to contempt.

Near a fortnight had passed before I attempted
to restrain their affliction; for premature consolation is but the remembrancer of sorrow. During
this interval my thoughts were employed on some
future means of supporting them; and at last a
small Cure of fifteen pounds a year was offered
me in a distant neighbourhood, where I could
still enjoy my principles without molestation.
With this proposal I joyfully closed, having determined to increase my salary by managing a little
farm.

Having taken this resolution, my next care was
to get together the wrecks of my fortune; and, all
debts collected and paid, out of fourteen thousand
pounds we had but four hundred remaining. My
chief attention, therefore, was now to bring down

the pride of my family to their circumstances ; for I well knew that aspiring beggary is wretchedness itself. "You cannot be ignorant, my children," cried I, "that no prudence of ours could have prevented our late misfortune ; but prudence may do much in disappointing its effects. We are now poor, my fondlings, and wisdom bids us conform to our humble situation. Let us, then, without repining, give up those splendours with which numbers are wretched, and seek in humbler circumstances that peace with which all may be happy. The poor live pleasantly without our help ; why, then, should not we learn to live without theirs ? No, my children, let us from this moment give up all pretensions to gentility: we have still enough left for happiness if we are wise, and let us draw upon content for the deficiencies of fortune."

As my eldest son was bred a scholar, I determined to send him to town, where his abilities might contribute to our support and his own. The separation of friends and families is, perhaps, one of the most distressful circumstances attendant on penury. The day soon arrived on which we were to disperse for the first time. My son, after taking leave of his mother and the rest, who mingled their tears with their kisses, came to ask a blessing from me. This I gave him from my heart, and which, added to five guineas, was all the patrimony I had now to bestow. "You are going, my boy," cried I, "to London on foot, in the manner Hooker, your great ancestor, travelled there before you. Take from me the same horse that was given him by the good Bishop Jewel—this staff; and take this book too; it will be your comfort on the way; these two lines in it are worth a million—*I have been young, and now am old; yet never saw I the righteous man forsaken, or his seed begging their bread.* Let this be your consolation as you travel on. Go, my boy; whatever be thy fortune, let me see thee once a year; still keep a good heart, and farewell." As he was possessed of integrity and honour, I was under no apprehensions from throwing him naked into the amphitheatre of life; for I knew he would act a good part, whether vanquished or victorious.

His departure only prepared the way for our own, which arrived a few days afterwards. The leaving a neighbourhood in which we had enjoyed so many hours of tranquillity was not without a tear, which scarce fortitude itself could suppress. Besides a journey of seventy miles, to a family that had hitherto never been above ten from home, filled us with apprehension; and the cries of the poor, who followed us for some miles, contributed to increase it. The first day's journey brought us in safety within thirty miles of our future retreat, and we put up for the night at an obscure inn in a village by the way. When we were shown a room, I desired the landlord, in my usual way, to let us have his company, to which he complied, as what he drank would increase the bill next morning. He knew, however, the whole neighbourhood to which I was removing,

particularly 'Squire Thornhill, who was to be my
landlord, and who lived within a few miles of the
place. This gentleman he described as one who
desired to know little more of the world than its
pleasures, being particularly remarkable for his
attachment for the fair sex. He observed that no
virtue was able to resist his arts and assiduity,
and that scarce a farmer's daughter within ten
miles round but what had found him successful
and faithless. Though this account gave me some
pain, it had a very different effect upon my
daughters, whose features seemed to brighten with
the expectation of an approaching triumph; nor
was my wife less pleased and confident of their
allurements and virtue. While our thoughts were
thus employed, the hostess entered the room to
inform her husband that the strange gentleman
who had been two days in the house wanted
money, and could not satisfy them for his reckoning. "Want money!" replied the host, "that must
be impossible; for it was no later than yesterday
he paid three guineas to our beadle to spare an
old broken soldier that was to be whipped through
the town for dog-stealing." The hostess, however,
still persisting in her first assertion, he was preparing to leave the room, swearing that he would
be satisfied one way or another, when I begged
the landlord would introduce me to the stranger
of so much charity as he described. With this he
complied, showing in a gentleman who seemed to
be about thirty, dressed in clothes that once were
laced. His person was well formed, and his face

marked with the lines of thinking. He had something short and dry in his address, and seemed not to understand ceremony, or to despise it. Upon the landlord's leaving the room, I could not avoid expressing my concern to the stranger at seeing a gentleman in such circumstances, and offered him my purse to satisfy the present demand. "I take it with all my heart, Sir," replied he, "and am glad that a late oversight in giving what money I had about me has shown me there are still some men like you. I must, however, previously entreat being informed of the name and residence of my benefactor, in order to repay him as soon as possible." In this I satisfied him fully, not only mentioning my name and late misfortunes, but the place to which I was going to remove. "This," cried he, "happens still more lucky than I hoped for, as I am going the same way myself, having been detained here two days by the floods, which I hope by to-morrow will be found passable." I testified the pleasure I should have in his company; and my wife and daughters joining in entreaty, he was prevailed upon to stay supper. The stranger's conversation, which was at once pleasing and instructive, induced me to wish for a continuance of it; but it was now high time to retire and take refreshment against the fatigues of the following day.

The next morning we all set forward together, my family on horseback, while Mr. Burchell, our new companion, walked along the footpath by the roadside, observing with a smile, that, as we were ill-mounted, he would be too generous to attempt leaving us behind. As the floods were not yet subsided, we were obliged to hire a guide, who trotted on before, Mr. Burchell and I bringing up the rear. We lightened the fatigues of the road with philosophical disputes, which he seemed to understand perfectly. But what surprised me most was, that though he was a money-borrower, he defended his opinions with as much obstinacy as if he had been my patron. He now and then also informed me to whom the different seats belonged that lay in our view as we travelled the road. "That," cried he, pointing to a very magnificent house which stood at some distance, "belongs to Mr. Thornhill, a young gentleman who enjoys a large fortune, though entirely dependent on the will of his uncle, Sir William Thornhill, a gentleman who, content with a little himself, permits his nephew to enjoy the rest, and chiefly resides in town."—"What!" cried I, "is my young landlord, then, the nephew of a man whose virtues, generosity, and singularities are so universally known? I have heard Sir William Thornhill represented as one of the most generous yet whimsical men in the kingdom—a man of consummate benevolence."—"Something, perhaps, too much so," replied Mr. Burchell; "at least he carried benevolence to an excess when young; for his passions were then strong, and as they all were upon the side of virtue, they led it up to a romantic extreme. He early began to aim at the qualifications of the soldier and the scholar, was soon distinguished in the army, and had some reputation among men of learning. Adulation ever follows the ambitious; for such alone receive most pleasure from flattery. He was surrounded with crowds, who showed him only one side of their character; so that he began to lose a regard for private interest in universal sympathy. He loved all mankind; for fortune prevented him from knowing that there were rascals. Physicians tell us of a disorder in which the whole body is so exquisitely sensible that the slightest touch gives pain. What some have thus suffered in their persons, this gentleman felt in his mind: the slightest distress, whether real or fictitious, touched him to the quick, and his soul laboured under a sickly sensibility of the miseries of others. Thus disposed to relieve, it will be easily conjectured he found numbers disposed to solicit; his profusions began to impair his fortune, but not his good-nature—that, indeed, was seen to increase as the other seemed to decay. He grew improvident as he grew poor; and though he talked like a man of sense, his actions were those of a fool. Still, however, being surrounded with importunity, and no longer able to satisfy every request that was made him, instead of *money* he gave *promises*. They were all he had to bestow, and he had not resolution enough to give any man pain by a denial. By this he drew round him crowds of dependants, whom he was sure to disappoint, yet wished to relieve. These hung upon him for a time, and left him with merited reproaches and contempt. But in proportion as he became contemptible to others, he became despicable to himself. His mind had leaned upon their adulation, and that support taken away, he could find no pleasure in the applause of his heart, which he had never learned to reverence. The world now began to wear a different aspect; the flattery of his friends began to dwindle into simple approbation; approbation soon took the more friendly form of advice; and advice, when rejected, produced their reproaches. He now, therefore, found that such friends as benefits had gathered round him were little estimable; he now found that a man's own heart must be ever given to gain that of another. I now found that—that— I forgot what I was going to observe; in short, sir, he resolved to respect himself, and laid down a plan of restoring his falling fortune. For this purpose, in his own whimsical manner, he travelled through Europe on foot; and now, though he has scarce attained the age of thirty, his circumstances are more affluent than ever. At present his bounties are more rational and moderate than before; but still he preserves the character of an humorist, and finds most pleasure in eccentric virtues.''

My attention was so much taken up by Mr. Burchell's account that I scarce looked forward as he went along, till we were alarmed by the cries of my family; when, turning, I perceived my youngest daughter in the midst of a rapid stream, thrown from her horse, and struggling with the torrent. She had sunk twice, nor was it in my power to disengage myself in time to bring her relief. My sensations were even too violent to permit my attempting her rescue. She must have certainly perished had not my companion, perceiving her danger, instantly plunged in to her relief, and with some difficulty brought her in safety to the opposite shore. By taking the current a little further up, the rest of the family got safely over, where we had an opportunity of joining our acknowledgments to hers. Her gratitude may be more readily imagined than described; she thanked her deliverer more with looks than with words, and continued to lean upon his arm, as if still willing to receive assistance. My wife also hoped one day to have the pleasure of returning his kindness at her own house. Thus, after we were refreshed at the next inn, and had dined together, as Mr. Burchell was going to a different part of the country, he took leave, and we pursued our journey, my wife observing as we went, that she liked him extremely, and protesting that if he had birth and fortune to entitle him to match into such a family as ours, she knew no man she would sooner fix upon. I could not but smile to hear her talk in this lofty strain; but I was never much displeased with those harmless delusions that tend to make us more happy.

CHAPTER IV

A PROOF THAT EVEN THE HUMBLEST FORTUNE MAY GRANT HAPPINESS, WHICH DEPENDS NOT ON CIRCUMSTANCES, BUT CONSTITUTION

THE place of our retreat was in a little neighbour-hood consisting of farmers, who tilled their own grounds, and were equal strangers to opulence and poverty. As they had almost all the conveniences of life within themselves, they seldom visited towns or cities in search of superfluity. Remote from the polite, they still retained the primeval simplicity of manners; and, frugal by habit, they scarce knew that temperance was a virtue. They wrought with cheerfulness on days of labour, but observed festivals as intervals of idleness and pleasure. They kept up the Christmas carol, sent true love-knots on Valentine morning, ate pancakes at Shrovetide, showed their wit on the first of April, and religiously cracked nuts on Michaelmas eve. Being apprised of our approach, the whole neighbourhood came out to meet their minister, dressed in their fine clothes, and preceded by a pipe and tabor. A feast also was provided for our reception, at which we sat cheerfully down; and what the conversation wanted in wit was made up in laughter.

Our little habitation was situated at the foot of a sloping hill, sheltered with a beautiful underwood behind, and a prattling river before ; on the one side a meadow, on the other a green. My farm consisted of about twenty acres of excellent land, having given an hundred pound for my predecessor's good-will. Nothing could exceed the neatness of my little enclosures, the elms and hedgerows appearing with inexpressible beauty. My house consisted of but one story, and was covered with thatch, which gave it an air of snugness ; the walls on the inside were nicely whitewashed, and my daughters undertook to adorn them with pictures of their own designing. Though the same room served us for parlour and kitchen, that only made it the warmer. Besides, as it was kept with the utmost neatness—the dishes, plates, and coppers being well scoured, and all disposed in bright rows on the shelves— the eye was agreeably relieved, and did not want richer furniture. There were three other apartments ; one for my wife and me, another for our two daughters within our own, and the third, with two beds, for the rest of the children.

The little republic to which I gave laws was regulated in the following manner :—By sunrise we all assembled in our common apartment, the fire being previously kindled by the servant. After we had saluted each other with proper ceremony —for I always thought fit to keep up some mechanical forms of breeding, without which freedom ever destroys friendship—we all bent in gratitude to that Being who gave us another day. This duty being performed, my son and I went to pursue our usual industry abroad, while my wife and daughters employed themselves in providing breakfast, which was always ready at a certain time. I allowed half an hour for this meal, and an hour for dinner, which time was taken up in innocent mirth between my wife and daughters, and in philosophical arguments between my son and me.

As we rose with the sun, so we never pursued our labours after it was gone down, but returned home to the expecting family, where smiling looks, a neat hearth, and pleasant fire were prepared for our reception. Nor were we without guests: sometimes Farmer Flamborough, our talkative neighbour, and often the blind piper, would pay us a visit, and taste our gooseberry wine, for the making of which we had lost neither the receipt nor the reputation. These harmless people had several ways of being good company; while one played, the other would sing some soothing ballad—Johnny Armstrong's Last Goodnight, or the cruelty of Barbara Allen. The night was concluded in the manner we began the morning, my youngest boys being appointed to read the lessons of the day; and he that read loudest, distinctest, and best was to have an halfpenny on Sunday to put into the poor's box.

When Sunday came, it was indeed a day of finery, which all my sumptuary edicts could not restrain. How well soever I fancied my lectures against pride had conquered the vanity of my daughters, yet I still found them secretly attached to all their former finery; they still loved laces, ribbons, bugles, and catgut; my wife herself retained a passion for her crimson paduasoy, because I formerly happened to say it became her.

The first Sunday, in particular, their behaviour served to mortify me. I had desired my girls the preceding night to be dressed early the next day; for I always loved to be at church a good while before the rest of the congregation. They punctually obeyed my directions; but when we were to assemble in the morning at breakfast, down came my wife and daughters dressed out in all their former splendour; their hair plastered up with pomatum, their faces patched to taste, their trains bundled up into a head behind, and rustling at every motion. I could not help smiling at their vanity, particularly that of my wife, from whom I expected more discretion. In this exigence, therefore, my only resource was to order my son, with an important air, to call our coach. The girls were amazed at the command; but I repeated it with more solemnity than before. "Surely, my dear, you jest," cried my wife; "we can walk it perfectly well; we want no coach to carry us now."—"You mistake, child," returned I, "we do want a coach; for if we walk to church in this trim, the very children in the parish will hoot after us."—"Indeed," replied my wife; "I always imagined that my Charles was fond of seeing his children neat and handsome about him."—"You may be as neat as you please," interrupted I, "and I shall love you the better for

"My only Resource was to order my Son, with an
Important Air, to call our Coach."

it; but all this is not neatness, but frippery. These rufflings, and pinkings and patchings will only make us hated by all the wives of our neighbours. No, my children," continued I, more gravely, "those gowns may be altered into something of a plainer cut; for finery is very unbecoming in us who want the means of decency. I do not know whether such flouncing and shredding is becoming even in the rich, if we consider, upon a moderate calculation, that the nakedness of the indigent world may be clothed from the trimmings of the vain."

This remonstration had the proper effect. They went with great composure, that very instant, to change their dress; and the next day I had the satisfaction of finding my daughters, at their own request, employed in cutting up their trains into Sunday waistcoats for Dick and Bill, the two little ones, and what was still more satisfactory, the gowns seemed improved by this curtailing.

CHAPTER V

AT a small distance from the house my predecessor had made a seat overshadowed by a hedge
of hawthorn and honeysuckle. Here, when the
weather was fine and our labour soon finished,
we usually sat together to enjoy an extensive
landscape, in the calm of the evening. Here, too,
we drank tea, which now was become an occa-
sional banquet; and as we had it but seldom, it
diffused a new joy, the preparations for it being
made with no small share of bustle and ceremony.
On these occasions our two little ones always read
for us, and they were regularly served after we
had done. Sometimes, to give a variety to our
amusements, the girls sung to the guitar; and
while they thus formed a little concert, my wife
and I would stroll down the sloping field, that was
embellished with blue-bells and centaury, talk of
our children with rapture, and enjoy the breeze
that wafted both health and harmony.

In this manner we began to find that every
situation in life may bring its own peculiar
pleasures: every morning waked us to a repeti-
tion of toil, but the evening repaid it with vacant
hilarity.

It was about the beginning of autumn, on a holiday—for I kept such as intervals of relaxation from labour—that I had drawn out my family to our usual place of amusement, and our young musicians began their usual concert. As we were thus engaged, we saw a stag bound nimbly by, within about twenty paces of where we were sitting, and by its panting it seemed pressed by the hunters. We had not much time to reflect upon the poor animal's distress, when we perceived the dogs and horsemen come sweeping along at some distance behind, and making the very path it had taken. I was instantly for returning in with my family, but either curiosity or surprise, or some more hidden motive, held my wife and daughters to their seats. The huntsman who rode foremost passed us with great swiftness, followed by four or five persons more, who seemed in equal haste. At last a young gentleman of more genteel appearance than the rest came forward, and for a while regarding us, instead of pursuing the chase, stopped short, and giving his horse to a servant who attended, approached us with a careless, superior air. He seemed to want no introduction, but was going to salute my daughters as one certain of a kind reception; but they had early learnt the lesson of looking presumption out of countenance, upon which he let us know that his name was Thornhill, and that he was owner of the estate that lay for some extent around us. He again, therefore, offered to salute the female part of the family, and such was the power of fortune and

"A Young Gentleman . . . approached us with a Careless and Superior Air."

fine clothes that he found no second repulse. As
his address, though confident, was easy, we soon
became more familiar; and perceiving musical
instruments lying near, he begged to be favoured
with a song. As I did not approve of such disproportioned acquaintances, I winked upon my
daughters in order to prevent their compliance;
but my hint was counteracted by one from their
mother; so that, with a cheerful air, they gave us
a favourite song of Dryden's. Mr. Thornhill
seemed highly delighted with their performance
and choice, and then took up the guitar himself.
He played but very indifferently; however, my
eldest daughter repaid his former applause with
interest, and assured him that his tones were
louder than even those of her master. At this compliment he bowed, which she returned with a
curtsey. He praised her taste, and she commended his understanding; an age could not have
made them better acquainted; while the fond
mother too, equally happy, insisted upon her
landlord's stepping in and tasting a glass of her
gooseberry. The whole family seemed earnest to
please him: my girls attempted to entertain him
with topics they thought most modern; while
Moses, on the contrary, gave him a question or
two from the ancients, for which he had the satisfaction of being laughed at. My little ones were
no less busy, and fondly stuck close to the
stranger. All my endeavours could scarce keep
their dirty fingers from handling and tarnishing
the lace on his clothes, and lifting up the flaps

of his pocket-holes to see what was there. At the approach of evening he took leave; but not till he had requested permission to renew his visit, which, as he was our landlord, we most readily agreed to.

As soon as he was gone, my wife called a council on the conduct of the day. She was of opinion that it was a most fortunate hit; for she had known even stranger things than that brought to bear. She hoped again to see the day in which we might hold up our heads with the best of them; and concluded, she protested she could see no reason why the two Miss Wrinklers should marry great fortunes, and her children get none. As this last argument was directed to me, I protested I could see no reason for it neither; nor why Mr. Simpkins got the ten thousand pound prize in the lottery, and we sat down with a blank. "I protest, Charles," cried my wife, "this is the way you always damp my girls and me when we are in spirits. Tell me, Sophy, my dear, what do you think of our new visitor? Don't you think he seemed to be good-natured?"—"Immensely so, indeed, mamma," replied she; "I think he has a great deal to say upon everything, and is never at a loss; and the more trifling the subject, the more he has to say."—"Yes," cried Olivia, "he is well enough for a man; but, for my part, I don't much like him; he is so extremely impudent and familiar; but on the guitar he is shocking." These two last speeches I interpreted by contraries. I found by this, that Sophia internally despised, as much as Olivia secretly admired him. "Whatever may be your opinions of him, my children," cried I, "to confess a truth, he has not prepossessed me in his favour. Disproportioned friendships ever terminate in disgust; and I thought, notwithstanding all his ease, that he seemed perfectly sensible of the distance between us. Let us keep to companions of our own rank. There is no character more contemptible than a man that is a fortune-hunter; and I can see no reason why fortune-hunting women should not be contemptible too. Thus, at best, we shall be contemptible if his views are honourable; but if they be otherwise !—I should shudder but to think of that. It is true, I have no apprehensions from the conduct of my children; but I think there are some from his character." I would have proceeded but for the interruption of a servant from the 'Squire, who, with his compliments, sent us a side of venison, and a promise to dine with us some days after. This well-timed present pleaded more powerfully in his favour than anything I had to say could obviate. I therefore continued silent, satisfied with just having pointed out danger, and leaving it to their own discretion to avoid it. That virtue which requires to be ever guarded is scarce worth the sentinel.

CHAPTER VI

THE HAPPINESS OF A COUNTRY FIRESIDE

As we carried on the former dispute with some degree of warmth, in order to accommodate matters, it was universally agreed that we should have a part of the venison for supper; and the girls undertook the task with alacrity. "I am sorry," cried I, "that we have no neighbour or stranger to take part in this good cheer; feasts of this kind acquire a double relish from hospitality."—"Bless me," cried my wife, "here comes our good friend Mr. Burchell, that saved our Sophia, and that run you down fairly in the argument."—"Confute me in argument, child!" cried I. "You mistake there, my dear; I believe there are but few that can do that. I never dispute your abilities at making a goose-pie, and I beg you'll leave argument to me." As I spoke, poor Mr. Burchell entered the house, and was welcomed by the family, who shook him heartily by the hand, while little Dick officiously reached him a chair.

I was pleased with the poor man's friendship for two reasons: because I knew that he wanted mine, and I knew him to be friendly as far as he was able. He was known in the neighbourhood by the character of the poor Gentleman, that would do no good when he was young, though he was not yet thirty. He would at intervals talk with great good sense, but in general he was fondest of the company of children, whom he used to call harmless little men. He was famous, I found, for singing them ballads and telling them stories, and seldom went out without something in his pockets for them—a piece of gingerbread or a halfpenny whistle. He generally came for a few days into our neighbourhood once a year, and lived upon the neighbours' hospitality. He sat down to supper among us, and my wife was not sparing of her gooseberry wine. The tale went round; he sung us old songs, and gave the children the story of the Buck of Beverland, with the history of Patient Grissel, the adventures of Catskin, and then Fair Rosamond's Bower. Our cock, which always crew at eleven, now told us it was time for repose; but an unforeseen difficulty started about lodging the stranger—all our beds were already taken up, and it was too late to send him to the next alehouse. In this dilemma little Dick offered him his part of the bed, if his brother Moses would let him lie with him. "And I," cried Bill, "will give Mr. Burchell my part, if my sisters will take me to theirs."—"Well done, my good children," cried I, "hospitality is one of the first Christian duties. The beast retires to its shelter, and the bird flies to its nest; but helpless man can only find refuge from his fellow-creature. The greatest stranger in this world was He that came to save it. He never had a house, as if willing to see what hospitality was left remaining among us. Deborah, my dear," cried I to my

"I COULD NOT AVOID OBSERVING THE ASSIDUITY OF
MR. BURCHELL IN ASSISTING MY DAUGHTER SOPHIA."

wife, "give those boys a lump of sugar each ; and
let Dick's be the largest, because he spoke first."

In the morning early I called out my whole
family to help at saving an after-growth of hay,
and our guest offering his assistance, he was
accepted among the number. Our labours went
on lightly ; we turned the swath to the wind. I
went foremost, and the rest followed in due suc-
cession. I could not avoid, however, observing
the assiduity of Mr. Burchell in assisting my
daughter Sophia in her part of the task. When he
had finished his own, he would join in hers, and
enter into a close conversation ; but I had too good
an opinion of Sophia's understanding, and was
too well convinced of her ambition, to be under
any uneasiness from a man of broken fortune.
When we were finished for the day, Mr. Burchell
was invited as on the night before, but he refused,
as he was to lie that night at a neighbour's, to
whose child he was carrying a whistle. When
gone, our conversation at supper turned upon our
late unfortunate guest. "What a strong instance,"
said I, "is that poor man of the miseries attending
a youth of levity and extravagance. He by no
means wants sense, which only serves to aggravate his former folly. Poor forlorn creature !
where are now the revellers, the flatterers, that
he could once inspire and command ? Gone, perhaps, to attend the bagnio pander, grown rich by
his extravagance. They once praised him, and
now they applaud the pander ; their former raptures at his wit are now converted into sarcasms

at his folly: he is poor, and perhaps deserves
poverty; for he has neither the ambition to be independent nor the skill to be useful." Prompted
perhaps by some secret reasons, I delivered this
observation with too much acrimony, which my
Sophia gently reproved. "Whatsoever his former
conduct may be, papa, his circumstances should
exempt him from censure now. His present indigence is a sufficient punishment for former folly;
and I have heard my papa himself say that we
should never strike our unnecessary blow at a
victim over whom Providence holds the scourge
of its resentment."—"You are right, Sophy,"
cried my son Moses; "and one of the ancients
finely represents so malicious a conduct by the
attempts of a rustic to flay Marsyas, whose skin,
the fable tells us, had been wholly stripped off by
another. Besides, I don't know if this poor man's
situation be so bad as my father would represent
it. We are not to judge of the feelings of others
by what we might feel in their place. However
dark the habitation of the mole to our eyes, yet
the animal itself finds the apartment sufficiently
lightsome. And, to confess a truth, this man's
mind seems fitted to his station; for I never heard
any one more sprightly than he was to-day, when
he conversed with you." This was said without
the least design; however, it excited a blush,
which she strove to cover by an affected laugh,
assuring him that she scarce took any notice of
what he said to her, but that she believed he might
once have been a very fine gentleman. The readi-

ness with which she undertook to vindicate herself, and her blushing, were symptoms I did not internally approve ; but I repressed my suspicions.

As we expected our landlord the next day, my wife went to make the venison pasty. Moses sat reading, while I taught the little ones. My daughters seemed equally busy with the rest, and I observed them for a good while cooking something over the fire. I at first supposed they were assisting their mother, but little Dick informed me in a whisper that they were making a wash for the face. Washes of all kinds I had a natural antipathy to ; for I knew that, instead of mending the complexion, they spoiled it. I therefore approached my chair by sly degrees to the fire, and grasping the poker as if it wanted mending, seemingly by accident overturned the whole composition, and it was too late to begin another.

CHAPTER VII

A TOWN WIT DESCRIBED—THE DULLEST FELLOWS
MAY LEARN TO BE COMICAL FOR A NIGHT OR TWO

WHEN the morning arrived on which we were to
entertain our young landlord, it may be easily
supposed what provisions were exhausted to make
an appearance. It may also be conjectured that
my wife and daughters expanded their gayest
plumage on this occasion. Mr. Thornhill came
with a couple of friends, his chaplain and feeder.
The servants, who were numerous, he politely
ordered to the next ale-house; but my wife on the
triumph of her heart, insisted on entertaining them
all; for which, by the by, our family was pinched
for three weeks after. As Mr. Burchell had hinted
to us the day before that he was making some
proposals of marriage to Miss Wilmot, my son
George's former mistress, this a good deal damped
the heartiness of his reception; but accident in
some measure relieved our embarrassment; for
one of the company, happening to mention her
name, Mr. Thornhill observed, with an oath, that
he never knew anything more absurd than calling
such a fright a beauty: "For, strike me ugly,"
continued he, "if I should not find as much
pleasure in choosing my mistress by the information of a lamp under the clock of St. Dunstan's."
At this he laughed, and so did we: the jests of

the rich are ever successful. Olivia, too, could not avoid whispering, loud enough to be heard, that he had an infinite fund of humour.

After dinner I began with my usual toast, the Church. For this I was thanked by the chaplain, as he said the church was the only mistress of his affections. "Come, tell us honestly, Frank," said the 'Squire, with his usual archness, "suppose the church, your present mistress, dressed in lawn sleeves, on the one hand, and Miss Sophia with no lawn about her, on the other, which would you be for?"—"For both, to be sure," cried the chaplain. "Right, Frank," cried the 'Squire; "for may this glass suffocate me, but a fine girl is worth all the priestcraft in the creation! For what are tithes and tricks but an imposition, all a confounded imposture?—and I can prove it."—"I wish you would," cried my son Moses; "and I think," continued he, "that I should be able to answer you."—"Very well, sir," cried the 'Squire, who immediately smoked him, and winked on the rest of the company to prepare us for the sport; "if you are for a cool argument on that subject, I am ready to accept the challenge. And, first, whether are you for managing it analogically or dialogically?"—"I am for managing it rationally," cried Moses, quite happy at being permitted to dispute.—"Good again," cried the 'Squire; "and firstly, of the first. I hope you'll not deny that whatever is, is. If you don't grant me that, I can go no further."—"Why," returned Moses, "I think I may grant that, and make the

best of it."—"I hope, too," returned the other,
"you'll grant that a part is less than the whole."
—"I grant that too," cried Moses, "it is but just
and reasonable."—"I hope," cried the 'Squire,
"you will not deny that the three angles of a
triangle are equal to two right ones."—"Nothing
can be plainer," returned t'other, and looked
round with his usual importance.—"Very well,"
cried the 'Squire, speaking very quick, "the
premisses being thus settled, I proceed to observe
that the concatenation of self-existences, proceed-
ing in a reciprocal duplicate ratio, naturally produces a problematical dialogism, which in some
measure proves that the essence of spirituality
may be referred to the second predicable."—
"Hold, hold!" cried the other, "I deny that. Do
you think that I can thus tamely submit to such
heterodox doctrines?"—"What!" replied the
'Squire, as if in a passion; "not submit! Answer
me one plain question: Do you think Aristotle
right when he says that relatives are related?"—
"Undoubtedly," replied the other.—"If so,
then," cried the 'Squire, "answer me directly to
what I propose: Whether do you judge the
analytical investigation of the first part of my
enthymem deficient secundum quoad, or quoad
minus; and give me your reasons—give me your
reasons, I say, directly."—"I protest," cried
Moses, "I don't rightly comprehend the force of
your reasoning; but if it be reduced to one simple
proposition, I fancy it may then have an answer."
—"Oh, sir," cried the 'Squire, "I am your most

humble servant; I find you want me to furnish
you with argument and intellects too. No, sir;
there I protest you are too hard for me." This
effectually raised the laugh against poor Moses,
who sat the only dismal figure in a group of merry
faces; nor did he offer a single syllable more
during the whole entertainment.

But though all this gave me no pleasure, it had
a very different effect upon Olivia, who mistook
it for humour, though but a mere act of the
memory. She thought him, therefore, a very fine
gentleman; and such as consider what powerful
ingredients a good figure, fine clothes, and fortune
are in that character, will easily forgive her. Mr.
Thornhill, notwithstanding his real ignorance,
talked with ease, and could expatiate upon the
common topics of conversation with fluency. It
is not surprising, then, that such talents should
win the affections of a girl, who by education was
taught to value an appearance in herself, and consequently to set a value upon it in another.

Upon his departure, we again entered into a
debate upon the merits of our young landlord.
As he directed his looks and conversation to
Olivia, it was no longer doubted but that she was
the object that induced him to be our visitor.
Nor did she seem to be much displeased at the
innocent raillery of her brother and sister upon
this occasion. Even Deborah herself seemed to
share the glory of the day, and exulted in her
daughter's victory as if it were her own. "And
now, my dear," cried she to me, "I'll fairly own

"THIS EFFECTUALLY RAISED THE LAUGH AGAINST POOR MOSES."

that it was I that instructed my girls to encourage our landlord's addresses. I had always some ambition, and you see that I was right; for who knows how this may end?"—"Ay, who knows that indeed!" answered I with a groan: "for my part, I don't much like it; and I could have been better pleased with one that was poor and honest, than this fine gentleman with his fortune and infidelity; for depend on't, if he be what I suspect him, no freethinker shall ever have a child of mine."

"Sure, father," cried Moses, "you are too severe in this; for heaven will never arraign him for what he thinks, but for what he does. Every man has a thousand vicious thoughts, which arise without his power to suppress. Thinking freely of religion may be involuntary with this gentleman; so that, allowing his sentiments to be wrong, yet as he is purely passive in his assent, he is no more to be blamed for his errors than the governor of a city without walls for the shelter he is obliged to afford an invading enemy."

"True, my son," cried I; "but if the governor invites the enemy there, he is justly culpable. And such is always the case with those who embrace error. The vice does not lie in assenting to the proofs they see, but in being blind to many of the proofs that offer; so that, though our erroneous opinions be involuntary when formed, yet, as we have been wilfully corrupt or very negligent in forming them, we deserve punishment for our vice or contempt for our folly."

My wife now kept up the conversation, though not the argument. She observed that several very prudent men of our acquaintance were free-thinkers, and made very good husbands; and she knew some sensible girls that had skill enough to make converts of their spouses. "And who knows, my dear," continued she, "what Olivia may be able to do? The girl has a great deal to say upon every subject, and to my knowledge is very well skilled in controversy."

"Why, my dear, what controversy can she have read?" cried I. "It does not occur to me that I ever put such books into her hands; you certainly overrate her merit."—"Indeed, papa," replied Olivia, "she does not; I have read a great deal of controversy. I have read the disputes between Thwackum and Square; the controversy between Robinson Crusoe and Friday the savage; and I am now employed in reading the controversy in Religious Courtship." "Very well," cried I, "that's a good girl; I find you are perfectly qualified for making converts, and so go help your mother to make the gooseberry pie."

CHAPTER VIII

AN AMOUR, WHICH PROMISES LITTLE GOOD FOR-
TUNE, YET MAY BE PRODUCTIVE OF MUCH

THE next morning we were again visited by Mr.
Burchell, though I began, for certain reasons, to
be displeased with the frequency of his return;
but I could not refuse him my company and fireside. It is true, his labour more than requited his
entertainment; for he wrought among us with
vigour, and, either in the meadow or at the hay-
rick, put himself foremost. Besides, he had
always something amusing to say that lessened
our toil, and was at once so out of the way, and
yet so sensible, that I loved, laughed at, and pitied
him. My only dislike arose from an attachment
he discovered to my daughter. He would, in a
jesting manner, call her his little mistress; and
when he bought each of the girls a set of ribbons,
hers was the finest. I knew not how, but he every
day seemed to become more amiable, his wit to
improve, and his simplicity to assume the superior
airs of wisdom.

Our family dined in the field, and we sat, or
rather reclined, round a temperate repast, our
cloth spread upon the hay, while Mr. Burchell
gave cheerfulness to the feast. To heighten our
satisfaction, two blackbirds answered each other

from opposite hedges, the familiar redbreast came
and pecked the crumbs from our hands, and every
sound seemed but the echo of tranquillity. "I
never sit thus," says Sophia, "but I think of the
two lovers, so sweetly described by Mr. Gay, who
were struck dead in each other's arms. There is
something so pathetic in the description, that I
have read it an hundred times with new rapture."
—"In my opinion," cried my son, "the finest
strokes in that description are much below those
in the Acis and Galatea of Ovid. The Roman
poet understands the use of *contrast* better ; and
upon that figure, artfully managed, all strength
in the pathetic depends."—"It is remarkable,"
cried Mr. Burchell, "that both the poets you mention have equally contributed to introduce a false
taste into their respective countries, by loading all
their lines with epithet. Men of little genius found
them most easily imitated in their defects ; and
English poetry, like that in the latter empire of
Rome, is nothing at present but a combination
of luxuriant images, without plot or connection—
a string of epithets that improve the sound without carrying on the sense. But perhaps, Madam,
while I thus reprehend others, you'll think it
just that I should give them an opportunity to
retaliate ; and, indeed, I have made this remark
only to have an opportunity of introducing to the
company a ballad, which, whatever be its other
defects, is, I think, at least free from those I have
mentioned."

A BALLAD

"Turn, gentle Hermit of the dale,
  And guide my lonely way
To where yon taper cheers the vale
  With hospitable ray.

"For here forlorn and lost I tread,
  With fainting steps and slow,
Where wilds, immeasurably spread,
  Seem lengthening as I go."

"Forbear, my son," the Hermit cries,
  "To tempt the dangerous gloom;
For yonder faithless phantom flies
  To lure thee to thy doom.

"Here to the houseless child of want
  My door is open still;
And, though my portion is but scant,
  I give it with good-will.

"Then turn to-night, and freely share
  Whate'er my cell bestows;
My rushy couch and frugal fare,
  My blessing and repose.

"No flocks that range the valley free
  To slaughter I condemn;
Taught by that Power that pities me,
  I learn to pity them:

"But from the mountain's grassy side
  A guiltless feast I bring;
A scrip with herbs and fruits supplied,
  And water from the spring.

"Then, pilgrim, turn, thy cares forego;
  All earth-born cares are wrong:
Man wants but little here below,
  Nor wants that little long."

Soft as the dew from heaven descends
  His gentle accents fell:
The modest stranger lowly bends,
  And follows to the cell.

83*

Far in a wilderness obscure
  The lonely mansion lay,
A refuge to the neighbouring poor,
  And strangers led astray.

No stores beneath its humble thatch
  Required a master's care;
The wicket, opening with a latch,
  Received the harmless pair.

And now, when busy crowds retire
  To take their evening rest,
The Hermit trimmed his little fire
  And cheered his pensive guest;

And spread his vegetable store,
  And gaily pressed and smiled,
And, skilled in legendary lore,
  The lingering hours beguiled.

Around, in sympathetic mirth,
  Its tricks the kitten tries,
The cricket chirrups on the hearth,
  The crackling faggot flies.

But nothing could a charm impart
  To soothe the stranger's woe;
For grief was heavy at his heart,
  And tears began to flow.

His rising cares the Hermit spied,
  With answering care oppressed;
And "Whence, unhappy youth," he cried,
  "The sorrows of thy breast?

"From better habitations spurned,
  Reluctant dost thou rove?
Or grieve for friendship unreturned,
  Or unregarded love?

"Alas! the joys that fortune brings
  Are trifling, and decay;
And those who prize the paltry things,
  More trifling still than they.

"And what is friendship but a name,
  A charm that lulls to sleep;

A shade that follows wealth or fame,
  But leaves the wretch to weep?

"And love is still an emptier sound,
  The modern fair one's jest;
On earth unseen, or only found
  To warm the turtle's nest.

"For shame, fond youth, thy sorrows hush,
  And spurn the sex," he said;
But while he spoke, a rising blush
  His love-lorn guest betrayed.

Surprised, he sees new beauties rise,
  Swift mantling to the view;
Like colours o'er the morning skies,
  As bright, as transient too.

The bashful look, the rising breast,
  Alternate spread alarms;
The lovely stranger stands confessed
  A maid in all her charms.

And, "Ah! forgive a stranger rude—
  A wretch forlorn," she cried;
"Whose feet unhallowed thus intrude
  Where Heaven and you reside.

"But let a maid thy pity share,
  Whom love has taught to stray;
Who seeks for rest, but finds despair
  Companion of her way.

"My father lived beside the Tyne,
  A wealthy lord was he;
And all his wealth was marked as mine—
  He had but only me.

"To win me from his tender arms
  Unnumbered suitors came,
Who praised me for imputed charms,
  And felt, or feigned, a flame.

"Each hour a mercenary crowd
  With richest proffers strove;
Amongst the rest young Edwin bowed,
  But never talked of love.

"In humble, simple habit clad,
 No wealth nor power had he;
Wisdom and worth were all he had,
 But these were all to me.

"And when, beside me in the dale,
 He carolled lays of love,
His breath lent fragrance to the gale
 And music to the grove.

"The blossom opening to the day,
 The dews of heaven refined,
Could nought of purity display
 To emulate his mind.

"The dew, the blossom on the tree,
 With charms inconstant shine:
Their charms were his, but, woe to me,
 Their constancy was mine.

"For still I tried each fickle art,
 Importunate and vain;
And while his passion touched my heart,
 I triumphed in his pain:

"Till, quite dejected with my scorn,
 He left me to my pride,
And sought a solitude forlorn,
 In secret, where he died.

"But mine the sorrow, mine the fault,
 And well my life shall pay;
I'll seek the solitude he sought,
 And stretch me where he lay.

"And there, forlorn, despairing, hid,
 I'll lay me down and die;
'Twas so for me that Edwin did,
 And so for him will I."

"Forbid it, Heaven!" the Hermit cried,
 And clasped her to his breast:
The wondering fair one turned to chide—
 'Twas Edwin's self that pressed!

"Turn, Angelina, ever dear,
  My charmer, turn to see
Thine own, thy long-lost Edwin here,
  Restored to love and thee.

"Thus let me hold thee to my heart,
  And every care resign:
And shall we never, never part,
  My life,—my all that's mine?

"No, never from this hour to part.
  We'll live and love so true,
The sigh that rends thy constant heart
  Shall break thy Edwin's too."

While this ballad was reading, Sophia seemed
to mix an air of tenderness with her approbation.
But our tranquillity was soon disturbed by the
report of a gun just by us, and immediately after
a man was seen bursting through the hedge to
take up the game he had killed. This sports-
man was the 'Squire's chaplain, who had shot
one of the blackbirds that so agreeably entertained us. So loud a report, and so near, startled
my daughters; and I could perceive that Sophia,
in the fright, had thrown herself into Mr. Burchell's arms for protection. The gentleman came
up and asked pardon for having disturbed us,
affirming that he was ignorant of our being so
near. He therefore sat down by my youngest
daughter, and, sportsman-like, offered her what
he had killed that morning. She was going to
refuse, but a private look from her mother soon
induced her to correct the mistake and accept his
present, though with some reluctance. My wife,
as usual, discovered her pride in a whisper,

observing that Sophy had made a conquest of the chaplain, as well as her sister had of the 'Squire. I suspected, however, with more probability, that her affections were placed upon a different object. The chaplain's errand was to inform us that Mr. Thornhill had provided music and refreshments, and intended that night giving the young ladies a ball by moonlight on the grass plot before our door. "Nor can I deny," continued he, "but I have an interest in being first to deliver this message, as I expect for my reward to be honoured with Miss Sophy's hand as a partner." To this my girl replied that she should have no objection if she could do it with honour. "But here," continued she, "is a gentleman," looking at Mr. Burchell, "who has been my companion in the task for the day, and it is fit he should share in its amusements." Mr. Burchell returned her a compliment for her intentions, but resigned her up to the chaplain; adding that he was to go that night five miles, being invited to a harvest supper. His refusal appeared to me a little extraordinary; nor could I conceive how so sensible a girl as my youngest could thus prefer a man of broken fortunes to one whose expectations were much greater. But as men are most capable of distinguishing merit in women, so the ladies often form the truest judgments of us. The two sexes seem placed as spies upon each other, and are furnished with different abilities, adapted for mutual inspection.

CHAPTER IX

MR. BURCHELL had scarce taken leave, and
Sophia consented to dance with the chaplain,
when my little ones came running out to tell us
that the 'Squire was come with a crowd of company. Upon our return, we found our landlord
with a couple of under gentleman and two young
ladies richly dressed, whom he introduced as
women of very great distinction and fashion from
town. We happened not to have chairs enough
for the whole company; but Mr. Thornhill immediately proposed, that every gentleman should sit
in a lady's lap. This I positively objected to,
notwithstanding a look of disapprobation from
my wife. Moses was therefore dispatched to borrow a couple of chairs; and as we were in want
of ladies to make up a set at country dances, the
two gentlemen went with him in quest of a
couple of partners. Chairs and partners were
soon provided. The gentlemen returned with my
neighbour Flamborough's rosy daughters, flaunt-
ing with red top-knots; but an unlucky circumstance was not adverted to—though the Miss
Flamboroughs were reckoned the very best
dancers in the parish, and understood the jig

and the round-about to perfection, yet they were
totally unacquainted with country dances. This at
first discomposed us; however, after a little
shoving and dragging they at last went merrily
on. Our music consisted of two fiddles, with a
pipe and tabor. The moon shone bright. Mr.
Thornhill and my eldest daughter led up the ball,
to the great delight of the spectators; for the
neighbours, hearing what was going forward,
came flocking about us. My girl moved with so
much grace and vivacity, that my wife could
not avoid discovering the pride of her heart by
assuring me that, though the little chit did it so
cleverly, all the steps were stolen from herself.
The ladies of the town strove hard to be equally
easy, but without success. They swam, sprawled,
languished, and frisked; but all would not do:
the gazers indeed owned that it was fine; but
neighbour Flamborough observed that Miss
Livy's feet seemed as pat to the music as its
echo. After the dance had continued about an
hour, the two ladies, who were apprehensive of
catching cold, moved to break up the ball. One
of them, I thought, expressed her sentiments
upon this occasion in a very coarse manner,
when she observed, that, by the *living jingo she
was all of a muck sweat*. Upon our return to
the house, we found a very elegant cold supper,
which Mr. Thornhill had ordered to be brought
with him. The conversation at this time was
more reserved than before. The two ladies threw
my girls into the shade; for they would talk of

nothing but high life, and high-lived company;
with other fashionable topics, such as pictures,
taste, Shakespeare, and the musical glasses. 'Tis
true they once or twice mortified us sensibly by
slipping out an oath; but that appeared to me
as the surest symptom of their distinction (though
I am since informed that swearing is perfectly
unfashionable). Their finery, however, threw a
veil over any grossness in their conversation.
My daughters seemed to regard their superior
accomplishments with envy; and what appeared
amiss, was ascribed to tip-top quality breeding.
But the condescension of the ladies was still
superior to their other accomplishments. One of
them observed, that had Miss Olivia seen a little
more of the world, it would greatly improve her;
to which the other added, that a single winter
in town would make her little Sophia quite
another thing. My wife warmly assented to both,
adding that there was nothing she more ardently
wished than to give her girls a single winter's
polishing. To this I could not help replying, that
their breeding was already superior to their fortune; and that greater refinement would only
serve to make their poverty ridiculous, and give
them a taste for pleasures they had no right to
possess. "And what pleasures," cried Mr. Thornhill, "do they not deserve to possess, who have
so much in their power to bestow? As for my
part," continued he, "my fortune is pretty
large; love, liberty, and pleasure are my maxims;
but curse me, if a settlement of half my estate

could give my charming Olivia pleasure, it
should be hers; and the only favour I would ask
in return would be to add myself to the benefit."
I was not such a stranger to the world as to be
ignorant that this was the fashionable cant to
disguise the insolence of the basest proposal; but
I made an effort to suppress my resentment.
"Sir," cried I, "the family which you now condescend to favour with your company has been
bred with as nice a sense of honour as you. Any
attempts to injure that may be attended with
very dangerous consequences. Honour, sir, is our
only possession at present, and of that last
treasure we must be particularly careful." I was
soon sorry for the warmth with which I had
spoken this, when the young gentleman, grasping
my hand, swore he commended my spirit, though
he disapproved my suspicions. "As to your
present hint," continued he, "I protest that
nothing was farther from my heart than such a
thought. No, by all that's tempting! the virtue
that will stand a regular siege was never to my
taste; for all my amours are carried by a coup-de-
main."

The two ladies, who affected to be ignorant of
the rest, seemed highly displeased with this last
stroke of freedom, and began a very discreet and
serious dialogue upon virtue; in this, my wife,
the chaplain, and I soon joined; and the 'Squire
himself was at last brought to confess a sense
of sorrow for his former excesses. We talked of
the pleasures of temperance, and of the sunshine

in the mind unpolluted with guilt. I was so well
pleased, that my little ones were kept up beyond
the usual time to be edified by so much good
conversation. Mr. Thornhill even went beyond
me, and demanded if I had any objection to
giving prayers. I joyfully embraced the proposal;
and in this manner the night was passed in the
most comfortable way, till at last the company
began to think of returning. The ladies seemed
very unwilling to part with my daughters, for
whom they had conceived a particular affection,
and joined in a request to have the pleasure of
their company home. The 'Squire seconded the
proposals, and my wife added her entreaties; the
girls, too, looked upon me as if they wished to go.
In this perplexity, I made two or three excuses,
which my daughters as readily removed: so that
at last I was obliged to give a peremptory refusal,
for which we had nothing but sullen looks and
short answers the whole day ensuing.

CHAPTER X

THE FAMILY ENDEAVOURS TO COPE WITH THEIR
BETTERS.—THE MISERIES OF THE POOR, WHEN
THEY ATTEMPT TO APPEAR ABOVE THEIR CIR-
CUMSTANCES

I now began to find that all my long and painful
lectures upon temperance, simplicity, and con-
tentment were entirely disregarded. The distinc-
tions lately paid us by our betters awaked that
pride which I had laid asleep, but not removed.
Our windows, again, as formerly, were filled with
washes for the neck and face. The sun was
dreaded as an enemy to the skin without doors,
and the fire as a spoiler of the complexion within. My wife observed that rising too early would
hurt her daughters' eyes, that working after
dinner would redden their noses; and she convinced me that the hands never looked so white
as when they did nothing. Instead therefore of
finishing George's shirts, we now had them new-
modelling their old gauzes, or flourishing upon
catgut. The poor Miss Flamboroughs, their
former gay companions, were cast off as mean
acquaintance, and the whole conversation ran
upon high life, and high-lived company, with
pictures, taste, Shakespeare, and the musical
glasses.

But we could have borne all this, had not a

fortune-telling gipsy come to raise us into perfect sublimity. The tawny sibyl no sooner
appeared, than my girls came running to me for
a shilling a-piece to cross her hand with silver.
To say the truth, I was tired of being always
wise, and could not help gratifying their request,
because I loved to see them happy. I gave each
of them a shilling; though for the honour of the
family it must be observed, that they never went
without money themselves, as my wife always
generously let them have a guinea each, to keep
in their pockets, but with strict injunctions never
to change it. After they had been closeted up
with the fortune-teller for some time, I knew by
their looks, upon their returning, that they had
been promised something great. "Well, my
girls, how have you sped? Tell me, Livy, has
the fortune-teller given thee a pennyworth?"
—"I protest, papa," says the girl, "I believe
she deals with somebody that's not right; for she
positively declared, that I am to be married to a
'Squire in less than a twelvemonth!"—"Well,
now, Sophy, my child," said I, "and what sort
of an husband are you to have?"—"Sir,"
replied she, "I am to have a Lord soon after
my sister has married the 'Squire"—"How!"
cried I, "is that all you are to have for your
two shillings? Only a Lord and a 'Squire for two
shillings? You fools, I could have promised you
a Prince and a Nabob for half the money."

This curiosity of theirs, however, was attended
with very serious effects: we now began to think

ourselves designed by the stars to something
exalted, and already anticipated our future
grandeur.

It has been a thousand times observed, and I
must observe it once more, that the hours we pass
with happy prospects in view, are more pleasing
than those crowned with fruition. In the first
case, we cook the dish to our own appetite; in
the latter Nature cooks it for us. It is impossible
to repeat the train of agreeable reveries we called
up for our entertainment. We looked upon our
fortunes as once more rising; and, as the whole
parish asserted that the 'Squire was in love with
my daughter, she was actually so with him; for
they persuaded her into the passion. In this agreeable interval my wife had the most lucky dreams
in the world, which she took care to tell us
every morning, with great solemnity and exact-
ness. It was one night a coffin and cross-bones,
the signs of an approaching wedding; at another
time she imagined her daughters' pockets filled
with farthings, a certain sign they would shortly
be stuffed with gold. The girls themselves had
their omens. They felt strange kisses on their lips;
they saw rings in the candle; purses bounced from
the fire, and true-love-knots lurked in the bottom
of every tea-cup.

Towards the end of the week we received a
card from the town ladies, in which, with their
compliments, they hoped to see all our family
at church the Sunday following. All Saturday
morning I could perceive, in consequence of this,

my wife and daughters in close conference together, and now and then glancing at me with
looks that betrayed a latent plot. To be sincere,
I had strong suspicions that some absurd proposal was preparing for appearing with splendour
the next day. In the evening they began their
operations in a very regular manner, and my wife
undertook to conduct the siege. After tea, when
I seemed in spirits, she began thus:—"I fancy,
Charles, my dear, we shall have a great deal of
good company at our church to-morrow."—
"Perhaps we may, my dear," returned I,
"though you need be under no uneasiness about
that; you shall have a sermon whether there be
or not."—"That is what I expect," returned
she; "but I think, my dear, we ought to appear
there as decently as possible, for who knows
what may happen?"—"Your precautions,"
replied I, "are highly commendable. A decent
behaviour and appearance in church is what
charms me. We should be devout and humble,
cheerful and serene."—"Yes," cried she, "I
know that; but I mean we should go there in as
proper a manner as possible; not altogether like
the scrubs about us."—"You are quite right, my
dear," returned I, "and I was going to make
the very same proposal. The proper manner of
going is to go there as early as possible, to have
time for meditation before the service begins."—
"Phoo, Charles," interrupted she, "all that is
very true; but not what I would be at; I mean
we should go there genteelly. You know the

church is two miles off, and I protest I don't like
to see my daughters trudging up to their pew all
blowzed and red with walking, and looking for
all the world as if they had been winners at a
smock race. Now, my dear, my proposal is this:
there are our two plough-horses, the colt that
has been in our family these nine years, and his
companion Blackberry, that has scarce done an
earthly thing for this month past. They are both
grown fat and lazy. Why should not they do
something as well as we? And let me tell you,
when Moses has trimmed them a little, they will
cut a very tolerable figure."

To this proposal I objected that walking would
be twenty times more genteel than such a paltry
conveyance, as Blackberry was wall-eyed, and
the colt wanted a tail; that they had never been
broke to the rein, but had a hundred vicious
tricks; and that we had but one saddle and
pillion in the whole house. All these objections,
however, were overruled; so that I was obliged
to comply. The next morning I perceived them
not a little busy in collecting such materials as
might be necessary for the expedition; but, as I
found it would be a business of time, I walked
on to the church before, and they promised
speedily to follow. I waited near an hour in the
reading desk for their arrival; but not finding
them come as expected, I was obliged to begin,
and went through the service, not without some
uneasiness at finding them absent. This was
increased, when all was finished, and no

appearance of the family. I therefore walked
back by the horse-way, which was five miles
round, though the footway was but two, and, but
when I got about half-way home, perceived the
procession marching slowly forward towards the
church; my son, my wife, and the two little ones
exalted on one horse, and my two daughters
upon the other. I demanded the cause of their
delay; but I soon found by their looks they had
met with a thousand misfortunes on the road.
The horses had at first refused to move from the
door, till Mr. Burchell was kind enough to beat
them forward for about two hundred yards with
his cudgel. Next, the straps of my wife's pillion
broke down, and they were obliged to stop to
repair them before they could proceed. After that,
one of the horses took it into its head to stand still,
and neither blows nor entreaties could prevail with
him to proceed. It was just recovering from this
dismal situation that I found them; but perceiving everything safe, I own their present mortification did not much displease me, as it would give
me many opportunities of future triumph, and
teach my daughters more humility.

"AND WHEN I GOT ABOUT HALF-WAY HOME, PERCEIVED THE PRO-
CESSION MARCHING SLOWLY FORWARD TOWARDS THE CHURCH."

CHAPTER XI

MICHAELMAS-EVE happening on the next day, we
were invited to burn nuts and play tricks at neighbour Flamborough's. Our late mortifications had
humbled us a little, or it is probable we might
have rejected such an invitation with contempt;
however, we suffered ourselves to be happy. Our
honest neighbour's goose and dumplings were
fine, and the lamb's-wool, even in the opinion of
my wife, who was a connoisseur, was excellent.
It is true, his manner of telling stories was not
quite so well. They were very long, and very dull,
and all about himself, and we had laughed at
them ten times before: however, we were kind
enough to laugh at them once more.

Mr. Burchell, who was of the party, was always
fond of seeing some innocent amusement going
forward, and set the boys and girls to blind-
man's buff. My wife, too, was persuaded to join
in the diversion, and it gave me pleasure to
think she was not yet too old. In the meantime,
my neighbour and I looked on, laughed at every
feat, and praised our own dexterity when we were
young. Hot cockles succeeded next, questions and
commands followed that, and last of all, they sat
down to hunt the slipper. As every person may

not be acquainted with this primeval pastime, it
may be necessary to observe, that the company
at this play plant themselves in a ring upon
the ground, all except one, who stands in the
middle, whose business it is to catch a shoe,
which the company shove about under their hams
from one to another, something like a weaver's
shuttle. As it is impossible, in this case, for
the lady who is up to face all the company at
once, the great beauty of the play lies in hitting
her a thump with the heel of the shoe on that
side least capable of making a defence. It was
in this manner that my eldest daughter was
hemmed in, and thumped about, all blowzed,
in spirits, and bawling for fair play, fair play,
with a voice that might deafen a ballad-singer,
when, confusion on confusion! who should
enter the room but our two great acquaintances
from town, Lady Blarney and Miss Carolina
Wilelmina Amelia Skeggs! Description would
but beggar, therefore it is unnecessary to describe,
this new mortification. Death! To be seen by
ladies of such high breeding in such vulgar attitudes! Nothing better could ensue from such
a vulgar play of Mr. Flamborough's proposing.
We seemed struck to the ground for some time,
as if actually petrified with amazement.

The two ladies had been at our house to see us,
and finding us from home, came after us hither,
as they were uneasy to know what accident could
have kept us from church the day before. Olivia
undertook to be our prolocutor, and delivered

the whole in a summary way, only saying, "We were thrown from our horses." At which account the ladies were greatly concerned; but being told the family received no hurt, they were extremely glad; but being informed that we were almost killed by the fright, they were vastly sorry; but hearing that we had a very good night, they were extremely glad again. Nothing could exceed their complaisance to my daughters: their professions the last evening were warm, but now they were ardent. They protested a desire of having a more lasting acquaintance. Lady Blarney was particularly attached to Olivia; Miss Carolina Wilelmina Amelia Skeggs (I love to give the whole name) took a greater fancy to her sister. They supported the conversation between themselves, while my daughters sat silent, admiring their exalted breeding. But as every reader, however beggarly himself, is fond of high-lived dialogues, with anecdotes of Lords, Ladies, and Knights of the Garter, I must beg leave to give him the concluding part of the present conversation.

"All that I know of the matter," cried Miss Skeggs, "is this, that it may be true or may not be true; but this I can assure your Ladyship, that the whole rout was in amaze; his Lordship turned all manner of colours, my Lady fell into a swound, but Sir Tomkyn drawing his sword, swore he was hers to the last drop of his blood."

"Well," replied our Peeress, "this I can say, that the Duchess never told me a syllable of the matter, and I believe her Grace would keep

nothing a secret from me. This you may depend
upon as fact, that the next morning my Lord
Duke cried out three times to his valet-de-
chambre, Jernigan! Jernigan! Jernigan! bring
me my garters."

But previously I should have mentioned the
very impolite behaviour of Mr. Burchell, who,
during this discourse, sat with his face turned to
the fire, and, at the conclusion of every sentence,
would cry out *fudge*, an expression which displeased us all, and in some measure damped the
rising spirit of the conversation.

"Besides, my dear Skeggs," continued our
Peeress, "there is nothing of this in the copy of
verses that Dr. Burdock made upon the occasion."—Fudge!

"I am surprised at that," cried Miss Skeggs:
"for he seldom leaves anything out, as he writes
only for his own amusement. But can your Ladyship favour me with a sight of them?"—*Fudge!*

"My dear creature," replied our Peeress, "do
you think I carry such things about me? Though
they are very fine, to be sure, and I think myself
something of a judge—at least I know what
pleases myself. Indeed, I was ever an admirer
of all Dr. Burdock's little pieces; for except what
he does, and our dear Countess at Hanover
Square, there's nothing comes out but the most
lowest stuff in nature; not a bit of high life among
them."—*Fudge!*

"Your Ladyship should except," says the
other, "your own things in the Lady's Magazine.

THE VERY IMPOLITE BEHAVIOUR OF MR. BURCHELL, WHO SAT
WITH HIS FACE TURNED TO THE FIRE, AND AT THE CON-
CLUSION OF EVERY SENTENCE WOULD CRY OUT "FUDGE!"

I hope you'll say there's nothing low-lived there?
But I suppose we are to have no more from that
quarter?"—*Fudge!*

"Why, my dear," says the lady, "you know
my reader and companion has left me, to be
married to Captain Roach, and as my poor eyes
won't suffer me to write myself, I have been for
some time looking out for another. A proper person is no easy matter to find; and, to be sure,
thirty pounds a year is a small stipend for a well-
bred girl of character, that can read, write, and
behave in company; as for the chits about town,
there is no bearing them about one."—*Fudge!*

"That I know," cried Miss Skeggs, "by experience. For of the three companions I had this
last half year, one of them refused to do plainwork an hour in the day; another thought twenty-
five guineas a year too small a salary; and I
was obliged to send away the third, because I
suspected an intrigue with the chaplain. Virtue,
my dear Lady Blarney, virtue is worth any
price; but where is that to be found?"—*Fudge!*

My wife had been, for a long time, all attention
to this discourse, but was particularly struck with
the latter part of it. Thirty pounds and twenty-
five guineas a year, made fifty-six pounds five
shillings English money, all which was in a
manner going a-begging, and might easily be
secured in the family. She for a moment studied
my looks for approbation; and, to own a truth,
I was of opinion, that two such places would fit
our two daughters exactly. Besides, if the 'Squire

had any real affection for my eldest daughter, this would be the way to make her every way qualified for her fortune. My wife, therefore, was resolved that we should not be deprived of such advantages for want of assurance, and undertook to harangue for the family. "I hope," cried she, "your Ladyships will pardon my present presumption. It is true, we have no right to pretend to such favours; but yet it is natural for me to wish putting my children forward in the world. And, I will be bold to say, my two girls have had a pretty good education and capacity; at least the country can't show better. They can read, write, and cast accounts; they understand their needle, broad-stitch, cross and change, and all manner of plainwork; they can pink, point, and frill, and know something of music; they can do up small clothes, work upon catgut; my eldest can cut paper, and my youngest has a very pretty manner of telling fortunes upon the cards."— *Fudge!*

When she had delivered this pretty piece of eloquence, the two ladies looked at each other a few minutes in silence, with an air of doubt and importance. At last Miss Carolina Wilelmina Amelia Skeggs condescended to observe that the young ladies, from the opinion she could form of them from so slight an acquaintance, seemed very fit for such employments. "But a thing of this kind, Madam," cried she, addressing my spouse, "requires a thorough examination into characters, and a more perfect knowledge of each other. Not, Madam," continued she, "that I in the least suspect the young ladies' virtue, prudence, and discretion: but there is a form in these things, Madam—there is a form."

My wife approved her suspicions very much, observing that she was very apt to be suspicious herself, but referred her to all the neighbours for a character; but this our Peeress declined as unnecessary, alleging that her cousin Thornhill's recommendation would be sufficient; and upon this we rested our petition.

CHAPTER XII

FORTUNE SEEMS RESOLVED TO HUMBLE THE FAMILY
OF WAKEFIELD.—MORTIFICATIONS ARE OFTEN
MORE PAINFUL THAN REAL CALAMITIES

WHEN we were returned home, the night was dedicated to schemes of future conquest. Deborah exerted much sagacity in conjecturing which of the two girls was likely to have the best place, and most opportunities of seeing good company. The only obstacle to our preferment was in obtaining the 'Squire's recommendation; but he had already shown us too many instances of his friendship to doubt of it now. Even in bed my wife kept up the usual theme: "Well, faith, my dear Charles, between ourselves I think we have made an excellent day's work of it."—"Pretty well!" cried I, not knowing what to say. "What, only pretty well!" returned she: "I think it is very well. Suppose the girls should come to make acquaintances of taste in town! This I am assured of, that London is the only place in the world for all manner of husbands. Besides, my dear, stranger things happen every day; and as ladies of quality are so taken with my daughters, what will not men of quality be? *Entre nous,* I protest I like my Lady Blarney vastly—so very obliging. However, Miss Carolina Wilelmina

Amelia Skeggs has my warm heart. But yet, when they came to talk of places in town, you saw at once how I nailed them. Tell me, my dear, don't you think I did for my children there?"—"Ay," returned I, not knowing well what to think of the matter; "Heaven grant they may be both the better for it this day three months!" This was one of those observations I usually made to impress my wife with an opinion of my sagacity: for if the girls succeeded, then it was a pious wish fulfilled; but if anything unfortunate ensued, then it might be looked upon as a prophecy. All this conversation, however, was only preparatory to another scheme; and indeed I dreaded as much. This was nothing less than that, as we were now to hold up our heads a little higher in the world, it would be proper to sell the Colt, which was grown old, at a neighbouring fair, and buy us a horse that would carry a single or double upon an occasion, and make a pretty appearance at church, or upon a visit. This at first I opposed stoutly; but it was stoutly defended. However, as I weakened, my antagonist gained strength, till at last it was resolved to part with him.

As the fair happened on the following day, I had intentions of going myself; but my wife persuaded me that I had got a cold, and nothing could prevail upon her to permit me from home. "No, my dear," said she, "our son Moses is a discreet boy, and can buy and sell to a very good advantage; you know all our great bargains are

"WE ALL FOLLOWED HIM SEVERAL PACES FROM THE DOOR,
BAWLING AFTER HIM 'GOOD LUCK! GOOD LUCK!' TILL WE
COULD SEE HIM NO LONGER."

84*

of his purchasing. He always stands out and
higgles, and actually tires them till he gets a
bargain.''

As I had some opinion of my son's prudence,
I was willing enough to entrust him with this
commission; and the next morning I perceived
his sisters mighty busy in fitting out Moses for
the fair: trimming his hair, brushing his buckles,
and cocking his hat with pins. The business of the
toilet being over, we had at last the satisfaction
of seeing him mounted upon the Colt, with a deal
box before him to bring home groceries in. He
had on a coat made of that cloth they call thunder-
and-lightning, which, though grown too short,
was much too good to be thrown away. His waistcoat was of gosling green, and his sisters had tied
his hair with a broad black ribbon. We all
followed him several paces from the door, bawling
after him, "Good luck! good luck!" till we could
see him no longer.

He was scarce gone, when Mr. Thornhill's
butler came to congratulate us upon our good
fortune, saying that he overheard his young
master mention our names with great commen-
dation.

Good fortune seemed not to come alone.
Another footman from the same family followed,
with a card for my daughters, importing that the
two ladies had received such pleasing accounts
from Mr. Thornhill of us all, that after a few
previous inquiries they hoped to be perfectly
satisfied. "Ay," cried my wife, "I now see it is

no easy matter to get into the families of the great; but when one once gets in, then, as Moses says, one may go to sleep." To this piece of humour, for she intended it for wit, my daughters assented with a loud laugh of pleasure. In short, such was her satisfaction at this message, that she actually put her hand in her pocket and gave the messenger sevenpence halfpenny.

This was to be our visiting day. The next that came was Mr. Burchell, who had been at the fair. He brought my little ones a pennyworth of gingerbread each, which my wife undertook to keep for them, and gave them by letters at a time. He brought my daughters also a couple of boxes, in which they might keep wafers, snuff, patches, or even money, when they got it. My wife was usually fond of a weasel-skin purse, as being the most lucky; but this by the by. We had still a regard for Mr. Burchell, though his late rude behaviour was in some measure displeasing; nor could we now avoid communicating our happiness to him, and asking his advice: although we seldom followed advice, we were all ready enough to ask it. When he read the note from the two ladies, he shook his head, and observed, that an affair of this sort demanded the utmost circumspection. This air of diffidence highly displeased my wife. "I never doubted, sir," cried she, "your readiness to be against my daughters and me. You have more circumspection than is wanted. However, I fancy when we come to ask advice, we will apply to persons who seem to have made

"HERE THEY ARE: A GROSS OF GREEN SPECTACLES, WITH
SILVER RIMS AND SHAGREEN CASES."

use of it themselves."—"Whatever my own conduct may have been, Madam," replied he, "is not the present question: though, as I have made no use of advice myself, I should in conscience give it to those that will." As I was apprehensive this answer might draw on a repartee, making up by abuse what it wanted in wit, I changed the subject, by seeming to wonder what could keep our son so long at the fair, as it was now almost nightfall. "Never mind our son," cried my wife; "depend upon it he knows what he is about. I'll warrant we'll never see him sell his hen on a rainy day. I have seen him buy such bargains as would amaze one. I'll tell you a good story about that, that will make you split your sides with laughing. —But, as I live, yonder comes Moses, without a horse, and the box at his back."

As she spoke, Moses came slowly on foot, and sweating under the deal box, which he had strapt round his shoulders like a pedlar. "Welcome, welcome, Moses! well, my boy, what have you brought us from the fair?"—"I have brought you myself," cried Moses, with a sly look, and resting the box on the dresser. "Ay, Moses," cried my wife, "that we know; but where is the horse?"—"I have sold him," cried Moses, "for three pounds five shillings and twopence."— "Well done, my good boy," returned she; "I knew you would touch them off. Between ourselves, three pounds five shillings and twopence is no bad day's work. Come, let us have it then." —"I have brought back no money," cried Moses again. "I have laid it all out in a bargain, and here it is," pulling out a bundle from his breast: "here they are; a gross of green spectacles, with silver rims and shagreen cases."—"A gross of green spectacles!" repeated my wife in a faint voice. "And you have parted with the Colt, and brought us back nothing but a gross of green paltry spectacles!"—"Dear mother," cried the boy, "why won't you listen to reason? I had them a dead bargain, or I should not have bought them. The silver rims alone will sell for double the money."—"A fig for the silver rims," cried my wife, in a passion: "I dare swear they won't sell for above half the money at the rate of broken silver, five shillings an ounce."—"You need be under no uneasiness," cried I, "about selling the rims, for they are not worth sixpence; for I perceive they are only copper varnished over."— "What!" cried my wife, "not silver! the rims not silver!"—"No," cried I, "no more silver than your saucepan."—"And so," returned she, "we have parted with the Colt, and have only got a gross of green spectacles, with copper rims and shagreen cases? A murrain take such trumpery! The blockhead has been imposed upon, and should have known his company better."— "There, my dear," cried I, "you are wrong; he should not have known them at all."—"Marry, hang the idiot!" returned she, "to bring me such stuff: if I had them, I would throw them in the fire."—"There again you are wrong, my dear," cried I; "for though they be copper, we will keep them by us, as copper spectacles, you know, are better than nothing.''

By this time the unfortunate Moses was undeceived. He now saw that he had indeed been imposed upon by a prowling sharper, who, observing his figure, had marked him for an easy prey. I therefore asked the circumstances of his deception. He sold the horse, it seems, and walked the fair in search of another. A reverend-looking man brought him to a tent, under the pretence of having one to sell. ''Here,'' continued Moses, ''we met another man, very well dressed, who desired to borrow twenty pounds upon these, saying that he wanted money, and would dispose of them for a third of the value. The first gentleman, who pretended to be my friend, whispered me to buy them, and cautioned me not to let so good an offer pass. I sent for Mr. Flamborough, and they talked him up as finely as they did me; and so at last we were persuaded to buy the two gross between us.''

CHAPTER XIII

MR. BURCHELL IS FOUND TO BE AN ENEMY, FOR HE
HAS THE CONFIDENCE TO GIVE DISAGREEABLE
ADVICE

OUR family had now made several attempts to
be fine; but some unforeseen disaster demolished
each as soon as projected. I endeavoured to take
the advantage of every disappointment to improve
their good sense, in proportion as they were
frustrated in ambition. "You see, my children,"
cried I, "how little is to be got by attempts to
impose upon the world in coping with our betters.
Such as are poor, and will associate with none
but the rich, are hated by those they avoid, and
despised by those they follow. Unequal combinations are always disadvantageous to the
weaker side, the rich having the pleasure, and the
poor the inconveniences that result from them.
But come, Dick, my boy, and repeat the fable
you were reading to-day, for the good of the
company."

"Once upon a time," cried the child, "a Giant
and a Dwarf were friends, and kept together.
They made a bargain that they would never forsake each other, but go seek adventures. The first
battle they fought was with two Saracens, and
the Dwarf, who was very courageous, dealt one
of the champions a most angry blow. It did the

Saracen but very little injury, who, lifting up his sword, fairly struck off the poor Dwarf's arm. He was now in a woful plight; but the Giant, coming to his assistance, in a short time left the two Saracens dead on the plain, and the Dwarf cut off the dead man's head out of spite. They then travelled on to another adventure. This was against three bloody-minded Satyrs, who were carrying away a damsel in distress. The Dwarf was not quite so fierce now as before, but for all that struck the first blow, which was returned by another that knocked out his eye; but the Giant was soon up with him, and had they not fled, would certainly have killed them every one. They were all very joyful for this victory, and the damsel, who was relieved, fell in love with the Giant, and married him. They now travelled far, and farther than I can tell, till they met with a company of robbers. The Giant, for the first time, was foremost now; but the Dwarf was not far behind. The battle was stout and long. Wherever the Giant came, all fell before him; but the Dwarf had liked to have been killed more than once. At last the victory declared for the two adventurers; but the Dwarf lost his leg. The Dwarf had now lost an arm, a leg, and an eye, while the Giant was without a single wound; upon which he cried out to his little companion, 'My little hero, this is glorious sport! let us get one victory more, and then we shall have honour for ever.'— 'No,' cries the Dwarf, who was by this time grown wiser, 'no, I declare off; I'll fight no more; for

I find in every battle that you get all the honour
and rewards, but all the blows fall upon me.' "

I was going to moralise this fable, when our
attention was called off to a warm dispute between
my wife and Mr. Burchell upon my daughters'
intended expedition to town. My wife very strenuously insisted upon the advantages that would
result from it; Mr. Burchell, on the contrary,
dissuaded her with great ardour; and I stood
neuter. His present dissuasions seemed but the
second part of those which were received with so
ill a grace in the morning. The dispute grew high;
while poor Deborah, instead of reasoning
stronger, talked louder, and at last was obliged
to take shelter from a defeat in clamour. The
conclusion of her harangue, however, was highly
displeasing to us all. She knew, she said, of some
who had their own secret reasons for what they
advised; but, for her part, she wished such to stay
away from her house for the future. "Madam,"
cried Burchell, with looks of great composure,
which tended to inflame her the more, "as for
secret reasons, you are right: I have secret
reasons, which I forbear to mention, because you
are not able to answer those of which I make no
secret; but I find my visits here are become
troublesome; I'll take my leave, therefore, now,
and perhaps come once more to take a final farewell when I am quitting the country." Thus saying, he took up his hat; nor could the attempts
of Sophia, whose looks seemed to upbraid his
precipitancy, prevent his going.

When gone, we all regarded each other for some minutes with confusion. My wife, who knew herself to be the cause, strove to hide her concern with a forced smile and an air of assurance, which I was willing to reprove. "How, woman," cried I to her, "is it thus we treat strangers? Is it thus we return their kindness? Be assured, my dear, that these were the harshest words, and to me the most unpleasing, that ever escaped your lips!"— "Why would be provoke me, then?" replied she; "but I know the motives of his advice perfectly well. He would prevent my girls from going to town that he may have the pleasure of my youngest daughter's company here at home. But, whatever happens, she shall choose better company than such low-lived fellows as he."—"Low-lived, my dear, do you call him?" cried I; "it is very possible we may mistake this man's character, for he seems, upon some occasions, the most finished gentleman I ever knew. Tell me, Sophia, my girl, has he ever given you any secret instances of his attachment?"—"His conversation with me, Sir," replied my daughter, "has ever been sensible, modest, and pleasing. As to ought else—no, never. Once, indeed, I remember to have heard him say, he never knew a woman who could find merit in a man that seemed poor."— "Such, my dear," cried I, "is the common cant of all the unfortunate or idle. But I hope you have been taught to judge properly of such men, and that it would be even madness to expect happiness from one who has been so very bad an economist

of his own. Your mother and I have now better
prospects for you. The next winter, which you
will probably spend in town, will give you opportunities of making a more prudent choice.''

What Sophia's reflections were upon this occasion I cannot pretend to determine ; but I was not
displeased at the bottom that we were rid of a
guest from whom I had much to fear. Our breach
of hospitality went to my conscience a little ; but
I quickly silenced that monitor by two or three
specious reasons, which served to satisfy and
reconcile me to myself. The pain which conscience
gives the man who has already done wrong is soon
got over. Conscience is a coward ; and those faults
it has not strength enough to prevent, it seldom
has justice enough to accuse.

CHAPTER XIV

FRESH MORTIFICATIONS, OR A DEMONSTRATION
THAT SEEMING CALAMITIES MAY BE REAL BLESSINGS

THE journey of my daughters to town was now resolved upon, Mr. Thornhill having kindly promised to inspect their conduct himself, and inform us by letter of their behaviour. But it was thought indispensably necessary that their appearance should equal the greatness of their expectations, which could not be done without expense. We debated therefore in full council what were the easiest methods of raising money, or, more properly speaking, what we could most conveniently sell. The deliberation was soon finished: it was found that our remaining horse was utterly useless for the plough without his companion, and equally unfit for the road, as wanting an eye: it was therefore determined that we should dispose of him, for the purposes above mentioned, at the neighbouring fair ; and to prevent imposition, that I should go with him myself. Though this was one of the first mercantile transactions of my life, yet I had no doubt about acquitting myself with reputation. The opinion a man forms of his own prudence is measured by that of the company he keeps : and as mine was most in the family way, I had conceived no unfavourable sentiments of my worldly wisdom. My wife, however, next morning, at parting, after I had got some paces from the door, called me back to advise me, in a whisper, to have all my eyes about me.

I had, in the usual forms, when I came to the fair, put my horse through all his paces, but for some time had no bidders. At last a chapman approached, and after he had for a good while examined the horse round, finding him blind of one eye, he would have nothing to say to him; a second came up, but observing that he had a spavin, declared he would not take him for the driving home; a third perceived he had a wind-gall, and would bid no money; a fourth knew by his eye that he had the botts; a fifth wondered what a plague I could do at the fair with a blind, spavined, galled hack, that was only fit to be cut up for a dog kennel. By this time, I began to have a most hearty contempt for the poor animal my-self, and was almost ashamed at the approach of every customer; for though I did not entirely believe all the fellows told me, yet I reflected that the number of witnesses was a strong presumption they were right; and St. Gregory, upon Good Works, professes himself to be of the same opinion.

I was in this mortifying situation, when a brother clergyman, an old acquaintance, who had also business at the fair, came up, and, shaking me by the hand, proposed adjourning to a public-house, and taking a glass of whatever we could get. I readily closed with the offer, and entering an alehouse, we were shown into a little back

"I BEGAN TO HAVE A HEARTY CONTEMPT FOR THIS POOR ANIMAL MYSELF, AND WAS ALMOST ASHAMED AT THE APPROACH OF EVERY CUSTOMER."

room, where was only a venerable old man, who
sat wholly intent over a large book, which he was
reading. I never in my life saw a figure that prepossessed me more favourably. His locks of silver
grey venerably shaded his temples, and his green
old age seemed to be the result of health and
benevolence. However, his presence did not interrupt our conversation: my friend and I dis-
coursed on the various turns of fortune we had
met; the Whistonian controversy, my last
pamphlet, the archdeacon's reply, and the hard
measure that was dealt me. But our attention was
in a short time taken off, by the appearance of a
youth, who, entering the room, respectfully said
something softly to the old stranger. "Make no
apologies, my child," said the old man; "to do
good is a duty we owe to all our fellow-creatures.
Take this, I wish it were more; but five pounds
will relieve your distress, and you are welcome."
The modest youth shed tears of gratitude, and
yet his gratitude was scarce equal to mine. I could
have hugged the good old man in my arms, his
benevolence pleased me so. He continued to read,
and we resumed our conversation, until my companion, after some time, recollecting that he had
business to transact in the fair, promised to be
soon back; adding, that he always desired to have
as much of Dr. Primrose's company as possible.
The old gentleman, hearing my name mentioned,
seemed to look at me with attention for some
time; and when my friend was gone, most respectfully demanded if I was any way related to

the great Primrose, that courageous monogamist, who had been the bulwark of the Church. Never did my heart feel sincerer rapture than at that moment. "Sir," cried I, "the applause of so good a man as I am sure you are, adds to that happiness in my breast which your benevolence has already excited. You behold before you, Sir, that Dr. Primrose, the monogamist, whom you have been pleased to call great. You here see that unfortunate divine, who has so long, and it would ill become me to say, successfully fought against the deuterogamy of the age."—"Sir," cried the stranger, struck with awe, "I fear I have been too familiar, but you'll forgive my curiosity, Sir: I beg pardon."—"Sir," cried I, grasping his hand, "you are so far from displeasing me by your familiarity, that I must beg you'll accept my friendship, as you have already my esteem."— "Then with gratitude I accept the offer," cried he, squeezing me by the hand, "thou glorious pillar of unshaken orthodoxy! and do I behold" ——I here interrupted what he was going to say; for though, as an author, I could digest no small share of flattery, yet now my modesty would permit no more. However, no lovers in romance ever cemented a more instantaneous friendship. We talked upon several subjects: at first I thought he seemed rather devout than learned, and began to think he despised all human doctrines as dross. Yet this no way lessened him in my esteem, for I had for some time begun privately to harbour such an opinion myself. I therefore took occasion to observe, that the world in general began to be blameably indifferent as to doctrinal matters, and followed human speculations too much. "Ay, Sir," replied he, as if he had reserved all his learning to that moment, "Ay, Sir, the world is in its dotage; and yet the cosmogony, or creation of the world, has puzzled philosophers of all ages. What a medley of opinions have they not broached upon the creation of the world ! Sanchoniathon, Manetho, Berosus, and Ocellus Lucanus, have all attempted it in vain. The latter has these words, *Anarchon ara kai atelutaion to pan,* which imply that all things have neither beginning nor end. Manetho also, who lived about the time of Nebuchadon-Asser—Asser being a Syriac word, usually applied as a surname to the kings of that country, as Teglat Phael-Asser, Nabon-Asser—he, I say, formed a conjecture equally absurd; for as we usually say, *ek to biblion kubernetes,* which implies that books will never teach the world; so he attempted to investigate—— But, Sir, I ask pardon, I am straying from the question."—That he actually was; nor could I, for my life, see how the creation of the world had anything to do with the business I was talking of; but it was sufficient to show me that he was a man of letters, and I now reverenced him the more. I was resolved, therefore, to bring him to the touchstone; but he was too mild and too gentle to contend for victory. Whenever I made an observation that looked like a challenge to controversy, he would smile, shake his head,

and say nothing; by which I understood he could
say much, if he thought proper. The subject,
therefore, insensibly changed from the business of
antiquity, to that which brought us both to the
fair: mine, I told him, was to sell a horse, and
very luckily, indeed, his was to buy one for one
of his tenants. My horse was soon produced; and,
in fine, we struck a bargain. Nothing now
remained but to pay me, and he accordingly
pulled out a thirty pound note, and bid me change
it. Not being in a capacity of complying with this
demand, he ordered his footman to be called up,
who made his appearance in a very genteel livery.
"Here, Abraham," cried he, "go and get gold for
this; you'll do it at neighbour Jackson's or anywhere." While the fellow was gone, he entertained
me with a pathetic harangue on the great scarcity
of silver, which I undertook to improve, by deploring also the great scarcity of gold; so that,
by the time Abraham returned, we had both
agreed that money was never so hard to be come
at as now. Abraham returned to inform us, that
he had been over the whole fair, and could not
get change, though he had offered half-a-crown
for doing it. This was a very great disappointment
to us all; but the old gentleman, having paused a
little, asked me if I knew one Solomon Flamborough in my part of the country. Upon replying
that he was my next-door neighbour: "If that
be the case, then," returned he, "I believe we
shall deal. You shall have a draft upon him,
payable at sight; and, let me tell you, he is as

warm a man as any within five miles round him.
Honest Solomon and I have been acquainted for
many years together. I remember I always beat
him at three jumps; but he could hop on one leg
further than I." A draft upon my neighbour was
to me the same as money; for I was sufficiently
convinced of his ability. The draft was signed,
and put into my hands, and Mr. Jenkinson, the
old gentleman, his man Abraham, and my horse,
old Blackberry, trotted off very well pleased with
each other.

After a short interval, being left to reflection, I
began to recollect that I had done wrong in taking
a draft from a stranger, and so prudently resolved
upon following the purchaser, and having back
my horse. But this was now too late; I therefore
made directly homewards, resolving to get the
draft changed into money at my friend's as fast
as possible. I found my honest neighbour smoking
his pipe at his own door, and informing him that
I had a small bill upon him, he read it twice over.
"You can read the name, I suppose," cried I—
"Ephraim Jenkinson."—"Yes," returned he,
"the name is written plain enough, and I know
the gentleman too—the greatest rascal under the
canopy of heaven. This is the very same rogue
who sold us the spectacles. Was he not a
venerable-looking man, with grey hair, and no
flaps to his pocket-holes? And did he not talk a
long string of learning about Greek, and cosmogony, and the world?" To this I replied with a
groan. "Ay," continued he, "he has but that one

piece of learning in the world, and he always talks
it away whenever he finds a scholar in company ;
but I know the rogue, and will catch him yet.''

Though I was already sufficiently mortified, my
greatest struggle was to come, in facing my wife
and daughters. No truant was ever more afraid
of returning to school, there to behold the master's
visage, than I was of going home. I was determined, however, to anticipate their fury, by first
falling into a passion myself.

But, alas ! upon entering, I found the family no
way disposed for battle. My wife and girls were
all in tears, Mr. Thornhill having been there that
day to inform them that their journey to town was
entirely over. The two ladies, having heard
reports of us from some malicious person about
us, were that day set out for London. He could
neither discover the tendency nor the author of
these ; but whatever they might be, or whoever
might have broached them, he continued to assure
our family of his friendship and protection. I
found, therefore, that they bore my disappointment with great resignation, as it was eclipsed in
the greatness of their own. But what perplexed us
most, was to think who could be so base as to
asperse the character of a family so harmless as
ours ; too humble to excite envy, and too inoffensive to create disgust.

CHAPTER XV

ALL MR. BURCHELL'S VILLAINY AT ONCE DETECTED.
—THE FOLLY OF BEING OVERWISE

THAT evening, and a part of the following day, was employed in fruitless attempts to discover our enemies: scarcely a family in the neighbour-hood but incurred our suspicions, and each of us had reasons for our opinions best known to our-selves. As we were in this perplexity, one of our little boys, who had been playing abroad, brought in a letter-case, which he found on the green. It was quickly known to belong to Mr. Burchell, with whom it had been seen, and, upon exam-ination, contained some hints upon different subjects; but what particularly engaged our attention was a sealed note, superscribed, *the copy of a letter to be sent to the ladies at Thornhill Castle*. It instantly occurred that he was the base informer, and we deliberated whether the note should not be broken open. I was against it; but Sophia, who said she was sure that of all men he would be the last to be guilty of so much baseness, insisted upon its being read. In this she was seconded by the rest of the family, and at their joint solicitation I read as follows:—

"Ladies,—The bearer will sufficiently satisfy you as to the person from whom this comes: one at least the friend of innocence, and ready to prevent its being seduced. I am informed for a truth, that you have some intention of bringing two ladies to town, whom I have some knowledge of, under the character of companions. As I would neither have simplicity imposed upon, nor virtue contaminated, I must offer it as my opinion, that the impropriety of such a step will be attended with dangerous consequences. It has never been my way to treat the infamous or the lewd with severity; nor should I now have taken this method of explaining myself, or reproving folly, did it not aim at guilt. Take, therefore, the admonition of a friend, and seriously reflect on the consequences of introducing infamy and vice into retreats where peace and innocence have hitherto resided.''

Our doubts were now at an end. There seemed, indeed, something applicable to both sides in this letter, and its censures might as well be referred to those to whom it was written, as to us; but the malicious meaning was obvious, and we went no farther. My wife had scarcely patience to hear me to the end, but railed at the writer with unrestrained resentment. Olivia was equally severe, and Sophia seemed perfectly amazed at his baseness. As for my part, it appeared to me one of the vilest instances of unprovoked ingratitude I had met with; nor could I account for it in any other manner than by imputing it to his desire of detaining my youngest daughter in the country, to have the more frequent opportunities of an interview. In this manner we all sat ruminating

upon schemes of vengeance, when our other little
boy came running in to tell us that Mr. Burchell
was approaching at the other end of the field. It
is easier to conceive than describe the complicated
sensations which are felt from the pain of a recent
injury, and the pleasure of approaching vengeance. Though our intentions were only to upbraid
him with his ingratitude, yet it was resolved to do
it in a manner that would be perfectly cutting.
For this purpose we agreed to meet him with our
usual smiles ; to chat in the beginning with more
than ordinary kindness, to amuse him a little ; and
then, in the midst of the flattering calm, to burst
upon him like an earthquake, and overwhelm him
with a sense of his own baseness. This being
resolved upon, my wife undertook to manage the
business herself, as she really had some talents for
such an undertaking. We saw him approach ; he
entered, drew a chair, and sat down. "A fine day,
Mr. Burchell."—"A very fine day, Doctor ;
though I fancy we shall have some rain by the
shooting of my corns."—"The shooting of your
horns !" cried my wife, in a loud fit of laughter,
and then asked pardon for being fond of a joke.
"Dear madam," replied he, "I pardon you with
all my heart, for I protest I should not have
thought it a joke had you not told me."—"Perhaps not, Sir," cried my wife, winking at us ;
"and yet I dare say you can tell us how many
jokes go to an ounce."—"I fancy, madam," returned Burchell, "you have been reading a jest
book this morning, that ounce of jokes is so very

good a conceit; and yet, madam, I had rather see half an ounce of understanding."—"I believe you might," cried my wife, still smiling at us, though the laugh was against her; "and yet I have seen some men pretend to understanding that have very little."—"And no doubt," returned her antagonist, "you have known ladies set up for wit that had none." I quickly began to find that my wife was likely to gain but little at this business; so I resolved to treat him in a style of more severity myself. "Both wit and understanding," cried I, "are trifles, without integrity; it is that which gives value to every character. The ignorant peasant without fault is greater than the philosopher with many; for what is genius or courage without an heart?

"'An honest man's the noblest work of God.'"

"I always held that hackneyed maxim of Pope," returned Mr. Burchell, "as very unworthy a man of genius, and a base desertion of his own superiority. As the reputation of books is raised, not by their freedom from defect, but the greatness of their beauties; so should that of men be prized, not for their exemption from fault but the size of those virtues they are possessed of. The scholar may want prudence, the statesman may have pride, and the champion ferocity; but shall we prefer to these the low mechanic, who laboriously plods on through life without censure or applause? We might as well prefer the tame correct paintings of the Flemish school to the

erroneous but sublime animations of the Roman
pencil."

"Sir," replied I, "your present observation is
just, when there are shining virtues and minute
defects ; but when it appears that great vices are
opposed in the same mind to as extraordinary
virtues, such a character deserves contempt."

"Perhaps," cried he, "there may be some such
monsters as you describe, of great vices joined to
great virtues ; yet in my progress through life, I
never yet found one instance of their existence :
on the contrary, I have ever perceived, that where
the mind was capacious, the affections were good.
And indeed Providence seems kindly our friend
in this particular, thus to debilitate the understanding where the heart is corrupt, and diminish
the power where there is the will to do mischief.
This rule seems to extend even to other animals :
the little vermin race are ever treacherous, cruel,
and cowardly, whilst those endowed with strength
and power are generous, brave, and gentle."

"These observations sound well," returned I,
"and yet it would be easy this moment to point
out a man," and I fixed my eye steadfastly upon
him, "whose head and heart form a most detest-
able contrast. Ay, Sir," continued I, raising my
voice, "and I am glad to have this opportunity
of detecting him in the midst of his fancied
security. Do you know this, Sir, this pocket-
book ?"—"Yes, Sir," returned he, with a face
of impenetrable assurance, "that pocket-book is
mine, and I am glad you have found it."—"And

do you know," cried I, "this letter? Nay, never
falter, man, but look me full in the face; I say
do you know this letter?"—"That letter?" returned he; "yes, it was I that wrote that letter."
—"And how could you," said I, "so basely, so
ungratefully presume to write this letter?"—"And
how came you," replied he, with looks of un-
paralleled effrontery, "so basely to presume to
break open this letter? Don't you know, now, I
could hang you all for this? All that I have to do
is to swear at the next justice's that you have been
guilty of breaking open the lock of my pocket-
book, and so hang you all up at his door." This
piece of unexpected insolence raised me to such
a pitch, that I could scarce govern my passion.
"Ungrateful wretch! begone, and no longer
pollute my dwelling with thy baseness! begone,
and never let me see thee again! Go from my
door, and the only punishment I wish thee is an
alarmed conscience, which will be a sufficient tor-
mentor!" So saying, I threw him his pocket-
book, which he took up with a smile, and shutting
the clasps with the utmost composure, left us,
quite astonished at the serenity of his assurance.
My wife was particularly enraged that nothing
could make him angry, or make him seem
ashamed of his villainies: "My dear," cried I,
willing to calm those passions that had been
raised too high among us, "we are not to be surprised that bad men want shame: they only blush
at being detected in doing good, but glory in their
vices.

"Guilt and Shame, says the allegory, were at first companions, and, in the beginning of their journey, inseparably kept together. But their union was soon found to be disagreeable and inconvenient to both. Guilt gave Shame frequent uneasiness, and Shame often betrayed the secret conspiracies of Guilt. After long disagreement, therefore, they at length consented to part for ever. Guilt boldly walked forward alone, to overtake Fate, that went before in the shape of an executioner; but Shame, being naturally timorous, returned back to keep company with Virtue, which in the beginning of their journey they had left behind. Thus, my children, after men have travelled through a few stages in vice, shame forsakes them, and returns back to wait upon the few virtues they have still remaining."

CHAPTER XVI

WHATEVER might have been Sophia's sensations, the rest of the family was easily consoled for Mr. Burchell's absence by the company of our landlord, whose visits now became more frequent, and longer. Though he had been disappointed in procuring my daughters the amusements of the town, as he designed, he took every opportunity of supplying them with those little recreations which our retirement would admit of. He usually came in the morning; and, while my son and I followed our occupations abroad, he sat with the family at home, and amused them by describing the town, with every part of which he was particularly acquainted. He could repeat all the observations that were retailed in the atmosphere of the play-houses, and had all the good things of the high wits by rote, long before they made their way into the jest books. The intervals between conversation were employed in teaching piquet, or sometimes in setting my two little ones to box, to make them *sharp*, as he called it: but the hopes of having him for a son-in-law in some measure blinded us to all his imperfections. It must be owned, that my wife laid a thousand schemes to entrap him; or to speak it more tenderly, used every art to magnify the merit of her daughter. If the cakes at tea ate short and crisp, they were made by Olivia; if the gooseberry wine was well knit, the gooseberries were of her gathering: it was her fingers which gave the pickles their peculiar green; and, in the composition of a pudding, it was her judgment that mixed the ingredients.

Then the poor woman would sometimes tell the 'Squire, that she thought him and Olivia extremely of a size, and would bid both stand up to see which was the tallest. These instances of cunning, which she thought impenetrable, yet which everybody saw through, were very pleasing to our benefactor, who gave every day some new proofs of his passion, which, though they had not arisen to proposals of marriage, yet we thought fell but little short of it; and his slowness was attributed sometimes to native bashfulness, and sometimes to his fear of offending his uncle. An occurrence, however, which happened soon after, put it beyond a doubt that he designed to become one of our family; my wife even regarded it as an absolute promise.

My wife and daughters happening to return a visit to neighbour Flamborough's, found that family had lately got their pictures drawn by a limner, who travelled the country, and took likeness for fifteen shillings a head. As this family and ours had long a sort of rivalry in point of taste, our spirit took the alarm at this stolen

"THEN THE POOR WOMAN WOULD SOMETIMES TELL THE 'SQUIRE THAT SHE THOUGHT HIM AND OLIVIA EXTREMELY OF A SIZE, AND WOULD BID BOTH STAND UP TO SEE WHICH WAS TALLEST."

march upon us; and, notwithstanding all I could say, and I said much, it was resolved that we should have our pictures done too.

Having, therefore, engaged the limner,—for what could I do?—our next deliberation was to show the superiority of our tastes in the attitudes. As for our neighbour's family, there were seven of them, and they were drawn with seven oranges, —a thing quite out of taste, no variety in life, no composition in the world. We desired to have something in a brighter style; and, after many debates, at length came to a unanimous resolution of being drawn together, in one large historical family piece. This would be cheaper, since one frame would serve for all, and it would be infinitely more genteel; for all families of any taste were now drawn in the same manner.

As we did not immediately recollect an historical subject to hit us, we were contented each with being drawn as independent historical figures. My wife desired to be represented as Venus, and the painter was desired not to be too frugal of his diamonds in her stomacher and hair. Her two little ones were to be as Cupids by her side; while I, in my gown and band, was to present her with my books on the Whistonian controversy. Olivia would be drawn as an Amazon, sitting upon a bank of flowers, dressed in a green joseph, richly laced in gold, and a whip in her hand. Sophia was to be a shepherdess, with as many sheep as the painter could put in for nothing; and Moses was to be dressed out with a hat and white feather. Our taste so much pleased the 'Squire, that he insisted on being put in as one of the family, in the character of Alexander the Great, at Olivia's feet. This was considered by us all as an indication of his desire to be introduced into the family, nor could we refuse his request. The painter was therefore set to work, and, as he wrought with assiduity and expedition, in less than four days the whole was completed. The piece was large, and, it must be owned, he did not spare his colours; for which my wife gave him great encomiums. We were all perfectly satisfied with his performance; but an unfortunate circumstance had not occurred till the picture was finished, which now struck us with dismay. It was so very large, that we had no place in the house to fix it. How we all came to disregard so material a point is inconceivable; but certain it is, we had been all greatly remiss. The picture, therefore, instead of gratifying our vanity, as we hoped, leaned, in a most mortifying manner, against the kitchen wall, where the canvas was stretched and painted, much too large to be got through any of the doors, and the jest of all our neighbours. One compared it to Robinson Crusoe's long-boat, too large to be removed; another thought it more resembled a reel in a bottle; some wondered how it could be got out, but still more were amazed how it ever got in.

But though it excited the ridicule of some, it effectually raised more malicious suggestions in

"Sophia was to be Shepherdess, with as many Sheep as the Painter could put in for Nothing."

many. The 'Squire's portrait being found united with ours was an honour too great to escape envy. Scandalous whispers began to circulate at our expense, and our tranquillity was continually disturbed by persons, who came as friends to tell us what was said of us by enemies. These reports we always resented with becoming spirit; but scandal ever improves by opposition.

We once again, therefore, entered into a consultation upon obviating the malice of our enemies, and at last came to a resolution which had too much cunning to give me entire satisfaction. It was this: as our principal object was to discover the honour of Mr. Thornhill's addresses, my wife undertook to sound him, by pretending to ask his advice in the choice of a husband for her eldest daughter. If this was not found sufficient to induce him to a declaration, it was then resolved to terrify him with a rival. To this last step, however, I would by no means give my consent, till Olivia gave me the most solemn assurances that she would marry the person provided to rival him upon this occasion, if he did not prevent it by taking her himself. Such was the scheme laid, which, though I did not strenuously oppose, I did not entirely approve.

The next time, therefore, that Mr. Thornhill came to see us, my girls took care to be out of the way, in order to give their mamma an opportunity of putting her scheme in execution; but they only retired to the next room, from whence

they could overhear the whole conversation. My
wife artfully introduced it, by observing that one
of the Miss Flamboroughs was like to have a very
good match of it in Mr. Spanker. To this the
'Squire assenting, she proceeded to remark, that
they who had warm fortunes were always sure of
getting good husbands: "But Heaven help,"
continued she, "the girls that have none! What
signifies beauty, Mr. Thornhill? or what signifies
all the virtue, and all the qualifications in the
world, in this age of self-interest? It is not, What
is she? but, What has she? is all the cry."

"Madam," returned he, "I highly approve the
justice, as well as the novelty, of your remarks;
and if I were a king, it should be otherwise. It
should then, indeed, be fine times with the girls
without fortunes: our two young ladies should be
the first for whom I would provide."

"Ah, Sir," returned my wife, "you are pleased
to be facetious: but I wish I were a queen, and
then I know where my eldest daughter should
look for a husband. But, now that you have put
it into my head, seriously, Mr. Thornhill, can't
you recommend me a proper husband for her!
She is now nineteen years old, well grown, and
well educated, and, in my humble opinion, does
not want for parts."

"Madam," replied he, "if I were to choose, I
would find out a person possessed of every accomplishment that can make an angel happy. One
with prudence, fortune, taste, and sincerity;
such, madam, would be, in my opinion, the pro-

per husband."—"Ay, Sir," said she, "but do you know of any such person?"—"No, madam," returned he, "it is impossible to know any person that deserves to be her husband: she's too great a treasure for one man's possession; she's a goddess! Upon my soul, I speak what I think—she's an angel!"—"Ah, Mr. Thornhill, you only flatter my poor girl: but we have been thinking of marrying her to one of your tenants, whose mother is lately dead, and who wants a manager; you know whom I mean, —farmer Williams; a warm man, Mr. Thornhill, able to give her good bread, and who has several times made her proposals" (which was actually the case); "but, Sir," concluded she, "I should be glad to have your approbation of our choice." "How, madam," replied he, "my approbation! —my approbation of such a choice! Never. What! sacrifice so much beauty, and sense, and goodness, to a creature insensible of the blessing! Excuse me, I can never approve of such a piece of injustice. And I have my reasons."—"Indeed, Sir," cried Deborah, "if you have your reasons, that's another affair; but I should be glad to know those reasons."—"Excuse me, madam," returned he, "they lie too deep for discovery" (laying his hand upon his bosom); "they remain buried, riveted here."

After he was gone, upon a general consultation, we could not tell what to make of these fine sentiments. Olivia considered them as instances of the most exalted passion; but I was not quite so sanguine : it seemed to me pretty plain, that they had more of love than matrimony in them ; yet, whatever they might portend, it was resolved to prosecute the scheme of farmer Williams, who, from my daughter's first appearance in the country, had paid her his addresses.

CHAPTER XVII

SCARCELY ANY VIRTUE FOUND TO RESIST THE
POWER OF LONG AND PLEASING TEMPTATION

As I only studied my child's real happiness, the
assiduity of Mr. Williams pleased me, as he was
in easy circumstances, prudent, and sincere. It
required but very little encouragement to revive
his former passion; so that in an evening or two
he and Mr. Thornhill met at our house, and sur-
veyed each other for some time with looks of
anger; but Williams owed his landlord no rent,
and little regarded his indignation. Olivia, on her
side, acted the coquette to perfection, if that might
be called acting which was her real character,
pretending to lavish all her tenderness on her
new lover. Mr. Thornhill appeared quite dejected
at this preference, and with a pensive air took
leave, though I own it puzzled me to find him
in so much pain as he appeared to be, when he
had it in his power so easily to remove the cause,
by declaring an honourable passion. But whatever uneasiness he seemed to endure, it could
easily be perceived that Olivia's anguish was still
greater. After any of these interviews between
her lovers, of which there were several, she
usually retired to solitude, and there indulged her
grief. It was in such a situation I found her one
evening, after she had been for some time sup-

porting a fictitious gaiety. "You now see, my child," said I, "that your confidence in Mr. Thornhill's passion was all a dream: he permits the rivalry of another, every way his inferior, though he knows it lies in his power to secure you to himself by a candid declaration."—"Yes, papa," returned she; "but he has his reasons for this delay: I know he has. The sincerity of his looks and words convinces me of his real esteem. A short time, I hope, will discover the generosity of his sentiments, and convince you that my opinion of him has been more just than yours." —"Olivia, my darling," returned I, "every scheme that has been hitherto pursued to compel him to a declaration has been proposed and planned by yourself; nor can you in the least say that I have constrained you. But you must not suppose, my dear, that I will ever be instrumental in suffering his honest rival to be the dupe of your ill-placed passion. Whatever time you require to bring your fancied admirer to an explanation shall be granted; but at the expiration of that term, if he is still regardless, I must absolutely insist that honest Mr. Williams shall be rewarded for his fidelity. The character which I have hitherto supported in life demands this from me, and my tenderness as a parent shall never influence my integrity as a man. Name, then, your day; let it be as distant as you think proper; and in the meantime, take care to let Mr. Thornhill know the exact time on which I design delivering you up to another. If he really loves you, his own good sense will readily suggest that there is but one method alone to prevent his losing you for ever.'' This proposal, which she could not avoid considering as perfectly just, was readily agreed to. She again renewed her most positive promise of marrying Mr. Williams, in case of the other's insensibility; and at the next opportunity, in Mr. Thornhill's presence, that day month was fixed upon for her nuptials with his rival.

Such vigorous proceedings seemed to redouble Mr. Thornhill's anxiety: but what Olivia really felt gave me some uneasiness. In this struggle between prudence and passion, her vivacity quite forsook her, and every opportunity of solitude was sought, and spent in tears. One week passed away; but Mr. Thornhill made no efforts to restrain her nuptials. The succeeding week he was still assiduous; but not more open. On the third he discontinued his visits entirely, and instead of my daughter testifying any impatience, as I expected, she seemed to retain a pensive tranquillity, which I looked upon as resignation. For my own part, I was now sincerely pleased with thinking that my child was going to be secured in a continuance of competence and peace, and frequently applauded her resolution in preferring happiness to ostentation.

It was within about four days of her intended nuptials, that my little family at night were gathered round a charming fire, telling stories of the past, and laying schemes for the future: busied in forming a thousand projects, and laugh-

ing at whatever folly came uppermost. "Well,
Moses," cried I, "we shall soon, my boy, have
a wedding in the family: what is your opinion of
matters and things in general?"—"My opinion,
father, is, that all things go on very well: and I
was just now thinking, that when sister Livy is
married to farmer Williams, we shall then have
the loan of his cider-press and brewing-tubs for
nothing."—"That we shall, Moses," cried I,
"and he will sing us *Death and the Lady,* to raise
our spirits into the bargain."—"He has taught
that song to our Dick," cried Moses; "and I
think he goes through it very prettily."—"Does
he so?" cried I, "then let us have it: where's
little Dick? let him up with it boldly."—"My
brother Dick," cried Bill, my youngest, "is just
gone out with sister Livy: but Mr. Williams has
taught me two songs, and I'll sing them for you,
papa. Which song do you choose, *The Dying
Swan,* or the *Elegy on the Death of a Mad Dog?*"
—"The elegy, child, by all means," said I; "I
never heard that yet: and Deborah, my life,
grief, you know, is dry; let us have a bottle of the
best gooseberry wine, to keep up our spirits. I
have wept so much at all sorts of elegies of late,
that without an enlivening glass I am sure this
will overcome me; and Sophy, love, take your
guitar, and thrum in with the boy a little."

AN ELEGY ON THE DEATH OF A MAD DOG

Good people all, of every sort,
  Give ear unto my song,
And if you find it wondrous short,
  It cannot hold you long.

In Islington there was a man,
  Of whom the world might say,
That still a godly race he ran,
  Whene'er he went to pray.

A kind and gentle heart he had,
  To comfort friends and foes;
The naked every day he clad,
  When he put on his clothes.

And in that town a dog was found,
  As many dogs there be,
Both mongrel, puppy, whelp, and hound,
  And curs of low degree.

This dog and man at first were friends;
  But when a pique began,
The dog, to gain some private ends,
  Went mad, and bit the man.

Around from all the neighbouring streets
  The wond'ring neighbours ran,
And swore the dog had lost his wits,
  To bite so good a man.

The wound it seemed both sore and sad
  To every Christian eye;
And while they swore the dog was mad,
  They swore the man would die.

But soon a wonder came to light,
  That showed the rogues they lied:
The man recovered of the bite—
  The dog it was that died.

"A very good boy, Bill, upon my word; and an elegy that may truly be called tragical. Come, my children, here's Bill's health, and may he one day be a bishop!"

"With all my heart," cried my wife; "and if he but preaches as well as he sings, I make no doubt of him. The most of his family, by the mother's side, could sing a good song: it was a common saying in our country, that the family of the Blenkinsops could never look straight before them, nor the Hugginsons blow out a candle; that there were none of the Grograms but could sing a song, or of the Marjorams but could tell a story."—"However that be," cried I, "the most vulgar ballad of them all generally pleases me better than the fine modern odes, and things that petrify us in a single stanza—productions that we at once detest and praise.—Put the glass to your brother, Moses.—The great fault of these elegiasts is, that they are in despair for griefs that give the sensible part of mankind very little pain. A lady loses her muff, her fan, or her lap-dog, and so the silly poet runs home to versify the disaster."

"That may be the mode," cried Moses, "in sublimer compositions: but the Ranelagh songs that come down to us are perfectly familiar, and all cast in the same mould: Colin meets Dolly, and they hold a dialogue together; he gives her a fairing to put in her hair, and she presents him with a nosegay; and then they go together to church, where they give good advice to young nymphs and swains to get married as fast as they can."

"And very good advice, too," cried I; "and I am told there is not a place in the world where advice can be given with so much propriety as there: for as it persuades us to marry, it also furnishes us with a wife; and surely that must be an excellent market, my boy, where we are told what we want, and supplied with it when wanting."

"Yes, Sir," returned Moses, "and I know but of two such markets for wives in Europe,—Ranelagh in England, and Fontarabia in Spain. The Spanish market is open once a year; but our English wives are saleable every night."

"You are right, my boy," cried his mother; "Old England is the only place in the world for husbands to get wives."—"And for wives to manage their husbands," interrupted I. "It is a proverb abroad, that if a bridge were built across the sea, all the ladies of the Continent would come over to take pattern with ours; for there are no such wives in Europe as our own. But let us have one bottle more, Deborah, my life; and, Moses, give us a good song. What thanks do we not owe to Heaven for thus bestowing tranquillity, health and competence! I think myself happier now than the greatest monarch upon earth. He has no such fireside, nor such pleasant faces about it. Yes, Deborah, we are now growing old; but the evening of our life is likely to be happy. We are descended from ancestors that knew no stain, and we shall leave a good and virtuous race of children behind us. While we live, they will be our support and our pleasure here: and when we die, they will transmit our honour untainted to posterity. Come, my son, we wait for a song: let us have a chorus. But where is my darling Olivia? that little cherub's voice is always sweetest in the concert."

Just as I spoke Dick came running in. "O papa, papa, she is gone from us, she is gone from us; my sister Livy is gone from us for ever!"—"Gone, child!"—"Yes, she is gone off with two gentlemen in a post-chaise, and one of them kissed her, and said he would die for her: and she cried very much, and was for coming back; but he persuaded her again, and she went into the chaise, and said, 'Oh, what will my poor papa do when he knows I am undone!'"—"Now, then," cried I, "my children, go and be miserable; for we shall never enjoy one hour more. And oh, may Heaven's everlasting fury light upon him and his!—thus to rob me of my child! And sure it will, for taking back my sweet innocent that I was leading up to Heaven. Such sincerity as my child was possessed of! But all our earthly happiness is now over! Go, my children, go and be miserable and infamous; for my heart is broken within me!"—"Father," cried my son, "is this your fortitude?"—"Fortitude, child? yes, he shall see I have fortitude! Bring me my pistols. I'll pursue the traitor—while he is on earth I'll pursue him. Old as I am, he shall find I can sting

him yet. The villain, the perfidious villain!" I
had by this time reached down my pistols, when
my poor wife, whose passions were not so strong
as mine, caught me in her arms. "My dearest,
dearest husband!" cried she, "the Bible is the
only weapon that is fit for your old hands now.
Open that, my love, and read our anguish into
patience, for she has vilely deceived us."—
"Indeed, Sir," resumed my son, after a pause,
"your rage is too violent and unbecoming. You
should be my mother's comforter, and you increase her pain. It ill suited you and your
reverend character thus to curse your greatest
enemy: you should not have cursed him, villain
as he is."—"I did not curse him, child, did I?"
—"Indeed, Sir, you did; you cursed him
twice."—"Then may Heaven forgive me and him
if I did! And now, my son, I see it was more
than human benevolence that first taught us to
bless our enemies: Blessed he His holy name for
all the good He hath given, and for all that He
hath taken away. But it is not—it is not a small
distress that can wring tears from these old eyes,
that have not wept for so many years. My child!
to undo my darling!—May confusion seize——
Heaven forgive me! what am I about to say!—
You may remember, my love, how good she was,
and how charming: till this vile moment all her
care was to make us happy. Had she but died!
But she is gone, the honour of our family contaminated, and I must look out for happiness in
other worlds than here. But, my child, you saw

them go off: perhaps he forced her away? If he forced her, she may yet be innocent."—"Ah, no, Sir," cried the child; "he only kissed her, and called her his angel, and she wept very much, and leaned upon his arm, and they drove off very fast."—"She's an ungrateful creature," cried my wife, who could scarcely speak for weeping, "to use us thus. She never had the least constraint put upon her affections. The vile strumpet has basely deserted her parents without any provocation, thus to bring your grey hairs to the grave; and I must shortly follow."

In this manner that night, the first of our real misfortunes, was spent in the bitterness of complaint, and ill-supported sallies of enthusiasm. I determined, however, to find out our betrayer, wherever he was, and reproach his baseness. The next morning we missed our wretched child at breakfast, where she used to give life and cheerfulness to us all. My wife, as before, attempted to ease her heart by reproaches. "Never," cried she, "shall that vilest stain of our family again darken these harmless doors. I will never call her daughter more. No, let the strumpet live with her vile seducer: she may bring us to shame, but she shall never more deceive us."

"Wife," said I, "do not talk thus hardly: my detestation of her guilt is as great as yours; but ever shall this house and this heart be open to a poor returning repentant sinner. The sooner she returns from her transgressions, the more welcome shall she be to me. For the first time the very best may err ; art may persuade, and novelty spread out its charm. The first fault is the child of simplicity, but every other, the offspring of guilt. Yes, the wretched creature shall be welcome to this heart and this house, though stained with ten thousand vices. I will again hearken to the music of her voice, again will I hang fondly on her bosom, if I find but repentance there. My son, bring hither my Bible and my staff: I will pursue her, wherever she is ; and though I cannot save her from shame, I may prevent the continuance of iniquity.''

CHAPTER XVIII

THE PURSUIT OF A FATHER TO RECLAIM A LOST CHILD TO VIRTUE

THOUGH the child could not describe the gentleman's person who handed his sister into the post-chaise, yet my suspicions fell entirely upon our young landlord, whose character for such intrigues was but too well known. I therefore directed my steps towards Thornhill Castle, resolving to upbraid him, and, if possible, to bring back my daughter: but before I had reached his seat, I was met by one of my parishioners, who said he saw a young lady resembling my daughter in a post-chaise with a gentleman, whom by the description I could only guess to be Mr. Burchell, and that they drove very fast. This information, however, did by no means satisfy me. I therefore went to the young 'Squire's, and, though it was yet early, insisted upon seeing him immediately. He soon appeared with the most open familiar air, and seemed perfectly amazed at my daughter's elopement, protesting, upon his honour, that he was quite a stranger to it. I now therefore condemned my former suspicions, and could turn them only on Mr. Burchell, who, I recollected, had of late several private conferences with her; but the appearance of another witness left me no room to doubt his villainy, who averred, that he and my daughter were actually gone towards the Wells, about thirty miles off, where there was a great deal of company.

Being driven to that state of mind in which we are all more ready to act precipitately than to reason right, I never debated with myself whether these accounts might not have been given by persons purposely placed in my way to mislead me, but resolved to pursue my daughter and her fancied deluder thither. I walked along with earnestness, and inquired of several by the way; but received no accounts, till entering the town, I was met by a person on horseback, whom I remembered to have seen at the 'Squire's, and he assured me that if I followed them to the races, which were about thirty miles farther, I might depend upon overtaking them; for he had seen them dance there the night before, and the whole assembly seemed charmed with my daughter's performance. Early the next day, I walked forward to the races, and about four in the afternoon I came upon the course. The company made a very brilliant appearance, all earnestly employed in one pursuit,—that of pleasure; how different from mine,—that of reclaiming a lost child to virtue! I thought I perceived Mr. Burchell at some distance from me; but, as if he dreaded an interview, upon my approaching him he mixed among a crowd, and I saw him no more.

I now reflected that it would be to no purpose to

continue my pursuit farther, and resolved to
return home to an innocent family, who wanted
my assistance. But the agitations of my mind,
and the fatigues I had undergone, threw me into
a fever, the symptoms of which I perceived before
I came off the course. This was another unexpected stroke, as I was more than seventy miles
distant from home: however, I retired to a little
ale-house by the road-side; and in this place, the
usual retreat of indigence and frugality, I laid me
down patiently to wait the issue of my disorder. I
languished here for near three weeks; but at last
my constitution prevailed, though I was unpro-
vided with money to defray the expenses of my
entertainment. It is possible the anxiety from this
last circumstance alone might have brought on a
relapse, had I not been supplied by a traveller,
who stopped to take a cursory refreshment. This
person was no other than the philanthropic book-
seller in St. Paul's Churchyard, who has written
so many little books for children: he called himself their friend, but he was the friend of all mankind. He was no sooner alighted, but he was in
haste to be gone; for he was ever on business of
the utmost importance, and was at that time
actually compiling materials for the history of
one Mr. Thomas Trip. I immediately recollected
this good-natured man's red pimpled face; for he
had published for me against the Deuterogamists
of the age; from him I borrowed a few pieces, to
be paid at my return. Leaving the inn, therefore,
as I was yet but weak, I resolved to return home

by easy journey of ten miles a day. My health
and usual tranquillity were almost restored, and
I now condemned that pride which had made me
refractory to the hand of correction. Man little
knows what calamities are beyond his patience to
bear, till he tries them: as in ascending the
heights of ambition, which look bright from
below, every step we rise shows us some new and
gloomy prospect of hidden disappointment: so in
our descent from the summits of pleasure, though
the vale of misery below may appear at first dark
and gloomy, yet the busy mind, still attentive to
its own amusement, finds, as we descend, something to flatter and to please. Still as we approach,
the darkest objects appear to brighten, and the
mental eye becomes adapted to its gloomy situation.

I now proceeded forward, and had walked
about two hours, when I perceived what appeared
at a distance like a waggon, which I was resolved
to overtake: but when I came up with it, found
it to be a strolling company's cart, that was carrying their scenes and other theatrical furniture to
the next village, where they were to exhibit. The
cart was attended only by the person who drove
it, and one of the company, as the rest of the
players were to follow the ensuing day. "Good
company upon the road," says the proverb, "is
the shortest cut." I therefore entered into conversation with the poor player; and as I once had
some theatrical powers myself, I dissertated on
such topics with my usual freedom; but as I was

pretty much unacquainted with the present state
of the stage, I demanded who were the present
theatrical writers in vogue—who the Drydens
and Otways of the day?—"I fancy, Sir," cried
the player, "few of our modern dramatists would
think themselves much honoured by being compared to the writers you mention. Dryden and
Rowe's manners, Sir, are quite out of fashion:
our taste has gone back a whole century;
Fletcher, Ben Jonson, and all the plays of
Shakespeare are the only things that go
down."—"How," cried I, "is it possible the
present age can be pleased with that antiquated
dialect, that obsolete humour, those overcharged
characters, which abound in the works you mention?"—"Sir," returned my companion, "the
public think nothing about dialect, or humour,
or character, for that is none of their business;
they only go to be amused, and find themselves
happy when they can enjoy a pantomime,
under the sanction of Jonson's or Shakespeare's
name."—"So then I suppose," cried I,"
"that our modern dramatists are rather imitators
of Shakespeare than of nature."—"To say the
truth," returned my companion, "I don't know
that they imitate anything at all; nor, indeed,
does the public require it of them; it is not the
composition of the piece, but the number of starts
and attitudes that may be introduced into it, that
elicits applause. I have known a piece, with not
one jest in the whole, shrugged into popularity,
and another saved by the poet's throwing in a

fit of the gripes. No, Sir, the works of Congreve
and Farquhar have too much wit in them for the
present taste; our modern dialect is much more
natural.''

By this time, the equipage of the strolling
company was arrived at the village, which, it
seems, had been apprised of our approach, and
was come out to gaze at us; for my companion
observed, that strollers always have more spectators without doors than within. I did not
consider the impropriety of my being in such
company, till I saw a mob gather about me. I
therefore took shelter, as fast as possible, in the
first ale-house that offered; and being shown into
the common room, was accosted by a well-dressed
gentleman, who demanded whether I was the real
chaplain of the company, or whether it was only
to be my masquerade character in the play?
Upon informing him of the truth, and that I did
not belong, in any sort, to the company, he was
condescending enough to desire me and the
player to partake in a bowl of punch, over which
he discussed modern politics with great earnestness and interest. I set him down, in my own mind,
for nothing less than a parliament-man at least;
but was almost confirmed in my conjectures,
when, upon asking what there was in the house
for supper, he insisted that the player and I should
sup with him at his house; with which request,
after some entreaties, we were prevailed on to
comply.

CHAPTER XIX

THE DESCRIPTION OF A PERSON DISCONTENTED WITH THE PRESENT GOVERNMENT, AND APPREHENSIVE OF THE LOSS OF OUR LIBERTIES

THE house where we were to be entertained lying at a small distance from the village, our inviter observed, that as the coach was not ready, he would conduct us on foot; and we soon arrived at one of the most magnificent mansions I had seen in that part of the country. The apartment into which we were shown was perfectly elegant and modern: he went to give orders for supper, while the player, with a wink, observed that we were perfectly in luck. Our entertainer soon returned; an elegant supper was brought in; two or three ladies in easy dishabille were introduced, and the conversation began with some sprightliness. Politics, however, were the subject on which our entertainer chiefly expatiated; for he asserted that liberty was at once his boast and his terror. After the cloth was removed, he asked me if I had seen the last *Monitor*? to which, replying in the negative, "What! nor the *Auditor*, I suppose?" cried he. "Neither, Sir," replied I. "That's strange, very strange!" replied my entertainer. "Now, I read all the politics that come out: the *Daily*, the *Public*, the *Ledger*, the *Chronicle*, the *London Evening*, the *Whitehall*

Evening, the seventeen Magazines, and the two Reviews; and, though they hate each other, I love them all. Liberty, Sir, liberty is the Briton's boast! and, by all my coal-mines in Cornwall, I reverence its guardians."—"Then, it is to be hoped," cried I, "you reverence the king?"—"Yes," returned my entertainer, "when he does what we would have him; but if he goes on as he has done of late, I'll never trouble myself more with his matters. I say nothing. I think only. I could have directed some things better. I don't think there has been a sufficient number of advisers: he should advise with every person willing to give him advice, and then we should have things done in another-guess manner."

"I wish," cried I, "that such intruding advisers were fixed in the pillory. It should be the duty of honest men to assist the weaker side of our constitution, that sacred power that has for some years been every day declining, and losing its due share of influence in the State. But these ignorants still continue the same cry of liberty, and, if they have any weight, basely throw it into the subsiding scale."

"How!" cried one of the ladies, "do I live to see one so base, so sordid, as to be an enemy to liberty, and a defender of tyrants? Liberty, that sacred gift of Heaven, that glorious privilege of Britons!"

"Can it be possible," cried our entertainer, "that there should be any found at present advocates for slavery? Any who are for meanly giving up the privileges of Britons? Can any, Sir, be so abject?"

"No, Sir," replied I, "I am for liberty! that attribute of gods! Glorious liberty! that theme of modern declamation! I would have all men kings! I would be a king myself. We have all naturally an equal right to the throne: we are all originally equal. This is my opinion, and was once the opinion of a set of honest men who were called Levellers. They tried to erect themselves into a community, where all should be equally free. But, alas! it would never answer: for there were some among them stronger, and some more cunning, than others, and these became masters of the rest: for, as sure as your groom rides your horses, because he is a cunninger animal than they, so surely will the animal that is cunninger or stronger than he, sit upon his shoulders in turn. Since, then, it is entailed upon humanity to submit, and some are born to command and others to obey, the question is, as there must be tyrants, whether it is better to have them in the same house with us, or in the same village, or, still farther off, in the metropolis. Now, Sir, for my own part, as I naturally hate the face of a tyrant, the farther off he is removed from me the better pleased am I. The generality of mankind also are of my way of thinking, and have unanimously created one king, whose election at once diminishes the number of tyrants, and puts tyranny at the greatest distance from the greatest number of people. Now the great, who were tyrants themselves before the election of one tyrant, are naturally averse to a power raised over them, and whose weight must ever lean heaviest on the subordinate orders. It is the interest of the great, therefore, to diminish kingly power as much as possible; because, whatever they take from that is naturally restored to themselves; and all they have to do in the state is to undermine the single tyrant, by which they resume their primeval authority. Now the state may be so circumstanced, or its laws may be so disposed, or its men of opulence so minded, as all to conspire in carrying on this business of undermining monarchy. For, in the first place, if the circumstances of our state be such as to favour the accumulation of wealth, and make the opulent still more rich, this will increase their ambition. An accumulation of wealth, however, must necessarily be the consequence, when, as at present, more riches flow in from external commerce than arise from internal industry; for external commerce can only be managed to advantage by the rich, and they have also at the same time all the emoluments arising from internal industry; so that the rich, with us, have two sources of wealth, whereas the poor have but one. For this reason, wealth, in all commercial states, is found to accumulate; and all such have hitherto in time become aristocratical.

"Again, the very laws also of this country

may contribute to the accumulation of wealth; as
when, by their means, the natural ties that bind
the rich and poor together are broken, and it is
ordained that the rich shall only marry with the
rich; or when the learned are held unqualified
to serve their country as counsellors, merely from
a defect of opulence, and wealth is thus made
the object of a wise man's ambition: by these
means, I say, and such means as these, riches
will accumulate. Now, the possessor of accumulated wealth, when furnished with the necessaries
and pleasures of life, has no other method to
employ the superfluity of his fortune but in
purchasing power. That is, differently speaking,
in making dependants, by purchasing the
liberty of the needy or the venal, of men who
are willing to bear the mortification of con-
tiguous tyranny for bread. Thus each very
opulent man generally gathers round him a
circle of the poorest of the people; and the polity
abounding in accumulated wealth may be compared to a Cartesian system, each orb with a
vortex of his own. Those, however, who are
willing to move in a great man's vortex, are
only such as must be slaves, the rabble of mankind, whose souls and whose education are
adapted to servitude, and who know nothing of
liberty except the name.

"But there must still be a large number of
the people without the sphere of the opulent man's
influence; namely, that order of men which sub-
sists between the very rich and the very rabble;

those men who are possessed of too large fortunes to submit to the neighbouring man in power, and yet are too poor to set up for tyranny themselves. In this middle order of mankind are generally to be found all the arts, wisdom, and virtues of society. This order alone is known to be the true preserver of freedom, and may be called THE PEOPLE. Now, it may happen that this middle order of mankind may lose all its influence in a state, and its voice be in a manner drowned in that of the rabble: for if the fortune sufficient for qualifying a person at present to give his voice in state affairs be ten times less than was judged sufficient upon forming the constitution, it is evident that great numbers of the rabble will thus be introduced into the political system, and they, ever moving in the vortex of the great, will follow where greatness shall direct. In such a state, therefore, all that the middle order has left, is to preserve the prerogative and privileges of the one principal governor with the most sacred circumspection. For he divides the power of the rich, and calls off the great from falling with tenfold weight on the middle order placed beneath them. The middle order may be compared to a town of which the opulent are forming the siege, and of which the governor from without is hastening the relief. While the besiegers are in dread of an enemy over them, it is but natural to offer the townsmen the most specious terms; to flatter them with sounds, and amuse them with privileges; but if they once defeat the governor from behind, the walls of the town will be but a small defence to its inhabitants. What they may then expect, may be seen by turning our eyes to Holland, Genoa, or Venice, where the laws govern the poor, and the rich govern the law. I am then for, and would die for, monarchy, sacred monarchy: for if there be anything sacred amongst men, it must be the anointed SOVEREIGN of his people; and every diminution of his power, in war or in peace, is an infringement upon the real liberties of the subject. The sounds of Liberty, Patriotism, and Britons, have already done much; it is to be hoped that the true sons of freedom will prevent their ever doing more. I have known many of those pretended champions for liberty in my time, yet do I not remember one that was not in his heart and in his family a tyrant."

My warmth, I found, had lengthened this harangue beyond the rules of good breeding; but the impatience of my entertainer, who often strove to interrupt it, could be restrained no longer. "What!" cried he, "then I have been all this while entertaining a Jesuit in parson's clothes! But, by all the coal-mines of Cornwall, out he shall pack, if my name be Wilkinson." I now found I had gone too far, and asked pardon for the warmth with which I had spoken. "Pardon!" returned he in a fury: "I think such principles demand ten thousand pardons. What! give up liberty, property, and as the *Gazetteer* says, lie down to be saddled with wooden shoes!

Sir, I insist upon your marching out of this house immediately, to prevent worse consequences: sir, I insist upon it." I was going to repeat my remonstrances, but just then we heard a footman's rap at the door, and the two ladies cried out, "As sure as death, there is our master and mistress come home!" It seems my entertainer was all this while only the butler, who, in his master's absence, had a mind to cut a figure, and be for a while the gentleman himself; and, to say the truth, he talked politics as well as most country gentlemen do. But nothing could now exceed my confusion upon seeing the gentleman and his lady enter; nor was their surprise, at finding such company and good cheer, less than ours. "Gentlemen," cried the real master of the house to me and my companion, "my wife and I are your most humble servants; but I protest this is so unexpected a favour, that we almost sink under the obligation." However unexpected our company might be to them, theirs, I am sure, was still more so to us, and I was struck dumb with the apprehension of my own absurdity, when whom should I next see enter the room but my dear Miss Arabella Wilmot, who was formerly designed to be married to my son George, but whose match was broken off, as already related. As soon as she saw me, she flew to my arms with the utmost joy. "My dear sir," cried she, "to what happy accident is it that we owe so unexpected a visit? I am sure my uncle and aunt will be in raptures when they find they

have the good Dr. Primrose for their guest."
Upon hearing my name, the old gentleman and
lady very politely stepped up, and welcomed me
with most cordial hospitality. Nor could they
forbear smiling, upon being informed of the
nature of my present visit: but the unfortunate butler, whom they at first seemed disposed to turn away, was at my intercession
forgiven.

Mr. Arnold and his lady, to whom the house
belonged, now insisted upon having the pleasure
of my stay for some days; and as their niece,
my charming pupil, whose mind in some measure
had been formed under my own instructions,
joined in their entreaties, I complied. That night
I was shown to a magnificent chamber; and the
next morning early Miss Wilmot desired to walk
with me in the garden, which was decorated in
the modern manner. After some time spent in
pointing out the beauties of the place, she inquired, with seeming unconcern, when last I had
heard from my son George.—"Alas! madam,"
cried I, "he has now been nearly three years
absent, without ever writing to his friends or me.
Where he is I know not; perhaps I shall never
see him or happiness more. No, my dear madam,
we shall never more see such pleasing hours as
were once spent by our fireside at Wakefield. My
little family are now dispersing very fast, and
poverty has brought not only want, but infamy
upon us." The good-natured girl let fall a tear at
this account; but as I saw her possessed of too

much sensibility, I forbore a more minute detail of our sufferings. It was, however, some consolation to me to find that time had made no alteration in her affections, and that she had rejected several matches that had been made her since our leaving her part of the country. She led me round all the extensive improvements of the place, pointing to the several walks and arbours, and at the same time catching from every object a hint for some new question relative to my son.

In this manner we spent the forenoon, till the bell summoned us in to dinner, where we found the manager of the strolling company that I mentioned before, who was come to dispose of tickets for the *Fair Penitent*, which was to be acted that evening: the part of Horatio by a young gentleman who had never appeared on any stage. He seemed to be very warm in the praises of the new performer, and averred that he never saw any who bid so fair for excellence. Acting, he observed, was not learned in a day; "but this gentleman," continued he, "seems born to tread the stage. His voice, his figure, and attitudes are all admirable. We caught him up accidentally in our journey down." This account in some measure excited our curiosity, and, at the entreaty of the ladies, I was prevailed upon to accompany them to the play-house, which was no other than a barn. As the company with which I went was incontestably the chief of the place, we were received with the greatest respect, and placed in the front seat of the theatre, where

we sat for some time with no small impatience
to see Horatio make his appearance. The new
performer advanced at last; and let parents
think of my sensations by their own, when I found
it was my unfortunate son! He was going to
begin; when, turning his eyes upon the audience,
he perceived Miss Wilmot and me, and stood at
once speechless and immovable.

The actors behind the scene, who ascribed this
pause to his natural timidity, attempted to encourage him; but instead of going on, he burst into a
flood of tears, and retired off the stage. I don't
know what were my feelings on this occasion,
for they succeeded with too much rapidity for
description; but I was soon awaked from this
disagreeable reverie by Miss Wilmot, who, pale,
and with a trembling voice, desired me to conduct her back to her uncle's. When got home,
Mr. Arnold, who was as yet a stranger to our
extraordinary behaviour, being informed that
the new performer was my son, sent his coach
and an invitation for him; and as he persisted
in his refusal to appear again upon the stage,
the players put another in his place, and we soon
had him with us. Mr. Arnold gave him the kindest
reception, and I received him with my usual
transport; for I could never counterfeit false
resentment. Miss Wilmot's reception was mixed
with seeming neglect, and yet I could perceive she
acted a studied part. The tumult in her mind
seemed not yet abated: she said twenty giddy
things that looked like joy, and then laughed loud

at her own want of meaning. At intervals she
would take a sly peep at the glass, as if happy in
the consciousness of unresisted beauty; and often
would ask questions, without giving any manner
of attention to the answers.

CHAPTER XX

AFTER we had supped, Mrs. Arnold politely offered
to send a couple of her footmen for my son's baggage, which he at first seemed to decline; but
upon her pressing the request, he was obliged
to inform her, that a stick and wallet were all the
movable things upon this earth that he could
boast of. "Why, ay, my son," cried I, "you left
me but poor, and poor I find you are come back:
and yet I make no doubt you have seen a great
deal of the world."—"Yes, Sir," replied my son,
"but travelling after Fortune is not the way to
secure her; and, indeed, of late I have desisted
from the pursuit."—"I fancy, Sir," cried Mrs.
Arnold, "that the account of your adventures
would be amusing; the first part of them I have
often heard from my niece; but could the company prevail for the rest, it would be an addi-
tional obligation."—"Madam," replied my son,
"I promise you the pleasure you have in hearing
will not be half so great as my vanity in repeating
them; yet in the whole narrative I can scarcely
promise you one adventure, as my account is
rather of what I saw than what I did. The first
misfortune of my life, which you all know, was
great; but though it distressed, it could not sink

me. No person ever had a better knack at hoping than I. The less kind I found Fortune at one time, the more I expected from her another; and being now at the bottom of her wheel, every new revolution might lift, but could not depress me. I proceeded, therefore, towards London in a fine morning, no way uneasy about to-morrow, but cheerful as the birds that carolled by the road; and comforted myself with reflecting, that London was the mart where abilities of every kind were sure of meeting distinction and reward.

"Upon my arrival in town, Sir, my first care was to deliver your letter of recommendation to our cousin, who was himself in little better circumstances than I. My first scheme, you know, Sir, was to be usher at an academy; and I asked his advice on the affair. Our cousin received the proposal with a true sardonic grin. 'Ay,' cried he, 'this is indeed a very pretty career that has been chalked out for you. I have been an usher at a boarding-school myself; and may I die by an anodyne necklace, but I had rather be an under-turnkey in Newgate. I was up early and late: I was browbeat by the master, hated for my ugly face by the mistress, worried by the boys within, and never permitted to stir out to meet civility abroad. But are you sure you are fit for a school? Let me examine you a little. Have you been bred apprentice to the business?'—'No.'—'Then you won't do for a school. Can you dress the boys' hair?'—'No.'—'Then you won't do for a school. Have you had the smallpox?' —'No.'—

'Then you won't do for a school. Can you lie three in a bed?'—'No.'—'Then you will never do for a school. Have you got a good stomach?'—'Yes.'—'Then you will by no means do for a school. No, sir: if you are for a genteel, easy profession, bind yourself seven years an apprentice to turn a cutler's wheel; but avoid a school by any means. Yet, come,' continued he, 'I see you are a lad of spirit and learning; what do you think of commencing author like me? You have read in books, no doubt, of men of genius starving at the trade. At present I'll show you forty very dull fellows about town that live by it in opulence; all honest, jog-trot men, who go on smoothly and dully, and write history and politics, and are praised—men, Sir, who, had they been bred cobblers, would all their lives have only mended shoes, but never made them.'

"Finding that there was no great degree of gentility affixed to the character of an usher, I resolved to accept his proposal; and having the highest respect for literature, hailed the *antiqua mater* of Grub Street with reverence. I thought it my glory to pursue a track which Dryden and Otway trod before me. I considered the goddess of this region as the parent of excellence; and however an intercourse with the world might give us good sense, the poverty she granted I supposed to be the nurse of genius! Big with these reflections, I sat down, and finding that the best things remained to be said on the wrong side, I resolved to write a book that should be wholly new. I therefore dressed up three paradoxes with some ingenuity. They were false, indeed, but they were new. The jewels of truth have been so often imported by others, that nothing was left for me to import but some splendid things that at a distance looked every bit as well. Witness, you powers, what fancied importance sat perched upon my quill while I was writing! The whole learned world, I made no doubt, would rise to oppose my systems; but then I was prepared to oppose the whole learned world. Like the porcupine, I sat self-collected, with a quill pointed against every opposer."

"Well said, my boy," cried I: "and what subject did you treat upon? I hope you did not pass over the importance of monogamy. But I interrupt: go on. You published your paradoxes; well, and what did the learned world say to your paradoxes?"

"Sir," replied my son, "the learned world said nothing to my paradoxes; nothing at all, Sir. Every man of them was employed in praising his friends or himself, and condemning his enemies; and unfortunately, as I had neither, I suffered the cruellest mortification—neglect.

"As I was meditating one day in a coffee-house on the fate of my paradoxes, a little man, happening to enter the room, placed himself in the box before me, and after some preliminary discourse, finding me to be a scholar, drew out a bundle of proposals, begging me to subscribe to a new edition he was going to give to the world of

Propertius, with Notes. This demand necessarily produced a reply that I had no money; and that concession led him to inquire into the nature of my expectations. Finding that my expectations were just as great as my purse—'I see,' cried he, 'you are unacquainted with the town: I'll teach you a part of it. Look at these proposals,—upon these very proposals I have subsisted very comfortably for twelve years. The moment a nobleman returns from his travels, a Creolian arrives from Jamaica, or a dowager from her country seat, I strike for a subscription. I first besiege their hearts with flattery, and then pour in my proposals at the breach. If they subscribe readily the first time, I renew my request to beg a dedication fee. If they let me have that, I smite them once more for engraving their coat-of-arms at the top. Thus,' continued he, 'I live by vanity, and laugh at it. But, between ourselves, I am now too well known; I should be glad to borrow your face a bit. A nobleman of distinction has just returned from Italy; my face is familiar to his porter; but if you bring this copy of verses, my life for it you succeed, and we divide the spoil.' "

"Bless us, George," cried I, "and is this the employment of poets now? Do men of their exalted talents thus stoop to beggary? Can they so far disgrace their calling as to make a vile traffic of praise for bread?"

"Oh no, Sir," returned he, "a true poet can never be so base; for wherever there is genius, there is pride. The creatures I now describe are only beggars in rhyme. The real poet, as he braves every hardship for fame, so he is equally a coward to contempt; and none but those who are unworthy protection, condescend to solicit it.

"Having a mind too proud to stoop to such indignities, and yet a fortune too humble to hazard a second attempt for fame, I was now obliged to take a middle course, and write for bread. But I was unqualified for a profession where mere industry alone was to ensure success. I could not suppress my lurking passion for applause; but usually consumed that time in efforts after excellence which takes up but little room, when it should have been more advantageously employed in the diffusive productions of fruitful mediocrity. My little piece would therefore come forth in the midst of periodical publications, unnoticed and unknown. The public were more importantly employed than to observe the easy simplicity of my style or the harmony of my periods. Sheet after sheet was thrown off to oblivion. My essays were buried among the essays upon liberty, Eastern tales, and cures for the bite of a mad dog; while Philautos, Philalethes, Philelutheros, and Philanthropos all wrote better, because they wrote faster than I.

" Now, therefore, I began to associate with none but disappointed authors like myself, who praised, deplored, and despised each other. The satisfaction we found in every celebrated writer's attempts was inversely as their merits.

I found that no genius in another could please me. My unfortunate paradoxes had entirely dried up that source of comfort. I could neither read nor write with satisfaction; for excellence in another was my aversion, and writing was my trade.

"In the midst of these gloomy reflections, as I was one day sitting on a bench in St James's Park, a young gentleman of distinction, who had been my intimate acquaintance at the university, approached me. We saluted each other with some hesitation; he almost ashamed of being known to one who made so shabby an appearance, and I afraid of repulse. But my suspicions soon vanished; for Ned Thornhill was at the bottom a very good-natured fellow."

"What did you say, George?" interrupted I. "Thornhill—was not that his name? It can certainly be no other than my landlord."—"Bless me," cried Mrs. Arnold, "is Mr. Thornhill so near a neighbour of yours? He has long been a friend in our family, and we expect a visit from him shortly."

"My friend's first care," continued my son, "was to alter my appearance by a very fine suit of his own clothes, and then I was admitted to his table, upon the footing of half friend, half underling. My business was to attend him at auctions, to put him in spirits when he sat for his picture, to take the left hand in his chariot when not filled by another, and to assist at tattering a kip, as the phrase was when he had a mind for a frolic. Besides this, I had twenty other little employments in the family. I was to do many small things without bidding: to carry the cork-screw; to stand godfather to all the butler's children; to sing when I was bid; to be never out of humour; always to be humble, and, if I could, to be very happy.

"In this honourable post, however, I was not without a rival. A captain of marines, who was formed for the place by nature, opposed me in my patron's affections. His mother had been a laundress to a man of quality, and thus he early acquired a taste for pimping and pedigree. As this gentleman made it the study of his life to be acquainted with lords, though he was dismissed from several for his stupidity, yet he found many of them, who were as dull as himself, that per-mitted his assiduities. As flattery was his trade, he practised it with the easiest address imagin-able; but it came awkward and stiff from me; and as every day my patron's desire of flattery increased, so every hour, being better acquainted with his defects, I became more unwilling to give it. Thus, I was once more fairly going to give the field to the captain, when my friend found occasion for my assistance. This was nothing less than to fight a duel for him with a gentle-man whose sister it was pretended he had used ill. I readily complied with this request; and though I see you are displeased at my conduct, yet, as it was a debt indispensably due to friend-ship, I could not refuse. I undertook the affair, disarmed my antagonist, and soon after had the pleasure of finding that the lady was only a woman of the town, and the fellow her bully and a sharper. This piece of service was repaid with the warmest professions of gratitude; but, as my friend was to leave town in a few days, he knew no other method of serving me but by recommending me to his uncle, Sir William Thornhill, and another nobleman of great distinction, who enjoyed a post under the government. When he was gone, my first care was to carry his recommendatory letter to his uncle, a man whose character for every virtue was universal, yet just. I was received by his servants with the most hospitable smiles; for the looks of the domestic ever transmit the master's benevolence. Being shown into a grand apartment, where Sir William soon came to me, I delivered my message and letter, which he read, and after pausing some minutes—'Pray, Sir,' cried he, 'inform me what you have done for my kinsman, to deserve this warm recommendation? But I suppose, Sir, I guess your merits: you have fought for him: and so you would expect a reward from me for being the instrument of his vices. I wish—sincerely wish—that my present refusal may be some punishment for your guilt; but still more, that it may be some inducement to your repentance.' The severity of this rebuke I bore patiently, because I knew it was just. My whole expectations now, therefore, lay in my letter to the great man.

As the doors of the nobility are almost ever beset
with beggars, all ready to thrust in some sly
petition, I found it no easy matter to gain
admittance. However, after bribing the servants
with half my worldly fortune, I was at last
shown into a spacious apartment, my letter being
previously sent up for his lordship's inspection.
During this anxious interval I had full time to
look round me. Everything was grand and of
happy contrivance; the paintings, the furniture,
the gildings, petrified me with awe, and raised my
idea of the owner. Ah, thought I to myself, how
very great must the possessor of all these things
be, who carries in his head the business of the
state, and whose house displays half the wealth
of a kingdom ! Sure his genius must be unfathom-
able ! During these awful reflections I heard a
step come heavily forward. Ah, this is the
great man himself ! No; it was only a chamber-
maid. Another foot was heard soon after. This
must be He ! No; it was only the great man's
valet-de-chambre. At last his lordship actually
made his appearance. 'Are you,' cried he, 'the
bearer of this here letter ?' I answered with a
bow. 'I learn by this,' continued he, 'as how
that ——' But just at that instant a servant
delivered him a card, and without taking further
notice, he went out of the room, and left me to
digest my own happiness at leisure. I saw no
more of him, till told by a footman that his lordship was going to his coach at the door. Down I
immediately followed, and joined my voice to

that of three or four more, who came, like me, to petition for favours. His lordship, however, went too fast for us, and was gaining his chariot door with large strides, when I hallooed out to know if I was to have any reply. He was by this time got in, and muttered an answer, half of which only I heard; the other half was lost in the rattling of his chariot wheels. I stood for some time with my neck stretched out, in the posture of one that was listening to catch the glorious sounds, till, looking round me, I found myself alone at his lordship's gate.

"My patience," continued my son, "was now quite exhausted. Stung with the thousand indignities I had met with, I was willing to cast myself away, and only wanted the gulf to receive me. I regarded myself as one of those vile things that Nature designed should be thrown by into her lumber-room, there to perish in obscurity. I had still, however, half a guinea left, and of that I thought Nature herself should not deprive me; but in order to be sure of this, I was resolved to go instantly and spend it while I had it, and then trust to occurrences for the rest. As I was going along with this resolution, it happened that Mr. Crispe's office seemed invitingly open to give me a welcome reception. In this office Mr. Crispe kindly offers all His Majesty's subjects a generous promise of £30 a year, for which promise all they give in return is their liberty for life, and permission to let him transport them to America as slaves. I was happy at finding a place where I could lose my fears in desperation, and entered this cell (for it had the appearance of one) with the devotion of a monastic. Here I found a number of poor creatures, all in circumstances like myself, expecting the arrival of Mr. Crispe, presenting a true epitome of English impatience. Each untractable soul, at variance with Fortune, wreaked her injuries on their own hearts; but Mr. Crispe at last came down, and all our murmurs were hushed. He deigned to regard me with an air of peculiar approbation, and indeed he was the first man who, for a month past, had talked to me with smiles. After a few questions, he found I was fit for everything in the world. He paused awhile upon the properest means of providing for me; and slapping his forehead as if he had found it, assured me that there was at that time an embassy talked of from the synod of Pennsylvania to the Chickasaw Indians, and that he would use his interest to get me made secretary. I knew in my own heart that the fellow lied, and yet his promise gave me pleasure, there was something so magnificent in the sound. I fairly, therefore, divided my half-guinea, one half of which went to be added to his thirty thousand pounds, and with the other half I resolved to go to the next tavern, to be there more happy than he.

"As I was going out with that resolution, I was met at the door by the captain of a ship with whom I had formerly some little acquaintance, and he agreed to be my companion over a bowl of punch. As I never chose to make a secret of

my circumstances, he assured me that I was upon
the very point of ruin, in listening to the office-
keeper's promises; for that he only designed to
sell me to the plantations. 'But,' continued he,
'I fancy you might, by a much shorter voyage,
be very easily put into a genteel way of bread.
Take my advice. My ship sails to-morrow for
Amsterdam: what if you go in her as a passen-
ger? The moment you land, all you have to do
is to teach the Dutchmen English, and I'll
warrant you'll get pupils and money enough. I
suppose you understand English,' added he, 'by
this time, or the deuce is in it.' I confidently
assured him of that; but expressed a doubt
whether the Dutch would be willing to learn
English. He affirmed, with an oath, that they
were fond of it to distraction; and upon that
affirmation I agreed with his proposal, and embarked the next day to teach the Dutch English
in Holland. The wind was fair, our voyage short;
and after having paid my passage with half my
movables, I found myself fallen as from the
skies, a stranger in one of the principal streets
of Amsterdam. In this situation I was unwilling
to let any time pass unemployed in teaching. I
addressed myself, therefore, to two or three of
those I met whose appearance seemed most
promising; but it was impossible to make ourselves mutually understood. It was not till this
very moment I recollected, that in order to teach
the Dutchmen English, it was necessary that they
should first teach me Dutch. How I came to over-

look so obvious an objection is to me amazing:
but certain it is I overlooked it.

"This scheme thus blown up, I had some
thoughts of fairly shipping back to England
again; but happening into company with an Irish
student, who was returning from Louvain, our
conversation turning upon topics of literature
(for, by the way, it may be observed that I always
forgot the meanness of my circumstances when
I could converse upon such subjects), from him
I learned that there were not two men in his whole
university who understood Greek. This amazed
me. I instantly resolved to travel to Louvain, and
there live by teaching Greek: and in this design
I was heartened by my brother student, who
threw out some hints that a fortune might be got
by it.

"I set boldly forward the next morning. Every
day lessened the burden of my movables, like
Æsop and his basket of bread; for I paid them
for my lodgings to the Dutch, as I travelled on.
When I came to Louvain, I was resolved not to
go sneaking to the lower professors, but openly
tendered my talents to the Principal himself. I
went, had admittance, and offered him my service as a master of the Greek language, which I
had been told was a desideratum in this university. The Principal seemed at first to doubt of my
abilities; but of these I offered to convince him,
by turning a part of any Greek author he should
fix upon into Latin. Finding me perfectly earnest
in my proposal, he addressed me thus: 'You see

me, young man; I never learned Greek, and I don't find that I have ever missed it. I have had a Doctor's cap and gown without Greek; I have ten thousand florins a year without Greek; I eat heartily without Greek; and, in short,' continued he, 'as I don't know Greek, I do not believe there is any good in it.'

"I was now too far from home to think of returning; so I resolved to go forward. I had some knowledge of music, with a tolerable voice, and now turned what was my amusement into a present means of subsistence. I passed among the harmless peasants of Flanders, and among such of the French as were poor enough to be very merry; for I ever found them sprightly in proportion to their wants. Whenever I approached a peasant's house towards night-fall, I played one of my most merry tunes, and that procured me not only a lodging, but subsistence for the next day. I once or twice attempted to play for the people of fashion, but they always thought my performance odious, and never re-warded me even with a trifle. This was to me the more extraordinary, as, whenever I used, in better days, to play for company, when playing was my amusement, my music never failed to throw them into raptures, and the ladies es-pecially; but as it was now my only means, it was received with contempt—a proof how ready the world is to underrate those talents by which a man is supported.

"In this manner I proceeded to Paris, with no

design but just to look about me, and then to go
forward. The people of Paris are much fonder of
strangers that have money, than those that have
wit. As I could not boast much of either, I was
no great favourite. After walking about the town
four or five days, and seeing the outsides of the
best houses, I was preparing to leave this retreat
of venal hospitality, when passing through one
of the principal streets, whom should I meet but
our cousin, to whom you first recommended me.
This meeting was very agreeable to me, and I
believe not displeasing to him. He inquired into
the nature of my journey to Paris, and informed
me of his own business there, which was to collect
pictures, medals, intaglios, and antiques of all
kinds for a gentleman in London who had just
stepped into taste and a large fortune. I was the
more surprised at seeing our cousin pitched upon
for this office, as he himself had often assured
me he knew nothing of the matter. Upon asking
how he had been taught the art of a cognoscento
so very suddenly, he assured me that nothing
was more easy. The whole secret consisted in a
strict adherence to two rules: the one, always to
observe that the picture might have been better
if the painter had taken more pains: and the
other, to praise the works of Pietro Perugino.
'But,' says he, 'as I once taught you how to be
an author in London, I'll now undertake to
instruct you in the art of picture-buying at
Paris.'

"With this proposal I very readily closed, as

it was living, and now all my ambition was to live. I went therefore to his lodgings, improved my dress by his assistance; and, after some time, accompanied him to auctions of pictures, where the English gentry were expected to be purchasers. I was not a little surprised at his intimacy with people of the best fashion, who referred themselves to his judgment upon every picture or medal, as an unerring standard of taste. He made very good use of my assistance upon these occasions; for, when asked his opinion, he would gravely take me aside and ask mine, shrug, look wise, return, and assure the company that he would give no opinion upon an affair of so much importance. Yet there was sometimes an occasion for a more supported assurance. I remember to have seen him, after giving his opinion that the colouring of a picture was not mellow enough, very deliberately take a brush with brown varnish, that was accidentally lying by, and rub it over the piece with great composure before all the company, and then asked if he had not improved the tints.

"When he had finished his commission in Paris, he left me strongly recommended to several men of distinction, as a person very proper for a travelling tutor; and after some time, I was employed in that capacity by a gentleman who brought his ward to Paris, in order to set him forward on his tour through Europe. I was to be the young gentleman's governor; but with a proviso, that he should always be permitted to govern himself. My pupil, in fact, understood the art of guiding in money concerns much better than I. He was heir to a fortune of about two hundred thousand pounds, left him by an uncle in the West Indies; and his guardians, to qualify him for the management of it, had bound him apprentice to an attorney. Thus avarice was his prevailing passion; all his questions on the road were, how money might be saved; which was the least expensive course of travel; whether anything could be bought that would turn to account when disposed of again in London? Such curiosities on the way as could be seen for nothing, he was ready enough to look at; but if the sight of them was to be paid for, he usually asserted that he had been told they were not worth seeing. He never paid a bill that he would not observe how amazingly expensive travelling was! and all this though he was not yet twenty-one. When arrived at Leghorn, as we took a walk to look at the port and shipping, he inquired the expense of the passage by sea home to England. This he was informed was but a trifle compared to his returning by land; he was therefore unable to withstand the temptation; so paying me the small part of my salary that was due, he took leave, and embarked with only one attendant for London.

"I now therefore was left once more upon the world at large; but then, it was a thing I was used to. However, my skill in music could avail me nothing in a country where every peasant was a better musician than I: but by this time I had acquired another talent, which answered my purpose as well, and this was a skill in disputation. In all the foreign universities and convents there are, upon certain days, philosophical theses maintained against every adventitious disputant; for which, if the champion opposes with any dexterity, he can claim a gratuity in money, a dinner, and a bed for one night. In this manner, therefore, I fought my way towards England; walked along from city to city; examined mankind more nearly; and, if I may so express it, saw both sides of the picture. My remarks, however, are but few: I found that monarchy was the best government for the poor to live in, and commonwealths for the rich. I found that riches in general were in every country another name for freedom; and that no man is so fond of liberty himself as not to be desirous of subjecting the will of some individuals in society to his own.

"Upon my arrival in England, I resolved to pay my respects first to you, and then to enlist as a volunteer in the first expedition that was going forward: but on my journey down, my resolutions were changed by meeting an old acquaintance, who I found belonged to a company of comedians that were going to make a summer campaign in the country. The company seemed not much to disapprove of me for an associate. They all, however, apprised me of the importance of the task at which I aimed; that the public was a many-headed monster, and that only such as had very good heads could please it;

that acting was not to be learned in a day; and that without some traditional shrugs, which had been on the stage, and only on the stage, these hundred years, I could never pretend to please. The next difficulty was in fitting me with parts, as almost every character was in keeping. I was driven for some time from one character to another, till at last Horatio was fixed upon, which the presence of the present company has happily hindered me from acting.''

CHAPTER XXI

THE SHORT CONTINUANCE OF FRIENDSHIP AMONG
THE VICIOUS, WHICH IS COEVAL ONLY WITH
MUTUAL SATISFACTION

MY son's account was too long to be delivered at
once; the first part of it was begun that night,
and he was concluding the rest after dinner the
next day, when the appearance of Mr. Thornhill's
equipage at the door seemed to make a pause in
the general satisfaction. The butler, who was now
become my friend in the family, informed me,
with a whisper, that the 'Squire had already made
some overtures to Miss Wilmot, and that her aunt
and uncle seemed highly to approve the match.
Upon Mr. Thornhill's entering, he seemed, at
seeing my son and me, to start back; but I readily
imputed that to surprise, and not displeasure.
However, upon our advancing to salute him, he
returned our greeting with the most apparent
candour; and after a short time his presence
served only to increase the general good humour.

After tea he called me aside to inquire after my
daughter; but upon my informing him that my
inquiry was unsuccessful, he seemed greatly surprised; adding that he had been since frequently
at my house in order to comfort the rest of my
family, whom he left perfectly well. He then
asked if I communicated her misfortune to Miss

Wilmot or my son; and upon my replying that I had not told them as yet, he greatly approved my prudence and precaution, desiring me by all means to keep it a secret: "For at best," cried he, "it is but divulging one's own infamy; and perhaps Miss Livy may not be so guilty as we all imagine." We were here interrupted by a servant who came to ask the 'Squire in, to stand up at country dances: so that he left me quite pleased with the interest he seemed to take in my concerns. His addresses, however, to Miss Wilmot were too obvious to be mistaken: and yet, she seemed not perfectly pleased, but bore them rather in compliance to the will of her aunt than from real inclination. I had even the satisfaction to see her lavish some kind looks upon my unfortunate son, which the other could neither extort by his fortune nor assiduity. Mr. Thornhill's seeming composure, however, not a little surprised me: we had now continued here a week at the pressing instances of Mr. Arnold; but each day the more tenderness Miss Wilmot showed my son, Mr. Thornhill's friendship seemed proportionably to increase for him.

He had formerly made us the most kind assurances of using his interest to serve the family; but now his generosity was not confined to promises alone. The morning I designed for my departure, Mr. Thornhill came to me with looks of real pleasure, to inform me of a piece of service he had done for his friend George. This was nothing less than his having procured him an ensign's commission in one of the regiments that was going to the West Indies, for which he had promised but one hundred pounds, his interest having been sufficient to get an abatement of the other two. "As for this trifling piece of service," continued the young gentleman, "I desire no other reward but the pleasure of having served my friend; and as for the hundred pounds to be paid, if you are unable to raise it yourselves, I will advance it, and you shall repay me at your leisure." This was a favour we wanted words to express our sense of; I readily, therefore, gave my bond for the money, and testified as much gratitude as if I never intended to pay.

George was to depart for town the next day, to secure his commission, in pursuance of his generous patron's directions, who judged it highly expedient to use despatch, lest in the meantime another should step in with more advantageous proposals. The next morning, therefore, our young soldier was early prepared for his departure, and seemed the only person among us that was not affected by it. Neither the fatigues and dangers he was going to encounter, nor the friends and mistress—for Miss Wilmot actually loved him—he was leaving behind, any way damped his spirits. After he had taken leave of the rest of the company, I gave him all I had, my blessing. "And now, my boy," cried I, "thou art going to fight for thy country; remember how thy brave grandfather fought for his sacred king, when loyalty among Britons was a virtue. Go, my boy, and imitate him in all but his misfortunes, if it was a misfortune to die with Lord Falkland. Go, my boy, and if you fall, though distant, exposed, and unwept by those that love you, the most precious tears are those with which Heaven bedews the unburied head of a soldier."

The next morning I took leave of the good family that had been kind enough to entertain me so long, not without several expressions of gratitude to Mr. Thornhill for his late bounty. I left them in the enjoyment of all that happiness which affluence and good breeding procure, and returned towards home, despairing of ever finding my daughter more, but sending a sigh to Heaven to spare and to forgive her.

I was now come within about twenty miles of home, having hired a horse to carry me, as I was yet but weak, and comforted myself with the hopes of soon seeing all I held dearest upon earth. But the night coming on, I put up at a little public-house by the road-side, and asked for the landlord's company over a pint of wine. We sat beside his kitchen fire, which was the best room in the house, and chatted on politics and the news of the country. We happened, among other topics, to talk of young 'Squire Thornhill, who, the host assured me, was hated as much as his uncle Sir William, who sometimes came down to the country, was loved. He went on to observe, that he made it his whole study to betray the daughters of such as received him to their houses, and, after a fortnight or three weeks' possession, turned

them out unrewarded, and abandoned to the
world. As we continued our discourse in this
manner, his wife, who had been out to get change,
returned, and perceiving that her husband was
enjoying a pleasure in which she was not a sharer,
she asked him in angry tone, what he did there?
to which he only replied, in an ironical way, by
drinking her health. "Mr. Symmonds," cried she,
"you use me very ill, and I'll bear it no longer.
Here three parts of the business is left for me to
do, and the fourth left unfinished, while you do
nothing but soak with the guests all day long;
whereas, if a spoonful of liquor were to cure me
of a fever, I never touch a drop." I now found
what she would be at, and immediately poured
her out a glass, which she received with a court-
sey; and, drinking towards my good health,
"Sir," resumed she, "it is not so much for the
value of the liquor I am angry, but one cannot
help it when the house is going out of the windows. If the customers or guests are to be dunned,
all the burden lies upon my back; he'd as lief
eat that glass as budge after them himself. There,
now, above stairs, we have a young woman who
has come to take up her lodging here, and I don't
believe she has got any money, by her over-
civility. I am certain she is very slow of payment,
and I wish she were put in mind of it."—"What
signifies minding her?" cried the host; "if she be
slow she is sure."—"I don't know that," replied
the wife; "but I know that I am sure she has been
here a fortnight, and we have not yet seen the

cross of her money."—"I suppose, my dear,"
cried he, "we shall have it all in a lump."—"In a
lump!" cried the other; "I hope we may get it
any way; and that I am resolved we will this very
night, or out she tramps, bag and baggage."
—"Consider, my dear," cried the husband, "she
is a gentlewoman, and deserves more respect."—
"As for the matter of that," returned the hostess,
"gentle or simple, out she shall pack with a
sussarara. Gentry may be good things where they
take; but, for my part, I never saw much good
of them at the sign of the Harrow."

Thus saying, she ran up a narrow flight of
stairs that went from the kitchen to a room over-
head; and I soon perceived, by the loudness of
her voice, and the bitterness of her reproaches,
that no money was to be had from her lodger.
I could hear her remonstrances very distinctly:
"Out, I say; pack out this moment! tramp, thou
infamous strumpet, or I'll give thee a mark thou
won't be the better for this three months. What!
you trumpery, to come and take up an honest
house without cross or coin to bless yourself with!
Come along I say;"—"Oh, dear madam," cried
the stranger, "pity me—pity a poor abandoned
creature, for one night, and death will soon do
the rest!" I instantly knew the voice of my poor
ruined child Olivia. I flew to her rescue, while
the woman was dragging her along by her hair,
and I caught the dear forlorn wretch in my arms.
"Welcome, any way welcome, my dearest lost one
—my treasure—to your poor old father's bosom!

"WELCOME, ANY WAY, WELCOME, MY DEAREST LOST ONE—MY
TREASURE—TO YOUR POOR OLD FATHER'S BOSOM."

Though the vicious forsake thee, there is yet one in the world that will never forsake thee; though thou hadst ten thousand crimes to answer for, he will forget them all!"—"Oh, my own dear,"— for minutes she could say no more—"my own dearest papa! Could angels be kinder? How do I deserve so much? The villain, I hate him and myself, to be a reproach to so much goodness! You can't forgive me, I know you cannot."— "Yes, my child, from my heart I do forgive thee: only repent, and we both shall yet be happy. We shall see many pleasant days yet, my Olivia."— "Ah! never, sir, never. The rest of my wretched life must be infamy abroad, and shame at home. But, alas! papa, you look much paler than you used to do. Could such a thing as I am give you so much uneasiness? Surely you have too much wisdom to take the miseries of my guilt upon yourself."—"Our wisdom, young woman," replied I.—"Ah, why so cold a name, papa?" cried she. "This is the first time you ever called me by so cold a name."—"I ask pardon, my darling," returned I; "but I was going to observe, that wisdom makes but a slow defence against trouble, though at last a sure one." The landlady now returned, to know if we did not choose a more genteel apartment; to which assenting, we were shown a room where we could converse more freely. After we had talked ourselves into some degree of tranquillity, I could not avoid desiring some account of the gradations that led her to her present wretched situation. "That villain, sir," said she, "from the first day of our meeting, made me honourable, though private proposals."

"Villain, indeed!" cried I; "and yet it in some measure surprises me how a person of Mr. Burchell's good sense and seeming honour could be guilty of such deliberate baseness, and thus step into a family to undo it."

"My dear papa," returned my daughter, "you labour under a strange mistake. Mr. Burchell never attempted to deceive me; instead of that, he took every opportunity of privately admonishing me against the artifices of Mr. Thornhill, who, I now find, was even worse than he represented him."—"Mr. Thornhill," interrupted I; "can it be?"—"Yes, Sir," returned she, "it was Mr. Thornhill who seduced me; who employed the two ladies as he called them, but who in fact were abandoned women of the town, without breeding or pity, to decoy us up to London. Their artifices, you may remember, would have certainly succeeded but for Mr. Burchell's letter, who directed those reproaches at them which we all applied to ourselves. How he came to have so much influence as to defeat their intentions still remains a secret to me; but I am convinced he was ever our warmest, sincerest friend."

"You amaze me, my dear," cried I; "but now I find my first suspicions of Mr. Thornhill's baseness were too well grounded. But he can triumph in security; for he is rich, and we are poor. But tell me, my child, sure it was no small temptation that could thus obliterate all the impressions of such an education and so virtuous a disposition as thine?"

"Indeed, Sir," replied she, "he owes all his triumph to the desire I had of making him, and not myself, happy. I knew that the ceremony of our marriage, which was privately performed by a popish priest, was in no way binding, and that I had nothing to trust to but his honour."—"What!" interrupted I, "and were you indeed married by a priest in orders?"—"Indeed, Sir, we were," replied she, "though we were both sworn to conceal his name."—"Why, then, my child, come to my arms again; and now you are a thousand times more welcome than before; for you are now his wife to all intents and purposes; nor can all the laws of man, though written upon tables of adamant, lessen the force of that sacred connection."

"Alas! papa," replied she, "you are but little acquainted with his villainies. He has been married already by the same priest to six or eight wives more, whom, like me, he has deceived and abandoned."

"Has he so?" cried I, "then we must hang the priest, and you shall inform against him to-morrow."—"But, Sir," returned she, "will that be right, when I am sworn to secrecy?"—"My dear," I replied, "if you have made such a promise, I cannot, nor will I attempt you to break it. Even though it may benefit the public, you must not inform against him. In all human insti-

tutions a smaller evil is allowed to procure a
greater good; as, in politics, a province may be
given away to secure a kingdom; in medicine, a
limb may be lopped off to preserve the body; but
in religion the law is written, and inflexible, *never*
to do evil. And this law, my child, is right; for
otherwise, if we commit a smaller evil to procure
a greater good, certain guilt would be thus incurred in expectation of contingent advantage.
And though the advantage should certainly
follow, yet the interval between commission and
advantage, which is allowed to be guilty, may be
that in which we are called away to answer for
the things we have done, and the volume of
human actions is closed for ever. But I interrupt
you, my dear; go on."

"The very next morning," continued she, "I
found what little expectation I was to have from
his sincerity. That very morning he introduced me
to two unhappy women more, whom, like me, he
had deceived, but who lived in contented prosti-
tution. I loved him too tenderly to bear such rivals
in his affections, and strove to forget my infamy
in a tumult of pleasures. With this view I danced,
dressed, and talked; but still was unhappy. The
gentlemen who visited there told me every
moment of the power of my charms, and this
only contributed to increase my melancholy, as
I had thrown all their power quite away. Thus
each day I grew more pensive, and he more insolent, till at last the monster had the assurance
to offer me to a young baronet of his acquain-

tance. Need I describe, Sir, how his ingratitude stung me? My answer to this proposal was almost madness. I desired to part. As I was going he offered me a purse: but I flung it at him with indignation, and burst from him in a rage, that for a while kept me insensible of the miseries of my situation. But I soon looked round me, and saw myself a vile, abject, guilty thing, without one friend in the world to apply to. Just in that interval, a stage coach happening to pass by, I took a place, it being my only aim to be driven at a distance from a wretch I despised and detested. I was set down here, where, since my arrival, my own anxiety and this woman's unkindness have been my only companions. The hours of pleasure that I have passed with my mamma and sister now grow painful to me. Their sorrows are much; but mine are greater than theirs, for mine are mixed with guilt and infamy."

"Have patience, my child," cried I, "and I hope things will yet be better. Take some repose to-night, and to-morrow I will carry you home to your mother and the rest of the family, from whom you will receive a kind reception. Poor woman! this has gone to her heart; but she loves you still, Olivia, and will forget it."

CHAPTER XXII

OFFENCES ARE EASILY PARDONED WHERE THERE IS
LOVE AT BOTTOM

THE next morning I took my daughter behind
me, and set out on my return home. As we
travelled along I strove, by every persuasion, to
calm her sorrows and fears, and to arm her with
resolution to bear the presence of her offended
mother. I took every opportunity, from the prospect of a fine country, through which we passed,
to observe how much kinder Heaven was to us
than we to each other; and that the misfortunes
of Nature's making were very few. I assured her,
that she should never perceive any change in my
affections, and that, during my life, which yet
might be long, she might depend upon a guardian
and an instructor. I armed her against the censure
of the world, showed her that books were sweet
unreproaching companions to the miserable, and
that, if they could not bring us to enjoy life, they
would at least teach us to endure it.

The hired horse that we rode was to be put up
that night at an inn by the way, within about five
miles from my house; and as I was willing to prepare my family for my daughter's reception, I determined to leave her that night at the inn, and to
return for her, accompanied by my daughter
Sophia, early the next morning. It was night

before we reached our appointed stage; however, after seeing her provided with a decent apartment, and having ordered the hostess to prepare proper refreshments, I kissed her, and proceeded towards home. And now my heart caught new sensations of pleasure, the nearer I approached that peaceful mansion. As a bird that had been frightened from its nest, my affections outwent my haste, and hovered round my little fireside with all the rapture of expectation. I called up the many fond things I had to say, and anticipated the welcome I was to receive. I already felt my wife's tender embrace, and smiled at the joy of my little ones. As I walked but slowly, the night waned apace. The labourers of the day were all retired to rest; the lights were out in every cottage; no sounds were heard but of the shrilling cock, and the deep-mouthed watch-dog, at hollow distance. I approached my little abode of pleasure, and, before I was within a furlong of the place, our honest mastiff came running to welcome me.

It was now near midnight that I came to knock at my door; all was still and silent; my heart dilated with unutterable happiness, when, to my amazement, I saw the house bursting out in a blaze of fire, and every aperture red with conflagration. I gave a loud convulsive outcry, and fell upon the pavement, insensible. This alarmed my son, who had, till this, been asleep; and he, perceiving the flames, instantly waked my wife and daughter; and all running out, naked, and wild with apprehension, recalled me to life with

their anguish. But it was only to objects of new
terror; for the flames had, by this time, caught
the roof of our dwelling, part after part continuing
to fall in, while the family stood, with silent
agony, looking on, as if they enjoyed the blaze.
I gazed upon them and upon it by turns, and then
looked round me for my two little ones; but they
were not to be seen. O misery! "Where," cried I,
"where are my little ones?"—"They are burnt to
death in the flames," said my wife calmly, "and
I will die with them." That moment I heard the
cry of the babes within, who were just awaked by
the fire, and nothing could have stopped me.
"Where, where are my children?" cried I, rush-
ing through the flames, and bursting the door of
the chamber in which they were confined!—
"Where are my little ones?"—"Here, dear papa,
here we are," cried they together, while the
flames were just catching the bed where they lay.
I caught them both in my arms, and snatched
them through the fire as fast as possible, while,
just as I got out, the roof sunk in. "Now," cried
I, holding up my children, "now let the flames
burn on, and all my possessions perish. Here they
are; I have saved my treasure. Here, my dearest,
here are our treasures, and we shall yet be
happy." We kissed our little darlings a thousand
times; they clasped us round the neck, and
seemed to share our transports, while their mother
laughed and wept by turns.

I now stood a calm spectator of the flames;
and, after some time, began to perceive that my

arm to the shoulder was scorched in a terrible manner. It was, therefore, out of my power to give my son any assistance, either in attempting to save our goods, or preventing the flames spreading to our corn. By this time the neighbours were alarmed, and came running to our assistance; but all they could do was to stand, like us —spectators of the calamity.

My goods, among which were the notes I had reserved for my daughters' fortunes, were entirely consumed, except a box with some papers that stood in the kitchen, and two or three things more of little consequence, which my son brought away in the beginning. The neighbours contributed, however, what they could to lighten our distress. They brought us clothes, and furnished one of our outhouses with kitchen utensils; so that by daylight we had another, though a wretched dwelling, to retire to. My honest next neighbour and his children were not the least assiduous in providing us with everything necessary, and offering whatever consolation untutored benevolence could suggest.

When the fears of my family had subsided, curiosity to know the cause of my long stay began to take place: having therefore informed them of every particular, I proceeded to prepare them for the reception of our lost one; and though we had nothing but wretchedness now to impart, I was willing to procure her a welcome to what we had. This task would have been more difficult but for our recent calamity, which had humbled my wife's pride, and blunted it by more poignant afflictions. Being unable to go for my poor child myself, as my arm grew very painful, I sent my son and daughter, who soon returned, supporting the wretched delinquent, who had not the courage to look up at her mother, whom no instructions of mine could persuade to a perfect reconciliation; for women have a much stronger sense of female error than men. "Ah, madam," cried her mother, "this is but a poor place you are come to after so much finery. My daughter Sophy and I can afford but little entertainment to persons who have kept company only with people of distinction. Yes, Miss Livy, your poor father and I have suffered very much of late; but I hope Heaven will forgive you." During this reception, the unhappy victim stood pale and trembling, unable to weep or to reply: but I could not continue a silent spectator of her distress; wherefore, assuming a degree of severity in my voice and manner which was ever followed with instant submission, "I entreat, woman, that my words may be now marked once for all: I have here brought you back a poor deluded wanderer; her return to duty demands the revival of our tenderness. The real hardships of life are now coming fast upon us; let us not, therefore, increase them by dissension among each other. If we live harmoniously together, we may yet be contented, as there are enough of us to shut out the censuring world and keep each other in countenance. The kindness of Heaven is promised to the penitent, and let ours be directed by the example. Heaven, we are assured, is much more pleased to view a repentant sinner, than ninety-nine persons who have supported a course of undeviating rectitude. And this is right; for that single effort by which we stop short in the down-hill path to perdition, is itself a greater exertion of virtue than an hundred acts of justice.''

CHAPTER XXIII

NONE BUT THE GUILTY CAN BE LONG AND COMPLETELY MISERABLE

SOME assiduity was now required to make our present abode as convenient as possible, and we were soon again qualified to enjoy our former serenity. Being disabled myself from assisting my son in our usual occupations, I read to my family from the few books that were saved, and particularly from such as, by amusing the imagination, contributed to ease the heart. Our good neighbours, too, came every day with the kindest condolence, and fixed a time in which they were all to assist at repairing my former dwelling. Honest Farmer Williams was not last among these visitors; but heartily offered his friendship. He would even have renewed his addresses to my daughter; but she rejected him in such a manner, as totally repressed his future solicitations. Her grief seemed formed for continuing; and she was the only person of our little society that a week did not restore to cheerfulness. She now lost that unblushing innocence which once taught her to respect herself, and to seek pleasure by pleasing. Anxiety now had taken strong possession of her mind; her beauty began to be impaired with her constitution, and neglect still more contributed to diminish it. Every tender epithet bestowed on her sister brought a pang to her heart, and a tear to her eye; and as one vice, though cured, ever plants others where it has been, so her former guilt, though driven out by repentance, left jealousy and envy behind. I strove a thousand ways to lessen her care, and even forgot my own pain in a concern for hers, collecting such amusing passages of history as a strong memory and some reading could suggest. "Our happiness, my dear," I would say, "is in the power of One who can bring it about in a thousand unforeseen ways, that mock our foresight. If example be necessary to prove this, I'll give you a story, my child, told us by a grave, though sometimes a romancing historian.

"Matilda was married very young to a Neapolitan nobleman of the first quality, and found herself a widow and a mother at the age of fifteen. As she stood one day caressing her infant son in the open window of an apartment which hung over the river Volturna, the child with a sudden spring leaped from her arms into the flood below, and disappeared in a moment. The mother, struck with instant surprise, and making an effort to save him, plunged in after; but far from being able to assist the infant, she herself with great difficulty escaped to the opposite shore, just when some French soldiers were plundering the country on that side, who immediately made her their prisoner.

"As the war was then carried on between the French and Italians with the utmost inhumanity, they were going at once to perpetrate those two extremes suggested by appetite and cruelty. This base resolution, however, was opposed by a young officer, who, though their retreat required the utmost expedition, placed her behind him, and brought her in safety to his native city. Her beauty at first caught his eye; her merit, soon after, his heart. They were married; he rose to the highest posts; they lived long together, and were happy. But the felicity of a soldier can never be called permanent; after an interval of several years, the troops which he commanded having met with a repulse, he was obliged to take shelter in the city where he had lived with his wife. Here they suffered a siege, and the city at length was taken. Few histories can produce more various instances of cruelty than those which the French and Italians at that time exercised upon each other. It was resolved by the victors, upon this occasion, to put all the French prisoners to death; but particularly the husband of the unfortunate Matilda, as he was principally instrumental in protracting the siege. Their determinations were, in general, executed almost as soon as resolved upon. The captive soldier was led forth, and the executioner with his sword stood ready, while the spectators in gloomy silence awaited the fatal blow, which was only suspended till the general who presided as judge should give the signal. It was in this interval of anguish and expectation that Matilda came to take her last farewell of her husband and deliverer, deploring her wretched situation, and the cruelty of fate, that had saved her from perishing by a premature death in the river Volturna, to be the spectator of still greater calamities. The general, who was a young man, was struck with surprise at her beauty, and pity at her distress; but with still stronger emotions when he heard her mention her former dangers. He was her son, the infant for whom she had encountered so much danger. He acknowledged her at once as his mother, and fell at her feet. The rest may be easily supposed; the captive was set free, and all the happiness that love, friendship, and duty could confer on each, were united.''

In this manner I would attempt to amuse my daughter: but she listened with divided attention; for her own misfortunes engrossed all the pity she once had for those of another, and nothing gave her ease. In company she dreaded contempt; and in solitude she only found anxiety. Such was the colour of her wretchedness, when we received certain information that Mr. Thornhill was going to be married to Miss Wilmot, for whom I always suspected he had a real passion, though he took every opportunity before me to express his contempt both of her person and fortune. This news only served to increase poor Olivia's affliction: such a flagrant breach of fidelity was more than her courage

could support. I was resolved, however, to get
more certain information, and to defeat, if
possible, the completion of his designs, by sending my son to old Mr. Wilmot's with instructions
to know the truth of the report, and to deliver
Miss Wilmot a letter, intimating Mr. Thornhill's
conduct in my family. My son went in pursuance
of my directions, and in three days returned,
assuring us of the truth of the account; but that
he had found it impossible to deliver the letter,
which he was therefore obliged to leave, as Mr.
Thornhill and Miss Wilmot were visiting round
the country. They were to be married, he said,
in a few days, having appeared together at church
the Sunday before he was there, in great splendour, the bride attended by six young ladies,
and he by as many gentlemen. Their approaching nuptials filled the whole country with
rejoicing, and they usually rode out together in
the grandest equipage that had been seen in the
country for many years. All the friends of both
families, he said, were there, particularly the
'Squire's uncle, Sir William Thornhill, who bore
so good a character. He added, that nothing but
mirth and feasting were going forward; that all
the country praised the young bride's beauty,
and the bridegroom's fine person, and that
they were immensely fond of each other;
concluding, that he could not help thinking Mr.
Thornhill one of the most happy men in the
world.

"Why, let him, if he can," returned I: "but,
88

my son, observe this bed of straw and unshelter-
ing roof; those mouldering walls and humid
floor; my wretched body thus disabled by fire,
and my children weeping round me for bread:
you have come home, my child, to all this; yet
here, even here, you see a man that would not for
a thousand worlds exchange situations. Oh, my
children, if you could but learn to commune with
your own hearts, and know what noble company you can make them, you would little regard
the elegance and splendour of the worthless.
Almost all men have been taught to call life a
passage, and themselves the travellers. The
similitude still may be improved, when we observe that the good are joyful and serene, like
travellers that are going towards home; the
wicked but by intervals happy, like travellers
that are going into exile."

My compassion for my poor daughter, over-
powered by this new disaster, interrupted what
I had further to observe. I bade her mother support her, and after a short time she recovered.
She appeared from that time more calm, and I
imagined had gained a new degree of resolution;
but appearances deceived me: for her tranquillity
was the languor of overwrought resentment. A
supply of provisions, charitably sent us by my
kind parishioners, seemed to diffuse new cheerfulness among the rest of the family, nor was I
displeased at seeing them once more sprightly and
at ease. It would have been unjust to damp their
satisfactions, merely to condole with resolute

melancholy, or to burden them with a sadness they did not feel. Thus once more the tale went round, and the song was demanded, and cheerfulness condescended to hover round our little habitation.

CHAPTER XXIV

FRESH CALAMITIES

THE next morning the sun arose with peculiar warmth for the season, so that we agreed to break-fast together on the honeysuckle bank; where, while we sat, my youngest daughter at my request joined her voice to the concert on the trees above us. It was in this place my poor Olivia first met her seducer, and every object served to recall her sadness. But that melancholy which is excited by objects of pleasure, or inspired by sounds of harmony, soothes the heart instead of corroding it. Her mother, too, upon this occasion, felt a pleasing distress, and wept, and loved her daughter as before. "Do, my pretty Olivia," cried she, "let us have that little melancholy air your papa was so fond of; your sister Sophy has already obliged us. Do, child; it will please your old father." She complied in a manner so exquisitely pathetic as moved me:

> When lovely woman stoops to folly,
>   And finds too late that men betray,
> What charm can soothe her melancholy?
>   What art can wash her guilt away?
>
> The only art her guilt to cover,
>   To hide her shame from every eye,
> To give repentance to her lover,
>   And wring his bosom, is—to die.

As she was concluding the last stanza, to which an interruption in her voice from sorrow gave peculiar softness, the appearance of Mr. Thornhill's equipage at a distance alarmed us all, but particularly increased the uneasiness of my eldest daughter, who, desirous of shunning her betrayer, returned to the house with her sister. In a few minutes he was alighted from his chariot, and making up to the place where I was still sitting, inquired after my health with his usual air of familiarity. "Sir," replied I, "your present assurance only serves to aggravate the baseness of your character; and there was a time when I would have chastised your insolence for presuming thus to appear before me. But now you are safe; for age has cooled my passions, and my calling restrains them."

"I vow, my dear Sir," returned he, "I am amazed at all this; nor can I understand what it means! I hope you don't think your daughter's late excursion with me had anything criminal in it?"

"Go," cried I, "thou art a wretch, a poor, pitiful wretch, and every way a liar: but your meanness secures you from my anger! Yet, Sir, I am descended from a family that would not have borne this!—And so, thou vile thing, to gratify a momentary passion, thou hast made one poor creature wretched for life, and polluted a family that had nothing but honour for their portion!"

"If she or you," returned he, "are resolved to

be miserable, I cannot help it. But you may still be happy; and whatever opinion you may have formed of me, you shall ever find me ready to contribute to it. We can marry her to another in a short time; and what is more, she may keep her lover beside; for I protest I shall ever continue to have a true regard for her."

I found all my passions alarmed at this new degrading proposal; for though the mind may often be calm under great injuries, little villainy can at any time get within the soul, and sting it into rage.—"Avoid my sight, thou reptile!" cried I, "nor continue to insult me with thy presence. Were my brave son at home, he would not suffer this; but I am old and disabled, and every way undone."

"I find," cried he, "you are bent upon obliging me to talk in a harsher manner than I intended. But as I have shown you what may be hoped from my friendship, it may not be improper to represent what may be the consequences of my resentment. My attorney, to whom your late bond has been transferred, threatens hard; nor do I know how to prevent the course of justice, except by paying the money myself, which, as I have been at some expenses lately previous to my intended marriage, is not so easy to be done. And then my steward talks of driving for the rent; it is certain he knows his duty; for I never trouble myself with affairs of that nature. Yet still I could wish to serve you, and even to have you and your daughter present at my marriage, which is shortly to be solemnized with Miss Wilmot; it is even the request of my charming Arabella herself, whom I hope you will not refuse."

"Mr. Thornhill," replied I, "hear me once for all: as to your marriage with any but my daughter, that I never will consent to; and though your friendship could raise me to a throne, or your resentment sink me to the grave yet would I despise both. Thou hast once woefully, irreparably deceived me. I reposed my heart upon thine honour, and have found its baseness. Never more, therefore, expect friendship from me. Go, and possess what fortune has given thee—beauty, riches, health, and pleasure. Go, and leave me to want, infamy, disease, and sorrow. Yet, humbled as I am, shall my heart still vindicate its dignity; and though thou hast my forgiveness, thou shalt ever have my contempt."

"If so," returned he, "depend upon it you shall feel the effects of this insolence; and we shall shortly see which is the fittest object of scorn, you or me."—Upon which he departed abruptly.

My wife and son, who were present at this interview, seemed terrified with apprehension. My daughters also, finding that he was gone, came out to be informed of the result of our conference, which, when known, alarmed them not less than the rest. But as to myself, I disregarded the utmost stretch of his malevolence: he had already struck the blow, and now I stood prepared to repel every new effort, like one of those instruments used in the art of war, which, however thrown, still presents a point to receive the enemy.

We soon, however, found that he had not threatened in vain; for the very next morning his steward came to demand my annual rent, which, by the train of accidents already related, I was unable to pay. The consequence of my incapacity was his driving my cattle that evening, and their being appraised and sold the next day for less than half their value. My wife and children now therefore entreated me to comply upon any terms, rather than incur certain destruction. They even begged of me to admit his visits once more, and used all their little eloquence to paint the calamities I was going to endure,—the terrors of a prison in so rigorous a season as the present, with the danger that threatened my health from the late accident that happened by the fire. But I continued inflexible.

"Why, my treasures," cried I, "why will you thus attempt to persuade me to the thing that is not right? My duty has taught me to forgive him; but my conscience will not permit me to approve. Would you have me applaud to the world what my heart must internally condemn? Would you have me tamely sit down and flatter our infamous betrayer; and, to avoid a prison, continually suffer the more galling bonds of mental confinement? No, never! If we are to be taken from this abode, only let us hold to the right; and wherever we are thrown, we can still

88*

retire to a charming apartment, when we can look round our own hearts with intrepidity and with pleasure !''

In this manner we spent that evening. Early the next morning, as the snow had fallen in great abundance in the night, my son was employed in clearing it away, and opening a passage before the door. He had not been thus engaged long, when he came running in, with looks all pale, to tell us that two strangers, whom he knew to be officers of justice, were making towards the house.

Just as he spoke they came in, and approaching the bed where I lay, after previously informing me of their employment and business, made me their prisoner, bidding me prepare to go with them to the county gaol, which was eleven miles off.

"My friends," said I, "this is severe weather in which you have come to take me to a prison ; and it is particularly unfortunate at this time, as one of my arms has lately been burnt in a terrible manner, and it has thrown me into a slight fever, and I want clothes to cover me, and I am now too weak and old to walk far in such deep snow ; but, if it must be so——"

I then turned to my wife and children, and directed them to get together what few things were left us, and to prepare immediately for leaving this place. I entreated them to be expeditious ; and desired my son to assist his eldest sister, who, from a consciousness that she was the cause of all our calamities, was fallen, and had lost anguish in insensibility. I encouraged my wife, who, pale and trembling, clasped our affrighted little ones in her arms, that clung to her bosom in silence, dreading to look round at the strangers. In the meantime my youngest daughter prepared for our departure, and as she received several hints to use despatch, in about an hour we were ready to depart.

CHAPTER XXV

WE set forward from this peaceful neighbourhood and walked on slowly. My eldest daughter being enfeebled by a slow fever, which had begun for some days to undermine her constitution, one of the officers who had an horse kindly took her behind him; for even these men cannot entirely divest themselves of humanity. My son led one of the little ones by the hand, and my wife the other, while I leaned upon my youngest girl, whose tears fell, not for her own, but my distresses.

We were now got from my late dwelling about two miles, when we saw a crowd running and shouting behind us, consisting of about fifty of my poorest parishioners. These, with dreadful imprecations, soon seized upon the two officers of justice, and swearing they would never see their minister go to gaol while they had a drop of blood to shed in his defence, were going to use them with great severity. The consequence might have been fatal, had I not immediately interposed, and with some difficulty rescued the officers from the hands of the enraged multitude. My children, who looked upon my delivery now as certain, appeared transported with joy, and were incapable of containing their raptures. But they were soon undeceived, upon hearing me address the poor deluded people, who came, as they imagined, to do me service.

"What! my friends," cried I, "and is this the way you love me? Is this the manner you obey the instructions I have given you from the pulpit? Thus to fly in the face of justice, and bring down ruin on yourselves and me? Which is your ringleader? Show me the man that has thus seduced you. As sure as he lives he shall feel my resentment. Alas! my dear deluded flock, return back to the duty you owe to God, to your country and to me. I shall yet perhaps one day see you in greater felicity here, and contribute to make your lives more happy. But, let it at least be my comfort, when I pen my fold for immortality, that not one here shall be wanting."

They now seemed all repentance, and melting into tears, came one after the other to bid me farewell. I shook each tenderly by the hand, and leaving them my blessing, proceeded forward without meeting any further interruption. Some hours before night, we reached the town, or rather village, for it consisted but of a few mean houses, having lost all its former opulence, and retaining no marks of its ancient superiority but the gaol.

Upon entering we put up at an inn, where we had such refreshments as could most readily be procured, and I supped with my family with my usual cheerfulness. After seeing them properly accommodated for that night, I next attended the sheriff's officers to the prison, which had formerly been built for the purposes of war, and consisted of one large apartment, strongly grated and paved with stone, common to both felons and debtors at certain hours in the four-and-twenty. Besides this, every prisoner had a separate cell, where he was locked in for the night.

I expected, upon my entrance, to find nothing but lamentations and various sounds of misery: but it was very different. The prisoners seemed all employed in one common design, that of forgetting thought in merriment or clamour. I was apprised of the usual perquisites required upon these occasions, and immediately complied with the demand, though the little money I had was very near being all exhausted. This was immediately sent away for liquor, and the whole prison was soon filled with riot, laughter, and profaneness.

"How," cried I to myself, "shall men so very wicked be cheerful, and shall I be melancholy? I feel only the same confinement with them, and I think I have more reason to be happy."

With such reflections I laboured to become cheerful; but cheerfulness was never yet produced by effort, which is itself painful. As I was sitting, therefore, in a corner of the gaol, in a pensive posture, one of my fellow-prisoners came up, and, sitting by me, entered into conversation. It was my constant rule in life never to avoid the conversation of any man who seemed to desire it; for if good, I might profit by his instruction; if bad, he might be assisted by mine. I found this to be a knowing man, of strong unlettered sense, but a thorough knowledge of the world, as it is called, or more properly speaking, of human nature on the wrong side. He asked me if I had taken care to provide myself with a bed, which was a circumstance I had never once attended to.

"That's unfortunate," cried he, "as you are allowed here nothing but straw, and your apartment is very large and cold. However, you seem to be something of a gentleman, and, as I have been one myself in my time, part of my bedclothes are heartily at your service."

I thanked him, professing my surprise at finding such humanity in a gaol in misfortunes; adding, to let him see that I was a scholar, "That the sage ancient seemed to understand the value of company in affliction, when he said, *Ton kosmon aire, ei dos ton etairon;* and, in fact," continued I, "what is the world if it affords only solitude?"

"You talk of the world, Sir," returned my fellow-prisoner; "the world is in its dotage: and yet the cosmogony or creation of the world has puzzled the philosophers of every age. What a medley of opinions have they not broached upon the creation of the world! Sanchoniathon, Manetho, Berosus, and Ocellus Lucanus, have all attempted it in vain. The latter has these words, *Anarchon ara kai atelutaion to pan,* which implies——" "I ask pardon, Sir," cried I, "for interrupting so much learning: but I think I have heard all this before. Have I not had the pleasure of once seeing you at Wellbridge fair, and is not your name Ephraim Jenkinson?" At this demand he only sighed. "I suppose you must recollect," resumed I, "one Doctor Primrose, from whom you bought a horse?"

He now at once recollected me; for the gloominess of the place and the approaching night had prevented his distinguishing my features before. "Yes, Sir," returned Mr. Jenkinson, "I remember you perfectly well; I bought a horse, but forgot to pay for him. Your neighbour Flamborough is the only prosecutor I am any way afraid of at the next assizes; for he intends to swear positively against me as a coiner. I am heartily sorry Sir, I ever deceived you, or indeed any man; for you see," continued he, showing his shackles, "what my tricks have brought me to."

"Well, Sir," replied I, "your kindness in offering me assistance when you could expect no return, shall be repaid with my endeavours to soften or totally suppress Mr. Flamborough's evidence, and I will send my son to him for that purpose the first opportunity; nor do I in the least doubt but he will comply with my request; and as to my own evidence, you need be under no uneasiness about that."

"Well, Sir," cried he, "all the return I can make shall be yours. You shall have more than half my bed-clothes to-night, and I'll take care

to stand your friend in the prison, where I think
I have some influence."

I thanked him, and could not avoid being
surprised at the present youthful change in his
aspect; for at the time I had seen him before, he
appeared at least sixty. "Sir," answered he,
"you are little acquainted with the world; I had
at that time, false hair, and have learnt the art
of counterfeiting every age from seventeen to
seventy. Ah, Sir! had I but bestowed half the
pains in learning a trade that I have in learning
to be a scoundrel, I might have been a rich man
at this day. But, rogue as I am, still I may be
your friend, and that, perhaps, when you least
expect it."

We were now prevented from further conversation by the arrival of the gaoler's servants, who
came to call over the prisoners' names, and lock
up for the night. A fellow also, with a bundle of
straw for my bed, attended, who led me along
a dark narrow passage, into a room paved like
the common prison, and in one corner of this
I spread my bed, and the clothes given me by
my fellow-prisoner; which done, my conductor,
who was civil enough, bade me a good night.
After my usual meditations, and having praised
my heavenly corrector, I laid myself down, and
slept with the utmost tranquillity till morning.

CHAPTER XXVI

A REFORMATION IN THE GAOL. TO MAKE LAWS COMPLETE THEY SHOULD REWARD AS WELL AS PUNISH

THE next morning early I was awakened by my family, whom I found in tears at my bedside. The gloomy strength of everything about us, it seems, had daunted them. I gently rebuked their sorrow, assuring them I had never slept with greater tranquillity; and next inquired after my eldest daughter, who was not among them. They informed me that yesterday's uneasiness and fatigue had increased her fever, and it was judged proper to leave her behind. My next care was to send my son to procure a room or two to lodge the family in, as near the prison as conveniently could be found. He obeyed; but could only find one apartment, which was hired at a small expense for his mother and sisters, the gaoler, with humanity, consenting to let him and his two little brothers lie in the prison with me. A bed was therefore prepared for them in a corner of the room, which I thought answered very conveniently. I was willing, however, previously to know whether my little children chose to lie in a place which seemed to fright them upon entrance.

"Well," cried I, "my good boys, how do you

like your bed? I hope you are not afraid to lie in this room, dark as it appears?"

"No, papa," says Dick, "I am not afraid to lie anywhere, where you are."

"And I," says Bill, who was yet but four years old, "love every place best that my papa is in."

After this I allotted to each of the family what they were to do. My daughter was particularly directed to watch her declining sister's health; my wife was to attend me; my little boys were to read to me: "And as for you, my son," continued I, "it is by the labour of your hands we must all hope to be supported. Your wages as a day-labourer will be fully sufficient, with proper frugality, to maintain us all, and comfortably too. Thou art now sixteen years old, and hast strength; and it was given thee, my son, for very useful purposes; for it must save from famine your helpless parents and family. Prepare then, this evening, to look out for work against to-morrow, and bring home every night what money you earn for our support."

Having thus instructed him, and settled the rest, I walked down to the common prison, where I could enjoy more air and room. But I was not long there when the execrations, lewdness, and brutality that invaded me on every side, drove me back to my apartment again. Here I sat for some time pondering upon the strange infatuation of wretches, who, finding all mankind in open arms against them, were labouring to make themselves a future and a tremendous enemy.

Their insensibility excited my highest compassion, and blotted my own uneasiness from my mind. It even appeared a duty incumbent upon me to attempt to reclaim them. I resolved, therefore, once more to return, and, in spite of their contempt, to give them my advice, and conquer them by my perseverance. Going, therefore, among them again, I informed Mr. Jenkinson of my design, at which he laughed heartily, but communicated it to the rest. The proposal was received with the greatest good humour, as it promised to afford a new fund of entertainment to persons who had now no other resource for mirth but what could be derived from ridicule or debauchery.

I therefore read them a portion of the service with a loud, unaffected voice, and found my audience perfectly merry upon the occasion. Lewd whispers, groans of contrition burlesqued, winking and coughing, alternately excited laughter. However, I continued with my natural solemnity to read on, sensible that what I did might mend some, but could itself receive no contamination from any.

After reading, I entered upon my exhortation, which was rather calculated at first to amuse them than to reprove. I previously observed, that no other motive but their welfare could induce me to this; that I was their fellow-prisoner, and now got nothing by preaching. I was sorry, I said, to hear them so very profane; because they got nothing by it, but might lose a great deal: "For be assured, my friends," cried I,—"for you are my friends, however the world may disclaim your friendship,—though you swore twelve thousand oaths in a day, it would not put one penny in your purse. Then what signifies calling every moment upon the devil, and courting his friendship, since you find how scurvily he uses you? He has given you nothing here, you find, but a mouthful of oaths and an empty belly; and, by the best accounts I have of him, he will give you nothing that's good hereafter.

"If used ill in our dealings with one man, we naturally go elsewhere. Were it not worth your while, then, just to try how you may like the usage of another master, who gives you fair promises at least to come to him? Surely, my friends, of all stupidity in the world, his must be the greatest, who, after robbing a house, runs to the thief-takers for protection. And yet, how are you more wise? You are all seeking comfort from one that has already betrayed you, applying to a more malicious being than any thief-taker of them all; for they only decoy and then hang you; but he decoys and hangs, and what is worst of all, will not let you loose after the hangman has done."

When I had concluded, I received the compliments of my audience, some of whom came and shook me by the hand, swearing that I was a very honest fellow, and that they desired my further acquaintance. I therefore promised to

repeat my lecture next day, and actually conceived some hopes of making a reformation
here; for it had ever been my opinion, that no
man was past the hour of amendment, every
heart lying open to the shafts of reproof; if the
archer could but take a proper aim. When I had
thus satisfied my mind, I went back to my
apartment, where my wife prepared a frugal
meal, while Mr. Jenkinson begged leave to add
his dinner to ours, and partake of the pleasure,
as he was kind enough to express it, of my
conversation. He had not yet seen my family;
for as they came to my apartment by a door in
the narrow passage already described, by this
means they avoided the common prison. Jenkinson, at the first interview, therefore, seemed not
a little struck with the beauty of my youngest
daughter, which her pensive air contributed to
heighten; and my little ones did not pass
unnoticed.

"Alas, Doctor," cried he, "these children are
too handsome and too good for such a place as
this!"

"Why, Mr. Jenkinson," replied I, "thank
Heaven, my children are pretty tolerable in
morals; and if they be good, it matters little for
the rest."

"I fancy, Sir," returned my fellow-prisoner,
"that it must give you great comfort to have all
this little family about you."

"A comfort, Mr. Jenkinson!" replied I; "yes,
it is indeed a comfort, and I would not be without

them for all the world; for they can make a dungeon seem a palace. There is but one way in this life of wounding my happiness, and that is by injuring them."

"I am afraid then, Sir," cried he, "that I am in some measure culpable; for I think I see here (looking at my son Moses) one that I have injured, and by whom I wish to be forgiven."

My son immediately recollected his voice and features, though he had before seen him in disguise, and taking him by the hand, with a smile, forgave him. "Yet," continued he, "I can't help wondering at what you could see in my face, to think me a proper mark for deception."

"My dear Sir," returned the other, "it was not your face, but your white stockings, and the black ribbon in your hair, that allured me. But, no disparagement to your parts, I have deceived wiser men than you in my time; and yet, with all my tricks, the blockheads have been too many for me at last."

"I suppose," cried my son, "that the narrative of such a life as yours must be extremely instructive and amusing."

"Not much of either," returned Mr. Jenkinson. "Those relations which describe the tricks and vices only of mankind, by increasing our suspicion in life, retard our success. The traveller that distrusts every person he meets, and turns back upon the appearance of every man that looks like a robber, seldom arrives in time at his journey's end.

"Indeed, I think, from my own experience, that the knowing one is the silliest fellow under the sun. I was thought cunning from my very childhood; when but seven years old, the ladies would say that I was a perfect little man; at fourteen, I knew the world, cocked my hat, and loved the ladies; at twenty, though I was perfectly honest, yet every one thought me so cunning, that no one would trust me. Thus I was at last obliged to turn sharper in my own defence, and have lived ever since, my head throbbing with schemes to deceive, and my heart palpitating with fears of detection. I used often to laugh at your honest simple neighbour Flamborough, and, one way or another, generally cheated him once a year. Yet still the honest man went forward without suspicion, and grew rich, while I still continued tricksy and cunning, and was poor, without the consolation of being honest. However," continued he, "let me know your case, and what has brought you here; perhaps, though I have not skill to avoid a gaol myself, I may extricate my friends."

In compliance with his curiosity, I informed him of the whole train of accidents and follies that had plunged me into my present troubles, and my utter inability to get free.

After hearing my story, and pausing some minutes, he slapped his forehead, as if he had hit upon something material, and took his leave, saying, he would try what could be done.

CHAPTER XXVII

THE SAME SUBJECT CONTINUED

THE next morning I communicated to my wife
and children the scheme I had planned of re-
forming the prisoners, which they received with
universal disapprobation, alleging the impossi-
bility and impropriety of it; adding that my endeavours would no way contribute to their
amendment, but might probably disgrace my
calling.

"Excuse me," returned I; "these people,
however fallen, are still men; and that is a very
good title to my affections. Good counsel rejected
returns to enrich the giver's bosom; and though
the instruction I communicate may not mend
them, yet it will assuredly mend myself. If these
wretches, my children, were princes, there would
be thousands ready to offer their ministry; but
in my opinion, the heart that is buried in a
dungeon is as precious as that seated upon a
throne. Yes, my treasures, if I can mend them,
I will: perhaps they will not all despise me.
Perhaps I may catch up even one from the gulf,
and that will be great gain; for is there upon
earth a gem so precious as the human soul?"

Thus saying, I left them, and descended to the
common prison, where I found the prisoners very
merry expecting my arrival; and each prepared

with some gaol trick to play upon the Doctor. Thus, as I was going to begin, one turned my wig awry, as if by accident, and then asked my pardon. A second, who stood at some distance, had a knack of spitting through his teeth, which fell in showers on my book. A third would cry Amen in such an affected tone as gave the rest great delight. A fourth had slyly picked my pocket of my spectacles. But there was one whose trick gave more universal pleasure than all the rest; for, observing the manner in which I had disposed my books on the table before me, he very dexterously displaced one of them, and put an obscene jest-book of his own in the place. However, I took no notice of all that this mischievous group of little beings could do, but went on, perfectly sensible that what was ridiculous in my attempt would excite mirth only the first or second time, while what was serious would be permanent. My design succeeded, and in less than six days some were penitent, and all attentive.

It was now that I applauded my perseverance and address, at thus giving sensibility to wretches divested of every moral feeling, and now began to think of doing them temporal services also, by rendering their situation somewhat more comfortable. Their time had hitherto been divided between famine and excess, tumultuous riot and bitter repining. Their only employment was quarrelling among each other, playing at cribbage, and cutting tobacco-stoppers. From this last mode of idle industry I took the hint of setting such as chose to work at cutting pegs for tobacconists and shoemakers, the proper wood being bought by a general subscription, and, when manufactured, sold by my appointment; so that each earned something every day—a trifle indeed, but sufficient to maintain him.

I did not stop here, but instituted fines for the punishment of immorality, and rewards for peculiar industry. Thus in less than a fortnight I had formed them into something social and humane, and had the pleasure of regarding myself as a legislator, who had brought men from their native ferocity into friendship and obedience.

And it were highly to be wished, that legislative power would thus direct the law rather to reformation than severity; that it would seem convinced that the work of eradicating crimes is not by making punishment familiar, but formidable. Then, instead of our present prisons, which find or make men guilty, which enclose wretches for the commission of one crime, and return them, if returned alive, fitted for the perpetration of thousands; we should see, as in other parts of Europe, places of penitence and solitude, where the accused might be attended by such as could give them repentance, if guilty, or new motives to virtue, if innocent. And this, but not the increasing punishments, is the way to mend a state. Nor can I avoid even questioning the validity of that right which social combinations have assumed, of capitally punishing offences of a slight nature. In cases of murder, their right is

obvious, as it is the duty of us all, from the law
of self-defence, to cut off that man who has shown
a disregard for the life of another. Against such,
all nature rises in arms; but it is not so against
him who steals my property. Natural law gives
me no right to take away his life, as, by that,
the horse he steals is as much his property as
mine. If, then, I have any right, it must be from
a compact made between us, that he who deprives
the other of his horse shall die. But this is a false
compact; because no man has a right to barter
his life no more than to take it away, as it is not
his own. And besides, the compact is inadequate,
and would be set aside, even in a court of modern
equity, as there is a great penalty for a very
trifling convenience, since it is far better that two
men should live than that one man should ride.
But a compact that is false between two men, is
equally so between a hundred or a hundred
thousand; for as ten millions of circles can never
make a square, so the united voice of myriads
cannot lend the smallest foundation to falsehood.
It is thus that reason speaks, and untutored nature
says the same thing. Savages, that are directed
by natural law alone, are very tender of the lives
of each other; they seldom shed blood but to
retaliate former cruelty.

Our Saxon ancestors, fierce as they were in war,
had but few executions in times of peace; and,
in all commencing governments that have the
print of nature still strong upon them, scarce any
crime is held capital.

It is among the citizens of a refined community that penal laws, which are in the hands of the rich, are laid upon the poor. Government, while it grows older, seems to acquire the moroseness of age, and, as if our property were become dearer in proportion as it increased—as if the more enormous our wealth the more extensive our fears—all our possessions are paled up with new edicts every day, and hung round with gibbets to scare every invader.

I cannot tell whether it is from the number of our penal laws, or the licentiousness of our people, that this country should show more convicts in a year than half the dominions of Europe united. Perhaps it is owing to both; for they mutually produce each other. When, by indiscriminate penal laws, a nation beholds the same punishment affixed to dissimilar degrees of guilt, from perceiving no distinction in the penalty, the people are led to lose all sense of distinction in the crime, and this distinction is the bulwark of all morality; thus the multitude of laws produce new vices, and new vices call for fresh restraints.

It were to be wished, then, that power, instead of contriving new laws to punish vice; instead of drawing hard the cords of society till a convulsion come to burst them; instead of cutting away wretches as useless before we have tried their utility; instead of converting correction into vengeance,—it were to be wished that we tried the restrictive arts of government, and made law the protector, but not the tyrant of the people. We should then find that creatures, whose souls are held as dross, only wanted the hand of a refiner: we should then find that wretches, now stuck up for long tortures, lest luxury should feel a momentary pang, might, if properly treated, serve to sinew the state in times of danger; that as their faces are like ours, their hearts are so too; that few minds are so base as that perseverance cannot amend; that a man may see his last crime without dying for it; and that very little blood will serve to cement our security.

CHAPTER XXVIII

HAPPINESS AND MISERY RATHER THE RESULT OF
PRUDENCE THAN OF VIRTUE IN THIS LIFE.
TEMPORAL EVILS OR FELICITIES BEING RE-
GARDED BY HEAVEN AS THINGS MERELY IN
THEMSELVES TRIFLING, AND UNWORTHY ITS
CARE IN THE DISTRIBUTION

I HAD now been confined more than a fortnight,
but had not since my arrival been visited by my
dear Olivia, and I greatly longed to see her.
Having communicated my wishes to my wife, the
next morning the poor girl entered my apartment, leaning on her sister's arm. The change
which I saw in her countenance struck me. The
numberless graces that once resided there were
now fled, and the hand of death seemed to have
moulded every feature to alarm me. Her temples
were sunk, her forehead was tense, and a fatal
paleness sat upon her cheek.

"I am glad to see thee, my dear," cried I;
"but why this dejection, Livy? I hope, my love,
you have too great a regard for me to permit
disappointment thus to undermine a life which I
prize as my own. Be cheerful, child, and we may
yet see happier days."

"You have ever, Sir," replied she, "been kind
to me, and it adds to my pain that I shall never
have an opportunity of sharing that happiness

89   257

you promise. Happiness, I fear, is no longer reserved for me here; and I long to be rid of a place where I have only found distress. Indeed, Sir, I wish you would make a proper submission to Mr. Thornhill; it may in some measure induce him to pity you, and it will give me relief in dying."

"Never, child," replied I; "never will I be brought to acknowledge my daughter a prostitute; for though the world may look upon your offence with scorn, let it be mine to regard it as a mark of credulity, not of guilt. My dear, I am no way miserable in this place, however dismal it may seem; and be assured, that while you continue to bless me by living, he shall never have my consent to make you more wretched by marrying another."

After the departure of my daughter, my fellow-prisoner, who was by at this interview, sensibly enough expostulated on my obstinacy in refusing a submission which promised to give me freedom. He observed that the rest of my family was not to be sacrificed to the peace of one child alone, and she the only one who had offended me. "Besides," added he, "I don't know if it be just thus to obstruct the union of man and wife, which you do at present, by refusing to consent to a match you cannot hinder, but may render unhappy."

"Sir," replied I, "you are unacquainted with the man that oppresses us. I am very sensible that no submission I can make could procure me liberty even for an hour. I am told that even in this very room a debtor of his, no later than last year, died for want. But though my submission and approbation could transfer me from hence to the most beautiful apartment he is possessed of, yet I would grant neither, as something whispers me that it would be giving a sanction to adultery. While my daughter lives, no other marriage of his shall ever be legal in my eye. Were she removed, indeed, I should be the basest of men, from any resentment of my own, to attempt putting asunder those who wish for a union. No, villain as he is, I should then wish him married, to prevent the consequences of his future debaucheries. But now, should I not be the most cruel of all fathers, to sign an instrument which must send my child to the grave, merely to avoid a prison myself; and thus, to escape one pang, break my child's heart with a thousand?''

He acquiesced in the justice of this answer, but could not avoid observing, that he feared my daughter's life was already too much wasted to keep me long a prisoner. ''However,'' continued he, ''though you refuse to submit to the nephew, I hope you have no objections to laying your case before the uncle, who has the first character in the kingdom for everything that is just and good. I would advise you to send him a letter by the post, intimating all his nephew's ill-usage; and my life for it, that in three days you shall have an answer.'' I thanked him for the hint, and instantly set about complying; but I wanted paper, and unluckily all our money had been laid out that morning in provisions: however, he supplied me.

For the three ensuing days I was in a state of anxiety to know what reception my letter might meet with; but in the meantime was frequently solicited by my wife to submit to any conditions rather than remain here, and every hour received repeated accounts of the decline of my daughter's health. The third day and the fourth arrived, but I received no answer to my letter: the complaints of a stranger against a favourite nephew were no way likely to succeed; so that these hopes soon vanished like all my former. My mind, however, still supported itself, though confinement and bad air began to make a visible alteration in my health, and my arm that had suffered in the fire grew worse. My children, however, sat by me, and while I was stretched on my straw, read to me by turns, or listened and wept at my instructions. But my daughter's health declined faster than mine: every message from her contributed to increase my apprehensions and pain. The fifth morning after I had written the letter which was sent to Sir William Thornhill, I was alarmed with an account that she was speechless. Now it was that confinement was truly painful to me; my soul was bursting from its prison to be near the pillow of my child, to comfort, to strengthen her, to receive her last wishes, and teach her soul the way to Heaven! Another account came: she was expiring, and I was debarred the small comfort of weeping by her. My fellow-prisoner, some time

after, came with the last account. He bade me be
patient: she was dead !——The next morning he
returned, and found me with my two little ones,
now my only companions, who were using all
their innocent efforts to comfort me. They entreated to read to me, and bade me not to cry,
for I was now too old to weep. "And is not my
sister an angel now, papa?" cried the eldest;
"and why, then, are you sorry for her? I wish I
were an angel out of this frightful place, if my
papa were with me."—"Yes," added my
youngest darling, "Heaven, where my sister is,
is a finer place than this, and there are none but
good people there, and the people here are very
bad."

Mr. Jenkinson interrupted their harmless prattle
by observing, that, now my daughter was no
more, I should seriously think of the rest of my
family, and attempt to save my own life, which
was every day declining for want of necessaries
and wholesome air. He added, that it was now
incumbent on me to sacrifice any pride or resentment of my own to the welfare of those who
depended on me for support; and that I was now,
both by reason and justice, obliged to try to reconcile my landlord.

"Heaven be praised," replied I, "there is no
pride left me now: I should detest my own heart
if I saw either pride or resentment lurking there.
On the contrary, as my oppressor has been once
my parishioner, I hope one day to present him
up an unpolluted soul at the eternal tribunal. No,

Sir, I have no resentment now; and though he has taken from me what I held dearer than all his treasures, though he has wrung my heart,—for I am sick almost to fainting, very sick, my fellow-prisoner,—yet that shall never inspire me with vengeance. I am now willing to approve his marriage; and, if this submission can do him any pleasure, let him know that if I have done him any injury I am sorry for it."

Mr. Jenkinson took pen and ink, and wrote down my submission nearly as I have expressed it, to which I signed my name. My son was employed to carry the letter to Mr. Thornhill, who was then at his seat in the country. He went, and, in about six hours, returned with a verbal answer. He had some difficulty, he said, to get a sight of his landlord, as the servants were insolent and suspicious: but he accidentally saw him as he was going out upon business, preparing for his marriage, which was to be in three days. He continued to inform us, that he stept up in the humblest manner, and delivered the letter, which, when Mr. Thornhill had read, he said that all submission was now too late and unnecessary; that he heard of our application to his uncle, which met with the contempt it deserved; and, as for the rest, that all future applications should be directed to his attorney, not to him. He observed, however, that as he had a very good opinion of the discretion of the two young ladies, they might have been the most agreeable intercessors.

"Well, Sir," said I to my fellow-prisoner, "you

now discover the temper of the man that oppresses me. He can at once be facetious and cruel: but, let him use me as he will, I shall soon be free, in spite of all his bolts to restrain me. I am now drawing towards an abode that looks brighter as I approach it: this expectation cheers my afflictions, and though I leave an helpless family of orphans behind me, yet they will not be utterly forsaken: some friend, perhaps, will be found to assist them for the sake of their poor father, and some may charitably relieve them for the sake of their heavenly Father."

Just as I spoke, my wife, whom I had not seen that day before, appeared with looks of terror, and making efforts, but unable, to speak. "Why, my love," cried I, "why will you thus increase my afflictions by your own? What though no submissions can turn our severe master, though he has doomed me to die in this place of wretchedness, and though we have lost a darling child, yet still you will find comfort in your other children when I shall be no more."—"We have indeed lost," returned she, "a darling child. My Sophia, my dearest, is gone; snatched from us, carried off by ruffians!"

"How, madam," cried my fellow-prisoner, "Miss Sophia carried off by villains! sure it cannot be?"

She could only answer by a fixed look, and a flood of tears. But one of the prisoners' wives who was present, and came in with her, gave us a more distinct account: she informed us, that as my

wife, my daughter, and herself were taking a
walk together on the great road, a little way out
of the village, a post-chaise and pair drove up to
them, and instantly stopped ; upon which a well-
dressed man, but not Mr. Thornhill, stepping out,
clasped my daughter round the waist, and forcing
her in, bade the postillion drive on, so that they
were out of sight in a moment.

"Now," cried I, "the sum of my miseries is
made up, nor is it in the power of anything on
earth to give me another pang. What ! not one
left !—not to leave me one !—The monster !—The
child that was next my heart !—she had the
beauty of an angel, and almost the wisdom of an
angel.—But support that woman, nor let her fall.
—Not to leave me one !"

"Alas ! my husband," said my wife, "you seem
to want comfort even more than I. Our distresses
are great, but I could bear this and more, if I saw
you but easy. They may take away my children,
and all the world, if they leave me but you."

My son, who was present, endeavoured to
moderate our grief ; he bade us take comfort, for
he hoped that we might still have reason to be
thankful. "My child," cried I, "look round the
world, and see if there be any happiness left me
now. Is not every ray of comfort shut out, while
all our bright prospects only lie beyond the
grave?"—"My dear father," returned he, "I
hope that there is still something that will give
you an interval of satisfaction ; for I have a letter
from my brother George."—"What of him,

child?" interrupted I; "does he know our misery? I hope my boy is exempt from any part of what this wretched family suffers?"—"Yes, Sir," returned he, "he is perfectly gay, cheerful, and happy. His letter brings nothing but good news; he is the favourite of his colonel, who promises to procure him the very next lieutenancy that becomes vacant."

"And are you sure of all this?" cried my wife: "are you sure that nothing ill has befallen my boy?"—"Nothing, indeed, madam," returned my son; "you shall see the letter, which will give you the highest pleasure; and if anything can procure you comfort, I am sure that will."— "But are you sure," still repeated she, "that the letter is from himself, and that he is really so happy?"—"Yes, madam," replied he, "it is certainly his, and he will one day be the credit and support of our family."—"Then, I thank Providence," cried she, "that my last letter to him has miscarried. Yes, my dear," continued she, turning to me, "I will now confess, that though the hand of Heaven is sore upon us in other instances, it has been favourable here. By the last letter I wrote my son, which was in the bitterness of anger, I desired him, upon his mother's blessing, and if he had the heart of a man, to see justice done his father and sister, and avenge our cause. But, thanks be to Him that directs all things, it has miscarried, and I am at rest."—"Woman!" cried I, "thou hast done very ill, and at another time, my reproaches might

89*

have been more severe. Oh! what a tremendous gulf hast thou escaped, that would have buried both thee and him in endless ruin; Providence, indeed, has here been kinder to us than we to ourselves. It has reserved that son to be the father and protector of my children when I shall be away. How unjustly did I complain of being stripped of every comfort, when still I hear that he is happy, and insensible of our afflictions; still kept in reserve to support his widowed mother, and to protect his brothers and sisters! But what sisters has he left? He has no sisters now: they are all gone, robbed from me, and I am undone." —"Father," interrupted my son, "I beg you will give me leave to read his letter—I know it will please you." Upon which, with my permission, he read as follows:

"HONOURED SIR,—I have called off my imagination a few moments from the pleasures that surround me, to fix it upon objects that are still more pleasing,—the dear little fireside at home. My fancy draws the harmless group, as listening to every line of this with great composure. I view those faces with delight, which never felt the deforming hand of ambition or distress! But, whatever your happiness may be at home, I am sure it will be some addition to it to hear that I am perfectly pleased with my situation, and every way happy here.

"Our regiment is countermanded, and is not to leave the kingdom. The colonel, who professes himself my friend, takes me with him to all companies where he is acquainted, and, after my first visit, I generally find myself received with increased respect upon repeating it. I danced last night with Lady G——, and could I forget you know whom, I might be perhaps successful. But it is my fate still to remember others, while I am myself forgotten by most of my absent friends; and in this number, I fear, Sir, that I must consider you; for I have long expected the pleasure of a letter from home, to no purpose. Olivia and Sophia too promised to write, but seem to have forgotten me. Tell them they are two arrant little baggages, and that I am at this moment in a most violent passion with them; yet still, I know not how, though I want to bluster a little, my heart is respondent only to softer emotions. Then tell them, Sir, that after all, I love them affectionately; and be assured of my ever remaining

Your dutiful Son.''

"In all our miseries," cried I, "what thanks have we not to return, that one at least of our family is exempted from what we suffer! Heaven be his guard, and keep my boy thus happy, to be the support of his widowed mother, and the father of these two babes, which is all the patrimony I can now bequeath him! May he keep their innocence from the temptations of want, and be their conductor in the paths of honour!" I had scarce said these words, when a noise like that of a tumult seemed to proceed from the prison below: it died away soon after, and a clanking of fetters was heard along the passage that led to my apartment. The keeper of the prison entered, holding a man all bloody, wounded, and fettered with the heaviest irons. I looked with compassion on the wretch as he approached me, but with horror, when I found it was my own son. "My George! my George! and do I behold thee thus? Wounded—fettered? Is this thy happiness? is this the manner you return to me? Oh that this sight could break my heart at once, and let me die!"

"Where, Sir, is your fortitude?" returned my son, with an intrepid voice. "I must suffer; my life is forfeited, and let them take it."

I tried to restrain my passions for a few minutes in silence, but I thought I should have died with the effort. "Oh, my boy, my heart weeps to behold thee thus, and I cannot, cannot help it. In the moment that I thought thee blest, and prayed for thy safety, to behold thee thus again! Chained—wounded; and yet the death of the youthful is happy. But I am old, a very old man, and have lived to see this day! To see my children all untimely falling about me, while I continue a wretched survivor in the midst of ruin! May all the curses that ever sunk a soul fall heavy upon the murderer of my children! May he live, like me, to see——"

"Hold, Sir," replied my son, "or I shall blush for thee. How, Sir! forgetful of your age, your holy calling, thus to arrogate the justice of

Heaven, and fling those curses upward that must soon descend to crush thy own grey head with destruction! No, Sir, let it be your care now to fit me for that vile death I must shortly suffer! to arm me with hope and resolution; to give me courage to drink of that bitterness which must shortly be my portion."

"My child, you must not die; I am sure no offence of thine can deserve so vile a punishment. My George could never be guilty of any crime to make his ancestors ashamed of him."

"Mine, Sir," returned my son, "is, I fear, an unpardonable one. When I received my mother's letter from home, I immediately came down, determined to punish the betrayer of our honour, and sent him an order to meet me, which he answered, not in person, but by despatching four of his domestics to seize me. I wounded one who first assaulted me, and I fear desperately; but the rest made me their prisoner. The coward is determined to put the law in execution against me; the proofs are undeniable; I have sent a challenge, and as I am the first transgressor upon the statute, I see no hope of pardon. But you have often charmed me with your lessons of fortitude; let me now, Sir, find them in your example."

"And, my son, you shall find them. I am now raised above this world, and all the pleasures it can produce. From this moment I break from my heart all the ties that held it down to earth, and will prepare to fit us both for eternity. Yes, my

son, I will point out the way, and my soul shall
guide yours in the ascent, for we will take our
flight together. I now see, and am convinced, you
can expect no pardon here; and I can only exhort
you to seek it at that greatest tribunal where we
both shall shortly answer. But let us not be nig-
gardly in our exhortation, but let all our fellow-
prisoners have a share. Good gaoler, let them be
permitted to stand here while I attempt to improve
them." Thus saying, I made an effort to rise
from my straw, but wanted strength, and was
able only to recline against the wall. The prisoners
assembled themselves according to my directions,
for they loved to hear my counsel: my son and
his mother supported me on either side; I looked
and saw that none were wanting, and then
addressed them with the following exhortation.

CHAPTER XXIX

THE EQUAL DEALINGS OF PROVIDENCE DEMON-
STRATED WITH REGARD TO THE HAPPY AND
THE MISERABLE HERE BELOW. THAT FROM THE
NATURE OF PLEASURE AND PAIN, THE
WRETCHED MUST BE REPAID THE BALANCE OF
THEIR SUFFERINGS IN THE LIFE HEREAFTER

"My friends, my children, and fellow-sufferers, when I reflect on the distribution of good and evil here below, I find that much has been given man to enjoy, yet still more to suffer. Though we should examine the whole world, we shall not find one man so happy as to have nothing left to wish for; but we daily see thousands who by suicide show us they have nothing left to hope. In this life, then, it appears that we cannot be entirely blest, but yet we may be completely miserable.

"Why man should thus feel pain; why our wretchedness should be requisite in the formation of universal felicity; why when all other systems are made perfect by the perfection of their subordinate parts, the great system should require for its perfection parts that are not only subordinate to others, but imperfect in themselves— these are questions that never can be explained, and might be useless if known. On this subject, Providence has thought fit to elude our curiosity, satisfied with granting us motives to consolation.

"In this situation man has called in the friendly assistance of philosophy; and Heaven, seeing the incapacity of that to console him, has given him the aid of religion. The consolations of philosophy are very amusing, but often fallacious; it tells us that life is filled with comforts, if we will but enjoy them; and, on the other hand, that though we unavoidably have miseries here, life is short, and they will soon be over. Thus do these consolations destroy each other; for, if life is a place of comfort, its shortness must be misery, and if it be long, our griefs are protracted. Thus philosophy is weak: but religion comforts in a higher strain. Man is here, it tells us, fitting up his mind, and preparing it for another abode. When the good man leaves the body, and is all a glorious mind, he will find he has been making himself a heaven of happiness here; while the wretch that has been maimed and contaminated by his vices, shrinks from his body with terror, and finds that he has anticipated the vengeance of Heaven. To religion, then, we must hold, in every circumstance of life, for our truest comfort: for if already we are happy, it is a pleasure to think that we can make that happiness unending; and if we are miserable, it is very consoling to think that there is a place of rest. Thus, to the fortunate, religion holds out a continuance of bliss; to the wretched, a change from pain.

"But though religion is very kind to all men, it has promised peculiar rewards to the unhappy: the sick, the naked, the houseless, the heavy-laden, and the prisoner, have ever most frequent promises in our sacred law. The Author of our religion everywhere professes himself the wretch's friend, and, unlike the false ones of this world, bestows all his caresses upon the forlorn. The unthinking have censured this as partiality, as a preference without merit to deserve it. But they never reflect, that it is not in the power even of Heaven itself to make the offer of unceasing felicity as great a gift to the happy as to the miserable. To the first, eternity is but a single blessing, since at most it but increases what they already possess. To the latter, it is a double advantage; for it diminishes their pain here, and rewards them with heavenly bliss hereafter.

"But Providence is in another respect kinder to the poor than to the rich, for as it thus makes the life after death more desirable, so it smooths the passage there. The wretched have had a long familiarity with every face of terror. The man of sorrows lays himself quietly down, without possessions to regret, and but few ties to stop his departure: he feels only nature's pang in the final separation, and this is no way greater than he has often fainted under before; for, after a certain degree of pain, every new breach that death opens in the constitution nature kindly covers with insensibility.

"Thus Providence has given the wretched two advantages over the happy in this life,—greater felicity in dying, and in heaven all that superiority of pleasure which arises from contrasted enjoyment. And this superiority, my friends, is no small advantage, and seems to be one of the pleasures of the poor man in the parable; for though he was already in heaven, and felt all the raptures it could give, yet it was mentioned as an addition to his happiness, that he had once been wretched, and now was comforted; that he had known what it was to be miserable, and now felt what it was to be happy.

"Thus, my friends, you see religion does what philosophy could never do: it shows the equal dealings of Heaven to the happy and the unhappy, and levels all human enjoyments to nearly the same standard. It gives to both rich and poor the same happiness hereafter, and equal hopes to aspire after it; but if the rich have the advantage of enjoying pleasure here, the poor have the end-less satisfaction of knowing what it was once to be miserable, when crowned with endless felicity hereafter; and even though this should be called a small advantage, yet, being an eternal one, it must make up by duration what the temporal happiness of the great may have exceeded by intenseness.

"These are, therefore, the consolations which the wretched have peculiar to themselves, and in which they are above the rest of mankind: in other respects, they are below them. They who would know the miseries of the poor, must see life and endure it. To declaim on the temporal advantages they enjoy, is only repeating what none either believe or practice. The men who have the necessaries of living are not poor; and they who want them must be miserable. Yes, my friends, we must be miserable. No vain efforts of a refined imagination can soothe the wants of nature, can give elastic sweetness to the dank vapour of a dungeon, or ease to the throbbings of a broken heart. Let the philosopher from his couch of softness tell us that we can resist all these: alas! the effort by which we resist them is still the greatest pain. Death is slight, and any man may sustain it; but torments are dreadful, and these no man can endure.

"To us, then, my friends, the promises of happiness in heaven should be peculiarly dear; for if our reward be in this life alone, we are then, indeed, of all men the most miserable. When I look round these gloomy walls, made to terrify as well as to confine us; this light, that only serves to show the horrors of the place; those shackles, that tyranny has imposed, or crime made neces- sary; when I survey these emaciated looks, and hear those groans—oh, my friends, what a glorious exchange would heaven be for these! To fly through regions unconfined as air—to bask in the sunshine of eternal bliss—to carol over endless hymns of praise—to have no master to threaten or insult us, but the form of Goodness himself for ever in our eyes!—when I think of these things, death becomes the messenger of very glad tidings; when I think of these things, his sharpest arrow becomes the staff of my support; when I think of these things, what is there in life worth having? when I think of these things, what is there that should not be spurned away? Kings in their palaces should groan for such advantages; but we, humbled as we are, should yearn for them.

"And shall these things be ours? Ours they will certainly be, if we but try for them; and, what is a comfort, we are shut out from many temptations that would retard our pursuit. Only let us try for them, and they will certainly be ours; and, what is still a comfort, shortly too: for if we look back on past life, it appears but a very short span, and whatever we may think of the rest of life, it will yet be found of less duration; as we grow older, the days seem to grow shorter, and our intimacy with Time ever lessens the perception of his stay. Then let us take comfort now, for we shall soon be at our journey's end; we shall soon lay down the heavy burden laid by Heaven upon us; and though death, the only friend of the wretched, for a little while mocks the weary traveller with the view, and like his horizon still flies before him; yet the time will certainly and shortly come, when we shall cease from our toil; when the luxurious great ones of the world shall no more tread us to the earth; when we shall think with pleasure of our sufferings below; when we shall be surrounded with all our friends, or such as deserved our friendship; when our bliss shall be unutterable, and still, to crown all, unending."

CHAPTER XXX

HAPPIER PROSPECTS BEGIN TO APPEAR. LET US BE
INFLEXIBLE AND FORTUNE WILL AT LAST
CHANGE IN OUR FAVOUR

WHEN I had thus finished, and my audience was
retired, the gaoler, who was one of the most
humane of his profession, hoped I would not be
displeased, as what he did was but his duty,
observing that he must be obliged to remove my
son into a stronger cell, but that he should be
permitted to revisit me every morning. I thanked
him for his clemency, and grasping my boy's
hand, bade him farewell, and be mindful of the
great duty that was before him.

I again therefore laid me down, and one of my
little ones sat by my bedside reading, when Mr.
Jenkinson entering, informed me that there was
news of my daughter; for that she was seen by
a person about two hours before in a strange
gentleman's company, and that they had stopped
at a neighbouring village for refreshment, and
seemed as if returning to town. He had scarcely
delivered this news when the gaoler came, with
looks of haste and pleasure, to inform me that
my daughter was found. Moses came running in
a moment after, crying out that his sister Sophy
was below, and coming up with our old friend
Mr. Burchell.

Just as he delivered this news, my dearest girl entered, and, with looks almost wild with pleasure, ran to kiss me, in a transport of affection. Her mother's tears and silence also showed her pleasure. "Here, papa," cried the charming girl, "here is the brave man to whom I owe my delivery; to this gentleman's intrepidity I am indebted for my happiness and safety——" A kiss from Mr. Burchell, whose pleasure seemed even greater than hers, interrupted what she was going to add.

"Ah! Mr. Burchell," cried I, "this is but a wretched habitation you now find us in; and we are now very different from what you last saw us. You were ever our friend: we have long discovered our errors with regard to you, and repented of our ingratitude. After the vile usage you then received at my hands, I am almost ashamed to behold your face; yet I hope you'll forgive me, as I was deceived by a base ungenerous wretch, who, under the mask of friendship, has undone me."

"It is impossible," cried Mr. Burchell, "that I should forgive you, as you never deserved my resentment. I partly saw your delusion then, and as it was out of my power to restrain, I could only pity it."

"It was ever my conjecture," cried I, "that your mind was noble; but now I find it so. But tell me, my dear child, how thou hast been relieved, or who the ruffians were who carried thee away?"

"Indeed, Sir," replied she, "as to the villain who carried me off, I am yet ignorant. For, as my mamma and I were walking out, he came behind us, and almost before I could call for help, forced me into the post-chaise, and in an instant the horses drove away. I met several on the road, to whom I cried out for assistance, but they disregarded my entreaties. In the meantime, the ruffian himself used every art to hinder me from crying out: he flattered and threatened by turns, and swore that, if I continued but silent, he intended no harm. In the meantime, I had broken the canvas that he had drawn up, and whom should I perceive at some distance but your old friend Mr. Burchell, walking along with his usual swiftness, with the great stick for which we used so much to ridicule him. As soon as we came within hearing, I called out to him by name, and entreated his help. I repeated my exclamations several times, upon which, with a very loud voice, he bid the postillion stop; but the boy took no notice, but drove on with still greater speed. I now thought he could never overtake us, when, in less than a minute, I saw Mr. Burchell come running up by the side of the horses, and, with one blow, knock the postillion to the ground. The horses, when he was fallen, soon stopped of themselves, and the ruffian, stepping out, with oaths and menaces, drew his sword, and ordered him, at his peril, to retire; but Mr. Burchell, running up, shivered his sword to pieces, and then pursued him for nearly a quarter of a mile; but he made his escape. I was at this time come out myself, willing to assist my deliverer; but he soon returned to me in triumph. The postillion, who was recovered, was going to make his escape too; but Mr. Burchell ordered him at his peril to mount again and drive back to town. Finding it impossible to resist, he reluctantly complied, though the wound he had received seemed, to me at least, to be dangerous. He continued to complain of the pain as we drove along, so that he at last excited Mr. Burchell's compassion, who, at my request, exchanged him for another, at an inn where we called on our return.''

"Welcome, then,'' cried I, "my child! and thou, her gallant deliverer, a thousand welcomes! Though our cheer is but wretched, yet our hearts are ready to receive you. And now, Mr. Burchell, as you have delivered my girl, if you think her a recompense, she is yours: if you can stoop to an alliance with a family so poor as mine, take her; obtain her consent,—as I know you have her heart,—and you have mine. And let me tell you, Sir, that I give you no small treasure: she has been celebrated for beauty, it is true, but that is not my meaning,—I give you up a treasure in her mind.''

"But I suppose, Sir,'' cried Mr. Burchell, "that you are apprised of my circumstances, and of my incapacity to support her as she deserves?''

"If your present objection,'' replied I, "be meant as an evasion of my offer, I desist; but I know no man so worthy to deserve her as you; and if I could give her thousands, and thousands sought her from me, yet my honest brave Burchell should be my dearest choice."

To all this his silence alone seemed to give a mortifying refusal: and, without the least reply to my offer, he demanded if he could not be furnished with refreshments from the next inn; to which being answered in the affirmative, he ordered them to send in the best dinner that could be provided upon such short notice. He bespoke also a dozen of their best wine, and some cordials for me; adding, with a smile, that he would stretch a little for once, and, though in a prison, asserted he was never better disposed to be merry. The waiter soon made his appearance with preparations for dinner; a table was lent us by the gaoler, who seemed remarkably assiduous; the wine was disposed in order, and two very well dressed dishes were brought in.

My daughter had not yet heard of her poor brother's melancholy situation, and we all seemed unwilling to damp her cheerfulness by the relation. But it was in vain that I attempted to appear cheerful: the circumstances of my unfortunate son broke through all efforts to dissemble; so that I was at last obliged to damp our mirth by relating his misfortunes, and wishing that he might be permitted to share with us in this little interval of satisfaction. After my guests were recovered from the consternation my account had produced, I requested also that Mr. Jenkinson, a

fellow-prisoner, might be admitted, and the
gaoler granted my request with an air of unusual
submission. The clanking of my son's irons was
no sooner heard along the passage, than his sister
ran impatiently to meet him, while Mr. Burchell,
in the meantime, asked me if my son's name
was George; to which replying in the affirmative, he still continued silent. As soon as my
boy entered the room, I could perceive he
regarded Mr. Burchell with a look of astonishment and reverence. "Come on," cried I, "my
son; though we are fallen very low, yet Providence has been pleased to grant us some small
relaxation from pain. Thy sister is restored to
us, and there is her deliverer: to that brave
man it is that I am indebted for yet having a
daughter: give him, my boy, the hand of friendship; he deserves our warmest gratitude."

My son seemed all this while regardless of what
I said, and still continued fixed at respectful distance. "My dear brother," cried his sister, "why
don't you thank my good deliverer? the brave
should ever love each other."

He still continued his silence and astonishment,
till our guest at last perceived himself to be known,
and, assuming all his native dignity, desired my
son to come forward. Never before had I seen
anything so truly majestic as the air he assumed
on this occasion. The greatest object in the
universe, says a certain philosopher, is a good
man struggling with adversity; yet there is still
a greater, which is the good man that comes to

relieve it. After he had regarded my son for some time with a superior air—"I again find," said he, "unthinking boy, that the same crime——" But here he was interrupted by one of the gaoler's servants, who came to inform us that a person of distinction, who had driven into town with a chariot and several attendants, sent his respects to the gentleman that was with us, and begged to know when he should think proper to be waited upon. "Bid the fellow wait," cried our guest, "till I shall have leisure to receive him;" and then turning to my son, "I again find, Sir," proceeded he, "that you are guilty of the same offence for which you once had my reproof, and for which the law is now preparing its justest punishments. You imagine, perhaps, that a contempt for your own life gives you a right to take that of another: but where, Sir, is the difference between a duellist, who hazards a life of no value, and the murderer who acts with greater security? Is it any diminution of the gamester's fraud, when he alleges that he has staked a counter?"

"Alas, Sir," cried I, "whoever you are, pity the poor misguided creature; for what he has done was in obedience to a deluded mother, who, in the bitterness of her resentment, required him, upon her blessing, to avenge her quarrel. Here, Sir, is the letter, which will serve to convince you of her imprudence, and diminish his guilt."

He took the letter, and hastily read it over. "This," says he, "though not a perfect excuse, is such a palliation of his fault as induces me to forgive him. And now, Sir," continued he, kindly taking my son by the hand, "I see you are surprised at finding me here; but I have often visited prisons upon occasions lest interesting. I am now come to see justice done a worthy man, for whom I have the most sincere esteem. I have long been a disguised spectator of thy father's benevolence. I have, at his little dwelling, enjoyed respect uncontaminated by flattery; and have received that happiness that courts could not give, from the amusing simplicity around his fireside. My nephew has been apprised of my intentions of coming here, and, I find, is arrived. It would be wronging him and you to condemn him without examination: if there be injury, there shall be redress; and this I may say, without boasting, that none have ever taxed the injustice of Sir William Thornhill."

We now found the personage whom we had so long entertained as an harmless amusing companion was no other than the celebrated Sir William Thornhill, to whose virtues and singularities scarce any were strangers. The poor Mr. Burchell was in reality a man of large fortune and great interest, to whom senates listened with applause, and whom party heard with conviction: who was the friend of his country, but loyal to his king. My poor wife, recollecting her former familiarity, seemed to shrink with apprehension; but Sophia, who a few moments before thought him her own, now perceiving the immense distance to which he was removed by fortune, was unable to conceal her tears.

"Ah! Sir," cried my wife, with a piteous aspect, "how is it possible that I can ever have your forgiveness? The slights you received from me the last time I had the honour of seeing you at our house, and the jokes which I audaciously threw out—these jokes, sir, I fear, can never be forgiven."

"My dear good lady," returned he with a smile, "if you had your joke, I had my answer: I'll leave it to all the company if mine were not as good as yours. To say the truth, I know nobody whom I am disposed to be angry with at present, but the fellow who so frighted my little girl here. I had not even time to examine the rascal's person so as to describe him in an advertisement. Can you tell me, Sophia, my dear, whether you should know him again?"

"Indeed, sir," replied she, "I can't be positive; yet now I recollect, he had a large mark over one of his eyebrows."—"I ask pardon, madam," interrupted Jenkinson, who was by, "but be so good as to inform me if the fellow wore his own red hair?"—"Yes, I think so," cried Sophia. "And did your honour," continued he, turning to Sir William, "observe the length of his legs?"—"I can't be sure of their length," cried the Baronet, "but I am convinced of their swiftness; for he outran me, which is what I thought few men in the kingdom could have done."—"Please your honour," cried Jenkinson, "I know the man: it is certainly the same: the best runner in England; he has beaten Pinwire of Newcastle: Timothy Baxter is his name; I know him perfectly, and the very place of his retreat this moment. If your honour will bid Mr. Gaoler let two of his men go with me, I'll engage to produce him to you in an hour at farthest.'' Upon this the gaoler was called, who instantly appearing, Sir William demanded if he knew him. ''Yes, please your honour,'' replied the gaoler, ''I know Sir William Thornhill well, and everybody that knows anything of him will desire to know more of him.'' ''Well, then,'' said the Baronet, ''my request is, that you will permit this man and two of your servants to go upon a message by my authority; and as I am in the commission of the peace, I undertake to secure you.''— ''Your promise is sufficient,'' replied the other, ''and you may, at a minute's warning, send them over England whenever your honour thinks fit.''

In pursuance of the gaoler's compliance, Jenkinson was despatched in search of Timothy Baxter, while we were amused with the assiduity of our youngest boy Bill, who had just come in and climbed up Sir William's neck in order to kiss him. His mother was immediately going to chastise his familiarity, but the worthy man prevented her; and taking the child, all ragged as he was, upon his knee, ''What, Bill, you chubby rogue,'' cried he, ''do you remember your old friend Burchell? and Dick, too, my honest veteran, are you here? you shall find I have not forgot you." So saying, he gave each a large piece of ginger-bread, which the poor fellows ate very heartily, as they had got that morning but a very scanty breakfast.

We now sat down to dinner, which was almost cold; but previously, my arm still continuing painful, Sir William wrote a prescription, for he had made the study of physic his amusement, and was more than moderately skilled in the profession: this being sent to an apothecary who lived in the place, my arm was dressed, and I found almost instantaneous relief. We were waited upon at dinner by the gaoler himself, who was willing to do our guest all the honour in his power. But before we had well dined, another message was brought from his nephew, desiring permission to appear in order to vindicate his innocence and honour; with which request the Baronet complied, and desired Mr. Thornhill to be introduced.

CHAPTER XXXI

FORMER BENEVOLENCE NOW REPAID WITH UNEXPECTED INTEREST

MR. THORNHILL made his appearance with a smile, which he seldom wanted, and was going to embrace his uncle, which the other repulsed with an air of disdain. "No fawning, Sir, at present," cried the Baronet, with a look of severity; "the only way to my heart is by the road of honour; but here I only see complicated instances of falsehood, cowardice, and oppression. How is it, Sir, that this poor man, for whom I know you professed a friendship, is used thus hardly? His daughter vilely seduced as a recompense for his hospitality, and he himself thrown into prison, perhaps but for resenting the insult? His son, too, whom you feared to face as a man——"

"Is it possible, Sir," interrupted his nephew, "that my uncle should object that as a crime, which his repeated instructions alone have persuaded me to avoid?"

"Your rebuke," cried Sir William, "is just; you have acted, in this instance, prudently and well, though not quite as your father would have done: my brother, indeed was the soul of honour; but thou——Yes, you have acted, in this instance, perfectly right, and it has my warmest approbation."

"And I hope," said his nephew, "that the rest of my conduct will not be found to deserve censure. I appeared, Sir, with this gentleman's daughter at some places of public amusement: thus, what was levity, scandal called by a harsher name, and it was reported I had debauched her. I waited on her father in person, willing to clear the thing to his satisfaction, and he received me only with insult and abuse. As for the rest, with regard to his being here, my attorney and steward can best inform you, as I commit the management of business entirely to them. If he has contracted debts, and is unwilling, or even unable to pay them, it is their business to proceed in this manner: and I see no hardship or injustice in pursuing the most legal means of redress."

"If this," cried Sir William, "be as you have stated it, there is nothing unpardonable in your offence; and though your conduct might have been more generous in not suffering this gentleman to be oppressed by subordinate tyranny, yet it has been at least equitable."

"He cannot contradict a single particular," replied the 'Squire; "I defy him to do so; and several of my servants are ready to attest what I say. Thus, Sir," continued he, finding that I was silent, for in fact I could not contradict him— "thus, Sir, my own innocence is vindicated: but though, at your entreaty, I am ready to forgive this gentleman every other offence, yet his attempts to lessen me in your esteem excite a resentment that I cannot govern. And this, too, at a time when his son was actually preparing to take away my life,—this, I say, was such guilt, that I am determined to let the law take its course. I have here the challenge that was sent me, and two witnesses to prove it: one of my servants has been wounded dangerously; and even though my uncle himself should dissuade me, which I know he will not, yet I will see public justice done, and he shall suffer for it."

"Thou monster!" cried my wife, "hast thou not had vengeance enough already, but must my poor boy feel thy cruelty? I hope that good Sir William will protect us; for my son is as innocent as a child: I am sure he is, and never did harm to man."

"Madam," replied the good man, "your wishes for his safety are not greater than mine; but I am sorry to find his guilt too plain; and if my nephew persists——" But the appearance of Jenkinson and the gaoler's two servants now called off our attention, who entered, hauling in a tall man, very genteely dressed, and answering the description already given of the ruffian who had carried off my daughter. "Here," cried Jenkinson, pulling him in, "here we have him; and if ever there was a candidate for Tyburn, this is one."

The moment Mr. Thornhill perceived the prisoner, and Jenkinson who had him in custody, he seemed to shrink back with terror. His face became pale with conscious guilt, and he would have withdrawn, but Jenkinson, who perceived

his design, stopped him. "What, 'Squire," cried
he, "are you ashamed of your two old acquaintances, Jenkinson and Baxter? But this is the
way that all great men forget their friends, though
I am resolved we will not forget you. Our
prisoner, please your honour," continued he,
turning to Sir William, "has already confessed
all. This is the gentleman reported to be so
dangerously wounded. He declares that it was
Mr. Thornhill who first put him upon this affair;
that he gave him the clothes he now wears, to
appear like a gentleman, and furnished him with
the post-chaise. The plan was laid between them,
that he should carry off the young lady to a
place of safety, and that there he should threaten
and terrify her; but Mr. Thornhill was to come
in, in the meantime, as if by accident, to her
rescue; and that they should fight awhile, and
then he was to run off,—by which Mr. Thornhill
would have the better opportunity of gaining her
affections himself, under the character of her
defender."

Sir William remembered the coat to have been
worn by his nephew, and all the rest the prisoner
himself confirmed by a more circumstantial
account: concluding, that Mr. Thornhill had
often declared to him that he was in love with
both sisters at the same time.

"Heavens!" cried Sir William, "what a viper
have I been fostering in my bosom! And so fond
of public justice, too, as he seemed to be! But
he shall have it; secure him, Mr. Gaoler—Yet,

hold ! I fear there is not legal evidence to detain him."

Upon this, Mr. Thornhill, with the utmost humility, entreated that two such abandoned wretches might not be admitted as evidences against him, but that his servants should be examined. "Your servants !" replied Sir William. "Wretch ! call them yours no longer : but come, let us hear what those fellows have to say ; let his butler be called."

When the butler was introduced, he soon perceived by his former master's looks that all his power was now over. "Tell me," cried Sir William, sternly, "have you ever seen your master and that fellow dressed up in his clothes, in company together ?"—"Yes, please your honour," cried the butler, "a thousand times : he was the man that always brought him his ladies." —"How !" interrupted young Mr. Thornhill, "this to my face ?" "Yes," replied the butler, "or to any man's face. To tell you a truth, Master Thornhill, I never either loved or liked you, and I don't care if I tell you now a piece of my mind."—"Now, then," cried Jenkinson, "tell his honour whether you know anything of me."—"I can't say," replied the butler, "that I know much good of you. The night that gentleman's daughter was deluded to our house, you were one of them."—"So then," cried Sir William, "I find you have brought a very fine witness to prove your innocence : thou stain to humanity ! to associate with such wretches ! But," continuing his examination, "you tell me, Mr. Butler, that this was the person who brought him this old gentleman's daughter."—"No, please your honour," replied the butler, "he did not bring her, for the 'Squire himself undertook that business; but he brought the priest that pretended to marry them."—"It is but too true," cried Jenkinson; "I cannot deny it; that was the employment assigned me, and I confess it to my confusion."

"Good heavens," exclaimed the Baronet, "how every new discovery of his villainy alarms me! All his guilt is now too plain, and I find his present prosecution was dictated by tyranny, cowardice, and revenge. At my request, Mr. Gaoler, set this young officer, now your prisoner, free, and trust to me for the consequences. I'll make it my business to set the affair in a proper light to my friend the magistrate, who has committed him. But where is the unfortunate young lady herself? Let her appear to confront this wretch: I long to know by what arts he has seduced her. Entreat her to come in. Where is she?"

"Ah! Sir," said I, "that question stings me to the heart: I was once indeed happy in a daughter, but her miseries——" Another interruption here prevented me; for who should make her appearance but Miss Arabella Wilmot, who was next day to have been married to Mr. Thornhill. Nothing could equal her surprise at seeing Sir William and his nephew here before her; for her arrival was quite accidental. It happened that she and the old gentleman, her father, were passing through the town, on the way to her aunt's, who had insisted that her nuptials with Mr. Thornhill should be consummated at her house; but stopping for refreshment, they put up at an inn at the other end of the town. It was there, from the window, that the young lady happened to observe one of my little boys playing in the street, and instantly sending a footman to bring the child to her, she learned from him some account of our misfortunes; but was still kept ignorant of young Mr. Thornhill's being the cause. Though her father made several remonstrances on the impropriety of going to a prison to visit us, yet they were ineffectual; she desired the child to conduct her, which he did, and it was thus she surprised us at a juncture so unexpected.

Nor can I go on without a reflection on those accidental meetings, which though they happen every day, seldom excite our surprise but upon some extraordinary occasion. To what a fortuitous concurrence do we not owe every pleasure and convenience of our lives! How many seeming accidents must unite before we can be clothed or fed! The peasant must be disposed to labour, shower must fall, the wind fill the merchant's sail, or numbers must want the usual supply.

We all continued silent for some moments, while my charming pupil, which was the name I generally gave this young lady, united in her looks compassion and astonishment, which gave new finishings to her beauty.—"Indeed, my dear Mr. Thornhill," cried she to the 'Squire, who she supposed was come here to succour, and not to oppress us, "I take it a little unkindly that you should come here without me, or never inform me of the situation of a family so dear to us both: you know I should take as much pleasure in contributing to the relief of my reverend old master here, whom I shall ever esteem, as you can. But I find that, like your uncle, you take a pleasure in doing good in secret."

"He find pleasure in doing good!" cried Sir William, interrupting her. "No, my dear, his pleasures are as base as he is. You see in him, madam, as complete a villain as ever disgraced humanity. A wretch, who, after having deluded this poor man's daughter, after plotting against the innocence of her sister, has thrown the father into prison, and the eldest son into fetters because he had the courage to face her betrayer. And give me leave, madam, now to congratulate you upon an escape from the embraces of such a monster."

"O goodness!" cried the lovely girl, "how have I been deceived! Mr. Thornhill informed me for certain that this gentleman's eldest son, Captain Primrose, was gone off to America with his new-married lady."

"My sweetest miss," cried my wife, "he has told you nothing but falsehood. My son George never left the kingdom, nor ever was married. Though you have forsaken him, he has always

loved you too well to think of anybody else; and
I have heard him say he would die a bachelor for
your sake." She then proceeded to expatiate
upon the sincerity of her son's passion: she set
his duel with Mr. Thornhill in a proper light; from
thence she made a rapid digression to the 'Squire's
debaucheries, his pretended marriages, and ended
with a most insulting picture of his cowardice.

"Good heavens!" cried Miss Wilmot, "how
very near have I been to the brink of ruin! But
how great is my pleasure to have escaped it! Ten
thousand falsehoods has this gentleman told me!
He had at last art enough to persuade me, that
my promise to the only man I esteemed was no
longer binding, since he had been unfaithful.
By his falsehoods I was taught to detest one
equally brave and generous!"

By this time my son was freed from the en-
cumbrances of justice, as the person supposed to
be wounded was detected to be an impostor. Mr.
Jenkinson, also, who had acted as his valet-de-
chambre, had dressed up his hair, and furnished
him with whatever was necessary to make a genteel appearance. He now therefore entered, hand-
somely dressed in his regimentals; and, without
vanity (for I am above it), he appeared as handsome a fellow as ever wore a military dress. As
he entered, he made Miss Wilmot a modest and
distant bow, for he was not as yet acquainted
with the change which the eloquence of his mother
had wrought in his favour. But no decorums
could restrain the impatience of his blushing mis-

90*

tress to be forgiven. Her tears, her looks, all contributed to discover the real sensations of her heart, for having forgotten her former promise, and having suffered herself to be deluded by an impostor. My son appeared amazed at her condescension, and could scarce believe it real.— "Sure, madam," cried he, "this is but delusion! I can never have merited this! To be blessed thus is to be too happy."—"No, sir," replied she; "I have been deceived, basely deceived, else nothing could have ever made me unjust to my promise. You know my friendship—you have long known it—but forget what I have done, and as you once had my warmest vows of constancy, you shall now have them repeated; and be assured, that, if your Arabella cannot be yours, she shall never be another's."—"And no other's you shall be," cried Sir William, "if I have any influence with your father."

This hint was sufficient for my son Moses, who immediately flew to the inn where the old gentleman was, to inform him of every circumstance that had happened. But in the meantime, the 'Squire, perceiving that he was on every side undone, now finding that no hopes were left from flattery or dissimulation, concluded that his wisest way would be to turn and face his pursuers. Thus, laying aside all shame, he appeared the open, hardy villain. "I find, then," cried he, "that I am to expect no justice here; but I am resolved it shall be done me. You shall know, Sir," turning to Sir William, "I am no longer a poor dependant upon your favours. I scorn them. Nothing can keep Miss Wilmot's fortune from me, which, I thank her father's assiduity, is pretty large. The articles, and a bond for her fortune, are signed, and safe in my possession. It was her fortune, not her person, that induced me to wish for this match; and, possessed of the one, let who will take the other."

This was an alarming blow. Sir William was sensible of the justice of his claims, for he had been instrumental in drawing up the marriage articles himself. Miss Wilmot, therefore, perceiving that her fortune was irretrievably lost, turning to my son, she asked if the loss of fortune could lessen her value to him? "Though fortune," said she, "is out of my power, at least I have my hand to give."

"And that, madam," cried her real lover, "was indeed all that you ever had to give; at least all that I ever thought worth the acceptance. And now I protest, my Arabella, by all that's happy, your want of fortune this moment increases my pleasure, as it serves to convince my sweet girl of my sincerity."

Mr. Wilmot now entering, he seemed not a little pleased at the danger his daughter had just escaped, and readily consented to a dissolution of the match. But finding that her fortune, which was secured to Mr. Thornhill by bond would not be given up, nothing could exceed his disappointment. He now saw that his money must all go to enrich one who had no fortune of his own.

He could bear his being a rascal, but to want an equivalent to his daughter's fortune was wormwood. He sat, therefore, for some minutes employed in the most mortifying speculations, till Sir William attempted to lessen his anxiety. "I must confess, Sir," cried he, "that your present disappointment does not entirely displease me. Your immoderate passion for wealth is now justly punished. But though the young lady cannot be rich, she has still a competence sufficient to give content. Here you see an honest young soldier, who is willing to take her without fortune: they have long loved each other; and for the friendship I bear his father, my interest shall not be wanting in his promotion. Leave, then, that ambition which disappoints you, and for once admit that happiness which courts your acceptance."

"Sir William," replied the old gentleman, "be assured I never yet forced her inclinations, nor will I now. If she still continues to love this young gentleman, let her have him, with all my heart. There is still, thank Heaven, some fortune left, and your promise will make it something more. Only let my old friend here" (meaning me) "give me a promise of settling six thousand pounds upon my girl if ever he should come to his fortune, and I am ready this night, to be the first to join them together."

As it now remained with me to make the young couple happy, I readily made a promise of making the settlement he required; which, to one who had such little expectations as I, was no great favour. We had now, therefore, the satisfaction of seeing them fly into each other's arms in a transport. "After all my misfortunes," cried my son George, "to be thus rewarded! Sure this is more than I could ever have presumed to hope for. To be possessed of all that's good, and after such an interval of pain! My warmest wishes could never rise so high!"

"Yes, my George," returned his lovely bride, "now let the wretch take my fortune; since you are happy without it, so am I. Oh, what an exchange have I made,—from the basest of men, to the dearest, best! Let him enjoy our fortune, I can now be happy even in indigence."—"And I promise you," cried the 'Squire, with a malicious grin, "that I shall be very happy with what you despise."—"Hold, hold, sir," cried Jenkinson, "there are two words to that bargain. As for the lady's fortune, Sir, you shall never touch a single stiver of it. Pray, your honour," continued he to Sir William, "can the 'Squire have this lady's fortune if he be married to another?" —"How can you make such a simple demand?" replied the Baronet: "undoubtedly he cannot."— "I am sorry for that," cried Jenkinson; "for as this gentleman and I have been old fellow-sporters, I have a friendship for him. But I must declare, well as I love him, that this contract is not worth a tobacco-stopper, for he is married already."—"You lie, like a rascal!" returned the 'Squire, who seemed roused by this insult; "I never was legally married to any woman."

"Indeed, begging your honour's pardon," replied the other, "you were: and I hope you will show a proper return of friendship to your own honest Jenkinson, who brings you a wife; and if the company restrain their curiosity a few minutes, they shall see her." So saying, he went off, with his usual celerity, and left us all unable to form any probable conjecture as to his design. "Ay, let him go," cried the 'Squire; "whatever else I may have done, I defy him there. I am too old now to be frightened with squibs."

"I am surprised," said the Baronet, "what the fellow can intend by this. Some low piece of humour, I suppose!"—"Perhaps, Sir," replied I, "he may have a more serious meaning. For when we reflect on the various schemes this gentleman has laid to seduce innocence, perhaps some one more artful than the rest has been found able to deceive him. When we consider what numbers he has ruined, how many parents now feel, with anguish, the infamy and the contamination which he has brought into their families, it would not surprise me if some one of them—— Amazement! Do I see my lost daughter? Do I hold her? It is, it is my life, my happiness! I thought thee lost, my Olivia, yet still I hold thee —and still thou shalt live to bless me." The warmest transports of the fondest lover were not greater than mine, when I saw him introduce my child, and held my daughter in my arms, whose silence only spoke her raptures.

"And art thou returned to me, my darling,"

cried I, "to be my comfort in age?"—"That she is," cried Jenkinson; "and make much of her, for she is your own honourable child, and as honest a woman as any in the whole room, let the other be who she will. And as for you, 'Squire, as sure as you stand there, this young lady is your lawful wedded wife: and to convince you that I speak nothing but the truth, here is the license by which you were married together." So saying, he put the license into the Baronet's hands, who read it, and found it perfect in every respect. "And now, gentlemen," continued he, "I find you are surprised at all this; but a few words will explain the difficulty. That there 'Squire of renown, for whom I have a great friendship (but that's between ourselves), has often employed me in doing odd little things for him. Among the rest, he commissioned me to procure him a false license and a false priest, in order to deceive this young lady. But as I was very much his friend, what did I do, but went and got a true license and a true priest, and married them both as fast as the cloth could make them. Perhaps you'll think it was generosity that made me do all this; but no; to my shame I confess it, my only design was to keep the license, and let the 'Squire know that I could prove it upon him whenever I thought proper, and so make him come down whenever I wanted money." A burst of pleasure now seemed to fill the whole apartment; our joy reached even to the common room, where the prisoners themselves sympathised,

. . . And shook their chains
In transport and rude harmony.

Happiness was expanded upon every face, and even Olivia's cheek seemed flushed with pleasure. to be thus restored to reputation, to friends, and fortune at once, was a rapture sufficient to stop the progress of decay, and restore former health and vivacity. But, perhaps, among all, there was not one who felt sincerer pleasure than I. Still holding the dear loved child in my arms, I asked my heart if these transports were not delusions. "How could you," cried I, turning to Mr. Jenkinson, "how could you add to my miseries by the story of her death? But it matters not; my pleasure at finding her again is more than a recompense for the pain."

"As to your question," replied Jenkinson, "that is easily answered. I thought the only probable means of freeing you from prison was by submitting to the 'Squire and consenting to his marriage with the other young lady. But these you had vowed never to grant while your daughter was living: there was therefore no other method to bring things to bear, but by persuading you that she was dead. I prevailed on your wife to join in the deceit, and we have not had a fit opportunity of undeceiving you till now."

In the whole assembly now there appeared only two faces that did not glow with transport. Mr. Thornhill's assurance had entirely forsaken him; he now saw the gulf of infamy and want before him, and trembled to take the plunge. He therefore fell on his knees before his uncle, and in a voice of piercing misery implored compassion. Sir William was going to spurn him away, but at my request he raised him, and, after pausing a few moments. "Thy vices, crimes, and ingratitude," cried he, "deserve no tenderness; yet thou shalt not be entirely forsaken—a bare competence shall be supplied to support the wants of life, but not its follies. This young lady, thy wife, shall be put in possession of a third part of that fortune which once was thine, and from her tenderness alone thou art to expect any extraordinary supplies for the future." He was going to express his gratitude for such kindness in a set speech; but the Baronet prevented him, by bidding him not aggravate his meanness, which was already but too apparent. He ordered him at the same time to be gone, and from all his former domestics to choose one, such as he should think proper, which was all that should be granted to attend him.

As soon as he left us, Sir William very politely stepped up to his new niece with a smile, and wished her joy. His example was followed by Miss Wilmot and her father. My wife, too, kissed her daughter with much affection; as, to use her own expression, she was now made an honest woman of. Sophia and Moses followed in turn; and even our benefactor Jenkinson desired to be admitted to that honour. Our satisfaction seemed scarcely capable of increase. Sir William, whose greatest pleasure was in doing good, now looked round with a countenance open as the sun, and saw nothing but joy in the looks of all except that of my daughter Sophia, who, for some reasons we could not comprehend, did not seem perfectly satisfied. "I think now," cried he, with a smile, "that all the company except one or two seem perfectly happy. There only remains an act of justice for me to do. You are sensible, Sir," continued he, turning to me, "of the obligations we both owe to Mr. Jenkinson; and it is but just we should both reward him for it. Miss Sophia will, I am sure, make him very happy, and he shall have from me five hundred pounds as her fortune; and upon this I am sure they can live very comfortably together. Come, Miss Sophia, what say you to this match of my making? Will you have him?" My poor girl seemed almost sinking into her mother's arms at the hideous proposal. "Have him, Sir!" cried she faintly; "no, Sir, never!"—"What!" cried he again, "not have Mr. Jenkinson, your benefactor, a handsome young fellow, with five hundred pounds, and good expectations?"— "I beg, Sir," returned she, scarce able to speak, "that you'll desist, and not make me so very wretched."—"Was ever such obstinacy known?" cried he again; "to refuse a man whom the family have such infinite obligations to, who has preserved your sister, and who has five hundred pounds! What! not have him!"—"No, Sir, never!" replied she angrily; "I'd sooner die first."—"If that be the case, then," cried he,

" if you will not have him—I think I must have
you myself." And, so saying, he caught her to
his breast with ardour. "My loveliest, my most
sensible of girls," cried he, "how could you ever
think your own Burchell could deceive you, or
that Sir William Thornhill could ever cease to
admire a mistress that loved him for himself
alone? I have for some years sought for a woman,
who, a stranger to my fortune, could think that
I had merit as a man. After having tried in vain,
even amongst the pert and ugly, how great at
last must be my rapture, to have made a conquest over such sense and such heavenly beauty."
Then turning to Jenkinson: "As I cannot, Sir,
part with this young lady myself, for she has
taken a fancy to the cut of my face, all the recompense I can make is to give you her fortune; and
you may call upon my steward to-morrow for
five hundred pounds." Thus we had all our compliments to repeat, and Lady Thornhill under-
went the same round of ceremony that her sister
had done before. In the meantime Sir William's
gentleman appeared to tell us that the equipages
were ready to carry us to the inn, where everything was prepared for our reception. My wife
and I led the van, and left those gloomy mansions
of sorrow. The generous Baronet ordered forty
pounds to be distributed among the prisoners,
and Mr. Wilmot, induced by his example, gave
half that sum. We were received below by the
shouts of the villagers, and I saw and shook by
the hand two or three of my honest parishioners,

who were among the number. They attended us
to our inn, where a sumptuous entertainment
was provided, and coarser provisions were distributed in great quantities among the populace.

After supper, as my spirits were exhausted by
the alternation of pleasure and pain which they
had sustained during the day, I asked permission
to withdraw; and, leaving the company in the
midst of their mirth, as soon as I found myself
alone, I poured out my heart in gratitude to the
Giver of joy as well as of sorrow, and then slept
undisturbed till morning.

CHAPTER XXXII

THE CONCLUSION

THE next morning, as soon as I awaked, I found my eldest son sitting by my bedside, who came to increase my joy with another turn of fortune in my favour. First having released me from the settlement that I had made the day before in his favour, he let me know that my merchant, who had failed in town, was arrested at Antwerp, and there had given up effects to a much greater amount than what was due to his creditors. My boy's generosity pleased me almost as much as this unlooked-for good fortune; but I had some doubts whether I ought, in justice, to accept his offer. While I was pondering upon this Sir William entered the room, to whom I communicated my doubts. His opinion was that, as my son was already possessed of a very affluent fortune by his marriage, I might accept his offer without any hesitation. His business, however, was to inform me, that as he had the night before sent for the licenses, and expected them every hour, he hoped that I would not refuse my assistance in making all the company happy that morning. A footman entered while we were speaking, to tell us that the messenger was returned; and as I was by this time ready, I went down, where I found the whole company as

merry as affluence and innocence could make
them. However, as they were now preparing for
a very solemn ceremony, their laughter entirely
displeased me. I told them of the grave, becoming, and sublime deportment they should assume
upon this mystical occasion, and read them two
homilies, and a thesis of my own composing, in
order to prepare them. Yet they still seemed perfectly refractory and ungovernable.

Even as we were going along to church, to
which I led the way, all gravity had quite forsaken them, and I was often tempted to turn
back in indignation. In church a new dilemma
arose, which promised no easy solution. This
was, which couple should be married first: my
son's bride warmly insisted that Lady Thornhill
(that was to be) should take the lead; but this
the other refused with equal ardour, protesting
she would not be guilty of such rudeness for the
world. The argument was supported for some
time between both, with equal obstinacy and
good breeding. But, as I stood all this time with
my book ready, I was at last quite tired of the
contest; and, shutting it, "I perceive," cried I,
"that none of you have a mind to be married,
and I think we had as good go back again; for
I suppose there will be no business done here
to-day." This at once reduced them to reason.
The Baronet and his lady were first married, and
then my son and his lovely partner.

I had previously, that morning, given orders
that a coach should be sent for my honest neigh-

"I PERCEIVE," CRIED I, "THAT NONE OF YOU HAVE A MIND
TO BE MARRIED."

bour Flamborough and his family; by which means, upon our return to the inn, we had the pleasure of finding the two Miss Flamboroughs alighted before us. Mr. Jenkinson gave his hand to the eldest, and my son Moses led up the other (and I have since found, that he has taken a real liking to the girl, and my consent and bounty he shall have whenever he thinks proper to demand them). We were no sooner returned to the inn, but numbers of my parishioners, hearing of my success, came to congratulate me; but, amongst the rest, were those who rose to rescue me, and whom I formerly rebuked with such sharpness. I told the story to Sir William, my son-in-law, who went out and reproved them with great severity; but finding them quite disheartened by his harsh reproof he gave them half-a-guinea apiece to drink his health, and raise their dejected spirits.

Soon after this we were called to a very genteel entertainment, which was dressed by Mr. Thornhill's cook.—And it may not be improper to observe with respect to that gentleman, that he now resides, in quality of companion, at a relation's house, being very well liked, and seldom sitting at the side-table, except when there is no room at the other; for they make no stranger of him. His time is pretty much taken up in keeping his relation, who is a little melancholy, in spirits, and in learning to blow the French horn. My eldest daughter, however, still remembers him with regret: and she has even told me, though I make a great secret of it, that when he reforms, she may be brought to relent.

But to return, for I am not apt to digress thus; when we were to sit down to dinner, our ceremonies were going to be renewed. The question was, whether my eldest daughter, as being a matron, should not sit above the two young brides; but the debate was cut short by my son George, who proposed that the company should sit indiscriminately, every gentleman by his lady. This was received with great approbation by all, excepting my wife, who, I could perceive, was not perfectly satisfied, as she expected to have had the pleasure of sitting at the head of the table, and carving all the meat for all the company. But notwithstanding this, it is impossible to describe our good humour. I can't say whether we had more wit among us now than usual; but I am certain we had more laughing, which answered the end as well. One jest I particularly remember: old Mr. Wilmot drinking to Moses, whose head was turned another way, my son replied, "Madam, I thank you." Upon which the old gentleman, winking upon the rest of the company, observed that he was thinking of his mistress. At which jest I thought the two Miss Flamboroughs would have died with laughing. As soon as dinner was over, according to my old custom, I requested that the table might be taken away to have the pleasure of seeing all my family assembled once more by a cheerful fireside. My two little ones sat upon each knee, the rest of the company by their partners. I had nothing now on this side of the grave to wish for: all my cares were over; my pleasure was unspeakable. It now only remained, that my gratitude in good fortune should exceed my former submission in adversity.

SHE
STOOPS TO CONQUER

SHE STOOPS TO CONQUER

BY

OLIVER GOLDSMITH

1933

DAILY EXPRESS PUBLICATIONS
LONDON

Editor's Note

GOLDSMITH'S play *She Stoops to Conquer* was produced in 1773—five years after his *Good-natured Man* and seven years after the publication of *The Vicar of Wakefield*. The idea of the play is supposed to be founded upon an amusing incident of the author's youth. Returning to school on a borrowed hack, and feeling lordly in the possession of an unexpected guinea, he loitered by the way until obliged to seek shelter for the night in Ardagh. He inquired, with a confident air, for the best house of entertainment; and a wag directed him respectfully to the residence of the great Squire Featherston as "the best house in Ardagh." Oliver rang the bell, gave his horse in charge, and was shown into the comfortable parlour of the Squire; who—unlike Mr. Hardcastle—is said to have seen the joke and furthered it. Oliver had supper; which gave him so much satisfaction that he ordered a bottle of wine to follow, not only insisting upon the landlord drinking with him, but also inviting his wife and pretty daughter. It was not until the next morning, when he took a parting look at his guinea before paying for his entertainment, that the truth was revealed by the good-natured Squire.

When *She Stoops to Conquer* was produced at Covent Garden on the 15th March, Johnson took a party of his cronies, including Burke and Reynolds. His verdict on the play was: "I know of no comedy for many years that has so much exhilarated an audience, that has answered so much the great end of comedy—making an audience merry." The play was an instant success, running for 12 nights; and it brought the poor author a very welcome £500. It has always maintained its popularity as an acting comedy.

TO

SAMUEL JOHNSON, LL.D.

DEAR SIR,

By inscribing this slight performance to you, I do not mean so much to compliment you as myself. It may do me some honour to inform the public, that I have lived many years in intimacy with you. It may serve the interests of mankind also to inform them, that the greatest wit may be found in a character, without impairing the most unaffected piety.

I have, particularly, reason to thank you for your partiality to this performance. The undertaking a comedy, not merely sentimental, was very dangerous; and Mr. Colman, who saw this piece in its various stages, always thought it so. However, I ventured to trust it to the public; and, though it was necessarily delayed till late in the season, I have every reason to be grateful.

I am, Dear Sir,

Your most sincere friend,

And admirer,

OLIVER GOLDSMITH.

PROLOGUE

BY DAVID GARRICK, ESQ.

Enter Mr. Woodward, *dressed in black, and holding a handkerchief to his eyes.*

Excuse me, sirs, I pray—I can't yet speak—
I'm crying now—and have been all the week.
" 'Tis not alone this mourning suit," good
    masters:
"I've that within"—for which there are no
    plasters!
Pray, would you know the reason why I'm
    crying?
The Comic Muse, long sick, is now a-dying!
And if she goes, my tears will never stop;
For as a player, I can't squeeze out one drop:
I am undone, that's all—shall lose my bread—
I'd rather, but that's nothing—lose my head.
When the sweet maid is laid upon the bier,
Shuter and I shall be chief mourners here.
To her a mawkish drab of spurious breed,
Who deals in sentimentals, will succeed!
Poor Ned and I are dead to all intents;
We can as soon speak Greek as sentiments!
But nervous grown, to keep our spirits up,
We now and then take down a hearty cup.
What shall we do? If Comedy forsake us,
They'll turn us out, and no one else will take us.
But why can't I be moral?—Let me try—

My heart thus pressing—fixed my face and
    eye—
With a sententious look, that nothing means,
(Faces are blocks in sentimental scenes)
Thus I begin: " All is not gold that glitters,
"Pleasure seems sweet, but proves a glass of
    bitters.
"When Ignorance enters, Folly is at hand:
"Learning is better far than house and land.
"Let not your virtue trip; who trips may stumble,
"And virtue is not virtue, if she tumble."

I give it up—morals won't do for me;
To make you laugh, I must play tragedy.
One hope remains—hearing the maid was ill,
A Doctor comes this night to show his skill.
To cheer her heart, and give your muscles motion,
He, in Five Draughts prepar'd, presents a
    potion;
A kind of magic charm—for be assur'd,
If you will swallow it, the maid is cur'd:
But desperate the Doctor, and her case is,
If you reject the dose, and make wry faces!
This truth he boasts, will boast it while he lives,
No poisonous drugs are mixed in what he gives.
Should he succeed, you'll give him his degree;
If not, within he will receive no fee!
The College *you*, must his pretensions back,
Pronounce him Regular, or dub him Quack.

DRAMATIS PERSONÆ

SIR CHARLES MARLOW.
YOUNG MARLOW (his son).
HARDCASTLE.
HASTINGS.
TONY LUMPKIN.
DIGGORY.

MRS. HARDCASTLE.
MISS HARDCASTLE.
MISS NEVILLE.
MAID.
LANDLORD, SERVANTS, &c.,
&c.

SHE STOOPS TO CONQUER

ACT THE FIRST.

SCENE I—*A Chamber in an old-fashioned House.*

Enter MRS. HARDCASTLE *and* MR. HARDCASTLE.

Mrs. Hard. I vow, Mr. Hardcastle, you're very particular. Is there a creature in the whole country but ourselves, that does not take a trip to town now and then, to rub off the rust a little? There's the two Miss Hoggs, and our neighbour Mrs. Grigsby, go to take a month's polishing every winter.

Hard. Ay, and bring back vanity and affectation to last them the whole year. I wonder why London cannot keep its own fools at home! In my time the follies of the town crept slowly among us, but now they travel faster than a stage-coach. Its fopperies come down not only as inside passengers, but in the very basket.

Mrs. Hard. Ay, your times were fine times indeed; you have been telling us of them for many a long year. Here we live in an old rumbling mansion, that looks for all the world like an inn, but that we never see company. Our best visitors are old Mrs. Oddfish, the curate's wife, and little Cripplegate, the lame dancing-master;

and all our entertainment your old stories of
Prince Eugene and the Duke of Marlborough. I
hate such old-fashioned trumpery.

Hard. And I love it. I love everything that's
old: old friends, old times, old manners, old
books, old wine; and I believe, Dorothy (*taking
her hand*), you'll own I have been pretty fond
of an old wife.

Mrs. Hard. Dear me, Mr. Hardcastle, you're
for ever at your Dorothy's and your old wife's.
You may be a Darby, but I'll be no Joan, I
promise you. I'm not so old as you'd make me,
by more than one good year. Add twenty to
twenty, and make money of that.

Hard. Let me see; twenty added to twenty
makes just fifty and seven.

Mrs. Hard. It's false, Mr. Hardcastle; I was
but twenty when Tony was born of my first marriage—my marriage with Mr. Lumpkin; and he's
not come to years of discretion yet.

Hard. Nor ever will, I dare answer for him.
Ay, you have taught him finely.

Mrs. Hard. No matter. Tony Lumpkin has a
good fortune. My son is not to live by his learning. I don't think a boy wants much learning to
spend fifteen hundred a year.

Hard. Learning, quotha! a mere composition
of tricks and mischief.

Mrs. Hard. Humour, my dear; nothing but
humour. Come, Mr. Hardcastle, you must allow
the boy a little humour.

Hard. I'd sooner allow him a horse-pond. If

burning the footmen's shoes, frightening the
maids, and worrying the kittens be humour, he
has it. It was but yesterday he fastened my wig
to the back of my chair, and when I went to make
a bow, I popt my bald head in Mrs. Frizzle's face.

Mrs. Hard. And am I to blame? The poor boy
was always too sickly to do any good. A school
would be his death. When he comes to be a little
stronger, who knows what a year or two's Latin
may do for him.

Hard. Latin for him! A cat and fiddle. No,
no; the alehouse and the stable are the only
schools he'll ever go to.

Mrs. Hard. Well, we must not snub the poor
boy now, for I believe we sha'n't have him long
among us. Anybody that looks in his face may
see he's consumptive.

Hard. Ay, if growing too fat be one of the
symptoms.

Mrs. Hard. He coughs sometimes.

Hard. Yes, when his liquor goes the wrong
way.

Mrs. Hard. I'm actually afraid of his lungs.

Hard. And truly so am I; for he sometimes
whoops like a speaking trumpet—(*Tony hallooing
behind the scenes*)—O, there he goes—a very
consumptive figure, truly.

Enter TONY, *crossing the stage.*

Mrs. Hard. Tony, where are you going, my
charmer! Won't you give papa and I a little of
your company, lovee?

Tony. I'm in haste, mother; I cannot stay.

Mrs. Hard. You sha'n't venture out this raw evening, my dear; you look most shockingly.

Tony. I can't stay, I tell you. The Three Pigeons expects me down every moment. There's some fun going forward.

Hard. Ay; the alehouse, the old place: I thought so.

Mrs. Hard. A low, paltry set of fellows.

Tony. Not so low, neither. There's Dick Muggins the exciseman, Jack Slang the horse doctor, little Aminadab that grinds the music box, and Tom Twist that spins the pewter platter.

Mrs. Hard. Pray, my dear, disappoint them for one night at least.

Tony. As for disappointing them, I should not so much mind; but I can't abide to disappoint myself.

Mrs. Hard. (*Detaining him.*) You sha'n't go.

Tony. I will, I tell you.

Mrs. Hard. I say you sha'n't.

Tony. We'll see which is strongest, you or I.
[*Exit, hauling her out.*

Hard. (*Solus.*) Aye, there goes a pair that only spoil each other. But is not the whole age in a combination to drive sense and discretion out of doors? There's my pretty darling Kate! the fashions of the times have almost infected her too. By living a year or two in town, she is as fond of gauze and French frippery as the best of them.

Enter MISS HARDCASTLE.

Hard. Blessings on my pretty innocence! drest out as usual, my Kate. Goodness! What a quantity of superfluous silk hast thou got about thee, girl! I could never teach the fools of this age, that the indigent world could be clothed out of the trimmings of the vain.

Miss Hard. You know our agreement, sir. You allow me the morning to receive and pay visits, and to dress in my own manner; and in the evening I put on my housewife's dress to please you.

Hard. Well, remember, I insist on the terms of our agreement; and, by the bye, I believe I shall have occasion to try your obedience this very evening.

Miss Hard. I protest, sir, I don't comprehend your meaning.

Hard. Then to be plain with you, Kate, I expect the young gentleman I have chosen to be your husband from town this very day. I have his father's letter, in which he informs me his son is set out, and that he intends to follow himself shortly after.

Miss Hard. Indeed! I wish I had known something of this before. Bless me, how shall I behave? It's a thousand to one I sha'n't like him; our meeting will be so formal, and so like a thing of business, that I shall find no room for friendship or esteem.

Hard. Depend upon it, child, I'll never control your choice ; but Mr. Marlow, whom I have pitched upon, is the son of my old friend, Sir Charles Marlow, of whom you have heard me talk so often. The young gentleman has been bred a scholar, and is designed for an employment in the service of his country. I am told he's a man of an excellent understanding.

Miss Hard. Is he?

Hard. Very generous.

Miss Hard. I believe I shall like him.

Hard. Young and brave.

Miss Hard. I'm sure I shall like him.

Hard. And very handsome.

Miss Hard. My dear papa, say no more (*kissing his hand*), he's mine ; I'll have him.

Hard. And, to crown all, Kate, he's one of the most bashful and reserved young fellows in all the world.

Miss Hard. Eh! you have frozen me to death again. That word *reserved* has undone all the rest of his accomplishments. A reserved lover, it is said, always makes a suspicious husband.

Hard. On the contrary, modesty seldom resides in a breast that is not enriched with nobler virtues. It was the very feature in his character that first struck me.

Miss Hard. He must have more striking features to catch me, I promise you. However, if he be so young, so handsome, and so everything as you mention, I believe he'll do still. I think I'll have him.

Hard. Ay, Kate, but there is still an obstacle.

It's more than an even wager he may not have you.

Miss Hard. My dear papa, why will you mortify one so? Well, if he refuses, instead of breaking my heart at his indifference, I'll only break my glass for its flattery, set my cap to some newer fashion, and look out for some less difficult admirer.

Hard. Bravely resolved! In the mean time I'll go prepare the servants for his reception: as we seldom see company, they want as much training as a company of recruits the first day's muster.

[*Exit.*

Miss Hard. (*Alone.*) Well, this news of papa's puts me all in a flutter. Young, handsome: these he put last; but I put them foremost. Sensible, good-natured; I like all that. But then reserved and sheepish; that's much against him. Yet can't he be cured of his timidity, by being taught to be proud of his wife? Yes, and can't I—But I vow I'm disposing of the husband before I have secured the lover.

Enter MISS NEVILLE.

Miss Hard. I'm glad you're come, Neville, my dear. Tell me, Constance, how do I look this evening? Is there anything whimsical about me? Is it one of my well-looking days, child? Am I in face to-day?

Miss Nev. Perfectly, my dear. Yet now I look again—bless me!—sure no accident has happened among the canary birds or the gold-fishes. Has your brother or the cat been meddling? or has the last novel been too moving?

Miss Hard. No; nothing of all this. I have been threatened—I can scarce get it out—I have been threatened with a lover.

Miss Nev. And his name—

Miss Hard. Is Marlow.

Miss Nev. Indeed!

Miss Hard. The son of Sir Charles Marlow.

Miss Nev. As I live, the most intimate friend of Mr. Hastings, my admirer. They are never asunder. I believe you must have seen him when we lived in town.

Miss Hard. Never.

Miss Nev. He's a very singular character, I assure you. Among women of reputation and virtue he is the modestest man alive; but his acquaintance give him a very different character among creatures of another stamp: you understand me.

Miss Hard. An odd character indeed. I shall never be able to manage him. What shall I do? Pshaw, think no more of him, but trust to occurrences for success. But how goes on your own affair, my dear? has my mother been courting you for my brother Tony as usual?

Miss Nev. I have just come from one of our agreeable *tête-à-têtes*. She has been saying a hundred tender things, and setting off her pretty monster as the very pink of perfection.

Miss Hard. And her partiality is such, that she actually thinks him so. A fortune like yours is no small temptation. Besides, as she has the sole management of it, I'm not surprised to see her unwilling to let it go out of the family.

Miss Nev. A fortune like mine, which chiefly consists in jewels, is no such mighty temptation. But at any rate, if my dear Hastings be but constant, I make no doubt to be too hard for her at last. However, I let her suppose that I am in love with her son; and she never once dreams that my affections are fixed upon another.

Miss Hard. My good brother holds out stoutly. I could almost love him for hating you so.

Miss Nev. It is a good-natured creature at bottom, and I'm sure would wish to see me married to anybody but himself. But my aunt's bell rings for our afternoon's walk round the improvements. *Allons!* Courage is necesary, as our affairs are critical.

Miss Hard. Would it were bed-time, and all were well.   [*Exeunt.*

SCENE II.—*An Alehouse Room. Several shabby Fellows with punch and tobacco.* TONY *at the head of the table, a little higher than the rest, a mallet in his hand.*

Omnes. Hurrea! hurrea! hurrea! bravo!

First Fel. Now, gentlemen, silence for a song. The 'squire is going to knock himself down for a song.

Omnes. Ay, a song, a song!

Tony. Then I'll sing you, gentlemen, a song I made upon this alehouse, the Three Pigeons.

SONG

Let schoolmasters puzzle their brain
    With grammar, and nonsense, and learning,
Good liquor, I stoutly maintain,
    Gives *genus* a better discerning.
Let them brag of their heathenish gods,
    Their Lethes, their Styxes, and Stygians,
Their Quis, and their Quæs, and their Quods,
    They're all but a parcel of Pigeons.
                Toroddle, toroddle, toroll.

When methodist preachers come down,
    A-preaching that drinking is sinful,
I'll wager the rascals a crown,
    They always preach best with a skinful. .
But when you come down with your pence,
    For a slice of their scurvy religion,
I'll leave it to all men of sense,
    But you, my good friend, are the Pigeon.
                Toroddle, toroddle, toroll.

Then come, put the jorum about,
    And let us be merry and clever,
Our hearts and our liquors are stout,
    Here's the Three Jolly Pigeons for ever.
Let some cry up woodcock or hare,
    Your bustards, your ducks, and your widgeons;
But of all the *gay* birds in the air,
    Here's a health to the Three Jolly Pigeons.
                Toroddle, toroddle, toroll.

Omnes. Bravo, bravo!

First Fel. The 'squire has got spunk in him.

Second Fel. I loves to hear him sing, bekeays he never gives us nothing that's low.

Third Fel. O hang anything that's low, I cannot bear it.

Fourth Fel. The genteel thing is the genteel thing any time: if so be that a gentleman bees in a concatenation accordingly.

Third Fel. I likes the maxum of it, Master Muggins. What, though I am obligated to dance a bear, a man may be a gentleman for all that. May this be my poison, if my bear ever dances but to the very genteelest of tunes; "Water Parted," or "The minuet in Ariadne."

Second Fel. What a pity it is the 'squire is not come to his own. It would be well for all the publicans within ten miles round of him.

Tony. Faith, and so it would, Master Slang. I'd then show what it was to keep choice of company.

Second Fel. O he takes after his own father for that. To be sure old 'Squire Lumpkin was the finest gentleman I ever set my eyes on. For winding the straight horn, or beating a thicket for a hare, or a wench, he never had his fellow. It was a saying in the place, that he kept the best horses, dogs, and girls, in the whole county.

Tony. Faith, and when I'm of age, I'll be no bastard, I promise you. I have been thinking of Bet Bouncer and the miller's grey mare to begin with. But come, my boys, drink about and be merry, for you pay no reckoning. Well, Stingo, what's the matter?

Enter Landlord.

Land. There be two gentlemen in a post-chaise at the door. They have lost their way upo' the forest; and they are talking something about Mr. Hardcastle.

Tony. As sure as can be, one of them must be the gentleman that's coming down to court my sister. Do they seem to be Londoners?

Land. I believe they may. They look woundily like Frenchmen.

Tony. Then desire them to step this way, and I'll set them right in a twinkling. (*Exit* Landlord.) Gentlemen, as they mayn't be good enough company for you, step down for a moment, and I'll be with you in the squeezing of a lemon.

[*Exeunt mob.*

Tony. (*Solus.*) Father-in-law has been calling me whelp and hound this half year. Now, if I pleased, I could be so revenged upon the old grumbletonian. But then I'm afraid—afraid of what? I shall soon be worth fifteen hundred a year, and let him frighten me out of *that* if he can.

Enter Landlord, *conducting* MARLOW *and* HASTINGS.

Mar. What a tedious uncomfortable day have we had of it! We were told it was but forty miles across the country, and we have come above threescore.

Hast. And all, Marlow, from that unaccountable reserve of yours, that would not let us inquire more frequently on the way.

Mar. I own, Hastings, I am unwilling to lay myself under an obligation to every one I meet, and often stand the chance of an unmannerly answer.

Hast. At present, however, we are not likely to receive any answer.

Tony. No offence, gentlemen. But I'm told you have been inquiring for one Mr. Hardcastle in these parts. Do you know what part of the country you are in?

Hast. Not in the least, sir, but should thank you for information.

Tony. Nor the way you came?

Hast. No, sir; but if you can inform us—

Tony. Why, gentlemen, if you know neither the road you are going, nor where you are, nor the road you came, the first thing I have to inform you is, that—you have lost your way.

Mar. We wanted no ghost to tell us that.

Tony. Pray, gentlemen, may I be so bold so as to ask the place from whence you came?

Mar. That's not necessary towards directing us where we are to go.

Tony. No offence; but question for question is all fair, you know. Pray, gentlemen, is not this same Hardcastle a cross-grained, old-fashioned, whimsical fellow, with an ugly face, a daughter, and a pretty son?

Hast. We have not seen the gentleman; but he has the family you mention.

Tony. The daughter, a tall, trapesing, trolloping, talkative maypole; the son, a pretty, well-bred, agreeable youth, that everybody is fond of.

Mar. Our information differs in this. The daughter is said to be well-bred and beautiful; the son an awkward booby, reared up and spoiled at his mother's apron-string.

Tony. He-he-hem!—Then, gentlemen, all I have to tell you is, that you won't reach Mr. Hardcastle's house this night, I believe.

Hast. Unfortunate!

Tony. It's a long, dark, boggy, dirty, dangerous way. Stingo, tell the gentlemen the way to Mr. Hardcastle's! (*Winking upon the* Landlord.) Mr. Hardcastle's, of Quagmire Marsh, you understand me.

Land. Master Hardcastle's! Lock-a-daisy, my masters, you're come a deadly deal wrong! When you came to the bottom of the hill, you should have crossed down Squash Lane.

Mar. Cross down Squash Lane!

Land. Then you were to keep straight forward, till you came to four roads.

Mar. Come to where four roads meet?

Tony. Ay; but you must be sure to take only one of them.

Mar. O, sir, you're facetious.

Tony. Then keeping to the right, you are to go sideways till you come upon Crackskull Common: then you must look sharp for the track of the wheel, and go forward till you come to Farmer Murrain's barn. Coming to the farmer's barn, you are to turn to the right, and then to the left, and then to the right about again, till you find out the old mill—

Mar. Why, man! we could as soon find out the longitude!

Hast. What's to be done, Marlow?

Mar. This house promises but a poor reception; though perhaps the landlord can accommodate us.

Land. Alack, master, we have but one spare bed in the whole house.

Tony. And to my knowledge, that's taken up by three lodgers already. (*After a pause, in which the rest seem disconcerted.*) I have hit it. Don't you think, Stingo, our landlady could accommodate the gentlemen by the fire-side, with —three chairs and a bolster?

Hast. I hate sleeping by the fire-side.

Mar. And I detest your three chairs and a bolster.

Tony. You do, do you? then, let me see— what if you go on a mile further, to the Buck's Head; the old Buck's Head on the hill, one of the best inns in the whole county?

Hast. O ho! so we have escaped an adventure for this night, however.

Land. (*Apart to* TONY.) Sure, you ben't sending them to your father's as an inn, be you?

Tony. Mum, you fool you. Let *them* find that out. (*To them.*) You have only to keep on straight forward, till you come to a large old house by the roadside. You'll see a pair of large horns over the door. That's the sign. Drive up the yard, and call stoutly about you.

Hast. Sir, we are obliged to you. The servants can't miss the way?

Tony. No, no: but I tell you, though, the landlord is rich, and going to leave off business; so he wants to be thought a gentleman, saving your presence, he! he! he! He'll be for giving you his company; and, 'faith, if you mind him, he'll persuade you that his mother was an alderman, and his aunt a justice of peace.

Land. A troublesome old blade, to be sure; but a keeps as good wines and beds as any in the whole country.

Mar. Well, if he supplies us with these, we shall want no further connection. We are to turn to the right, did you say?

Tony. No, no; straight forward. I'll just step myself, and show you a piece of the way. (*To the* Landlord.) Mum!

Land. Ah! bless your heart, for a sweet, pleasant—mischievous rascal.

[*Exeunt.*

ACT THE SECOND

SCENE—*An old-fashioned House.*

Enter HARDCASTLE, *followed by three or four awkward* Servants.

Hard. Well, I hope you are perfect in the table exercise I have been teaching you these three days. You all know your posts and your places, and can show that you have been used to good company, without ever stirring from home.

Omnes. Ay, ay.

Hard. When company comes you are not to pop out and stare, and then run in again, like frighted rabbits in a warren.

Omnes. No, no.

Hard. You, Diggory, whom I have taken from the barn, are to make a show at the side-table; and you, Roger, whom I have advanced from the plough, are to place yourself behind my chair. But you're not to stand so, with your hands in your pockets. Take your hands from your pockets, Roger; and from your head, you blockhead you. See how Diggory carries his hands. They're a little too stiff, indeed, but that's no great matter.

Dig. Ay, mind how I hold them. I learned to

hold my hands this way when I was upon drill for the militia. And so being upon drill—

Hard. You must not be so talkative, Diggory. You must be all attention to the guests. You must hear us talk, and not think of talking; you must see us drink, and not think of drinking; you must see us eat, and not think of eating.

Dig. By the laws, your worship, that's parfectly unpossible. Whenever Diggory sees yeating going forward, he's always wishing for a mouthful himself.

Hard. Blockhead! Is not a bellyful in the kitchen as good as a bellyful in the parlour? Stay your stomach with that reflection.

Dig. I thank your worship, I'll make a shift to stay my stomach with a slice of cold beef in the pantry.

Hard. Diggory, you are too talkative.—Then, if I happen to say a good thing, or tell a good story at table, you must not all burst out a-laughing, as if you made part of the company.

Dig. Then your worship must not tell the story of Ould Grouse in the gun-room: I can't help laughing at that—he! he! he!—for the soul of me. We have laughed at that these twenty years —ha! ha! ha!

Hard. Ha! ha! ha! The story is a good one. Well, honest Diggory, you may laugh at that— but still remember to be attentive. Suppose one of the company should call for a glass of wine, how will you behave? A glass of wine, sir, if you please (*to* DIGGORY).—Eh, why don't you move?

Dig. Your worship, I never have courage till I see the eatables and drinkables brought upo' the table, and then I'm as bauld as a lion.

Hard. What, will nobody move?

First Serv. I'm not to leave this pleace.

Second Serv. I'm sure it's no pleace of mine.

Third Serv. Nor mine, for sartin.

Dig. And I'm sure it canna be mine.

Hard. You numskulls! and so while, like your betters, you are quarrelling for places, the guests must be starved. O you dunces! I find I must begin all over again—But don't I hear a coach drive into the yard? To your posts, you block-heads. I'll go in the mean time and give my old friend's son a hearty reception at the gate.

[*Exit* HARDCASTLE.

Dig. By the elevens, my pleace is gone quite out of my head.

Rog. I know that my pleace is to be every-where.

First Serv. Where is mine?

Second Serv. My pleace is to be nowhere at all; and so Is' go about my business.

[*Exeunt* Servants, *running about as if frighted, different ways.*

Enter Servant *with candles, showing in* MARLOW *and* HASTINGS.

Serv. Welcome, gentlemen, very welcome! This way.

Hast. After the disappointments of the day, welcome once more, Charles, to the comforts of a clean room and a good fire. Upon my word, a very well-looking house; antique but creditable.

Mar. The usual fate of a large mansion. Having first ruined the master by good housekeeping, it at last comes to levy contributions as an inn.

Hast. As you say, we passengers are to be taxed to pay all these fineries. I have often seen a good sideboard, or a marble chimney-piece, though not actually put in the bill, inflame a reckoning confoundedly.

Mar. Travellers, George, must pay in all places: the only difference is, that in good inns you pay dearly for luxuries; in bad inns you are fleeced and starved.

Hast. You have lived very much among them. In truth, I have been often surprised, that you who have seen so much of the world, with your natural good sense, and your many opportunities, could never yet acquire a requisite share of assurance.

Mar. The Englishman's malady. But tell me, George, where could I have learned that assurance you talk of? My life has been chiefly spent in a college or an inn, in seclusion from that lovely part of the creation that chiefly teach men confidence. I don't know that I was ever familiarly acquainted with a single modest woman—except my mother—But among females of another class, you know—

Hast. Ay, among them you are impudent enough of all conscience.

Mar. They are of *us,* you know.

Hast. But in the company of women of reputation I never saw such an idiot, such a trembler; you look for all the world as if you wanted an opportunity of stealing out of the room.

Mar. Why, man, that's because I do want to steal out of the room. Faith, I have often formed a resolution to break the ice, and rattle away at any rate. But I don't know how, a single glance from a pair of fine eyes has totally overset my resolution. An impudent fellow may counterfeit modesty; but I'll be hanged if a modest man can ever counterfeit impudence.

Hast. If you could but say half the fine things to them that I have heard you lavish upon the bar-maid of an inn, or even a college bed-maker—

Mar. Why, George, I can't say fine things to them; they freeze, they petrify me. They may talk of a comet, or a burning mountain, or some such bagatelle; but, to me, a modest woman, drest out in all her finery, is the most tremendous object of the whole creation.

Hast. Ha! ha! ha! At this rate, man, how can you ever expect to marry?

Mar. Never; unless, as among kings and princes, my bride were to be courted by proxy. If, indeed, like an Eastern bridegroom, one were to be introduced to a wife he never saw before, it might be endured. But to go through all the terrors of a formal courtship, together with the

episode of aunts, grandmothers, and cousins, and
at last to blurt out the broad staring question of,
Madam, will you marry me? No, no, that's a
strain much above me, I assure you.

Hast. I pity you. But how do you intend be-
having to the lady you are come down to visit
at the request of your father.

Mar. As I behave to all other ladies. Bow very
low, answer yes or no to all her demands—But
for the rest—I don't think I shall venture to look
in her face till I see my father's again.

Hast. I'm surprised that one who is so warm
a friend can be so cool a lover.

Mar. To be explicit, my dear Hastings, my chief
inducement down was to be instrumental in for-
warding your happiness, not my own. Miss
Neville loves you, the family don't know you;
as my friend you are sure of a reception, and let
honour do the rest.

Hast. My dear Marlow! But I'll suppress the
emotion. Were I a wretch, meanly seeking to
carry off a fortune, you should be the last man in
the world I would apply to for assistance. But
Miss Neville's person is all I ask, and that is
mine, both from her deceased father's consent,
and her own inclination.

Mar. Happy man! You have talents and art
to captivate any woman. I'm doomed to adore
the sex, and yet to converse with the only part
of it I despise. This stammer in my address, and
this awkward prepossessing visage of mine, can
never permit me to soar above the reach of a

milliner's 'prentice, or one of the duchesses of Drury-lane. Pshaw! this fellow here to interrupt us.

Enter HARDCASTLE.

Hard. Gentlemen, once more you are heartily welcome. Which is Mr. Marlow? Sir, you are heartily welcome. It's not my way, you see, to receive my friends with my back to the fire. I like to give them a hearty reception in the old style at my gate. I like to see their horses and trunks taken care of.

Mar. (*Aside.*) He has got our names from the servants already. (*To him.*) We approve your caution and hospitality, sir. (*To Hastings.*) I have been thinking, George, of changing our travelling dresses in the morning. I am grown confoundedly ashamed of mine.

Hard. I beg, Mr. Marlow, you'll use no ceremony in this house.

Hast. I fancy, Charles, you're right; the first blow is half the battle. I intend opening the campaign with the white and gold.

Hard. Mr. Marlow—Mr. Hastings—gentlemen pray be under no restraint in this house. This is Liberty-hall, gentlemen. You may do just as you please here.

Mar. Yet, George, if we open the campaign too fiercely at first, we may want ammunition before it is over. I think to reserve the embroidery to secure a retreat.

Hard. Your talking of a retreat, Mr. Marlow,

puts me in mind of the Duke of Marlborough, when he went to besiege Denain. He first summoned the garrison—

Mar. Don't you think the *ventre d'or* waistcoat will do with the plain brown?

Hard. He first summoned the garrison, which might consist of about five thousand men—

Hast. I think not: brown and yellow mix but very poorly.

Hard. I say, gentlemen, as I was telling you, he summoned the garrison, which might consist of about five thousand men—

Mar. The girls like finery.

Hard. Which might consist of about five thousand men, well appointed with stores, ammunition, and other implements of war. Now, says the Duke of Marlborough to George Brooks, that stood next to him—you must have heard of George Brooks—I'll pawn my dukedom, says he, but I take that garrison without spilling a drop of blood. So—

Mar. What, my good friend, if you give us a glass of punch in the meantime; it would help us to carry on the siege with vigour.

Hard. Punch, sir! (*Aside.*) This is the most unaccountable kind of modesty I ever met with.

Mar. Yes, sir, punch. A glass of warm punch, after our journey, will be comfortable. This is Liberty-hall, you know.

Hard. Here's a cup, sir.

Mar. (*Aside.*) So this fellow, in his Liberty-hall, will only let us have just what he pleases.

Hard. (*Taking the cup.*) I hope you'll find it to your mind. I have prepared it with my own hands, and I believe you'll own the ingredients are tolerable. Will you be so good as to pledge me, sir? Here, Mr. Marlow, here is to our better acquaintance.

[*Drinks.*

Mar. (*Aside.*) A very impudent fellow this! but he's a character, and I'll humour him a little. Sir, my service to you.

[*Drinks.*

Hast. (*Aside.*) I see this fellow wants to give us his company, and forgets that he's an innkeeper, before he has learned to be a gentleman.

Mar. From the excellence of your cup, my old friend, I suppose you have a good deal of business in this part of the country. Warm work, now and then, at elections, I suppose.

Hard. No, sir, I have long given that work over. Since our betters have hit upon the expedient of electing each other, there is no business "for us that sell ale."

Hast. So, then, you have no turn for politics, I find.

Hard. Not in the least. There was a time, indeed, I fretted myself about the mistakes of government, like other people; but finding myself every day grow more angry, and the government growing no better, I left it to mend itself. Since that, I no more trouble my head about Hyder Ally, or Ally Cawn, than about Ally Croaker. Sir, my service to you.

Hast. So that with eating above stairs, and drinking below, with receiving your friends within, and amusing them without, you lead a good pleasant bustling life of it.

Hard. I do stir about a great deal, that's certain. Half the differences of the parish are adjusted in this very parlour.

Mar. (*After drinking.*) And you have an argument in your cup, old gentleman, better than any in Westminster-hall.

Hard. Ay, young gentleman, that, and a little philosophy.

Mar. (*Aside.*) Well, this is the first time I ever heard of an innkeeper's philosophy.

Hast. So then, like an experienced general, you attack them on every quarter. If you find their reason manageable, you attack it with your philosophy; if you find they have no reason, you attack them with this. Here's your health, my philosopher.

[*Drinks.*

Hard. Good, very good, thank you; ha! ha! Your generalship puts me in mind of Prince Eugene, when he fought the Turks at the battle of Belgrade. You shall hear.

Mar. Instead of the battle of Belgrade, I believe it's almost time to talk about supper. What has your philosophy got in the house for supper?

Hard. For supper, sir? (*Aside.*) Was ever such a request to a man in his own house?

Mar. Yes, sir, supper, sir; I begin to feel an

appetite. I shall make fine work to-night in the larder, I promise you.

Hard. (*Aside.*) Such a brazen dog sure never my eyes beheld. [*To him.*] Why, really, sir, as for supper I can't well tell. My Dorothy and the cook-maid settle these things between them. I leave these kind of things entirely to them.

Mar. You do, do you?

Hard. Entirely. By the bye, I believe they are in actual consultation upon what's for supper this moment in the kitchen.

Mar. Then I beg they'll admit me as one of their privy council. It's a way I have got. When I travel, I always choose to regulate my own supper. Let the cook be called. No offence, I hope, sir.

Hard. O no, sir, none in the least; yet I don't know how; our Bridget, the cook-maid, is not very communicative upon these occasions. Should we send for her, she might scold us all out of the house.

Hast. Let's see your list of the larder then. I ask it as a favour. I always match my appetite to my bill of fare.

Mar. [*To* HARDCASTLE, *who looks at them with surprise.*] Sir, he's very right, and it's my way too.

Hard. Sir, you have a right to command here. Here, Roger, bring us the bill of fare for to-night's supper: I believe it's drawn out—Your manner, Mr. Hastings, puts me in mind of my uncle, Colonel Wallop. It was a saying of his, that no man was sure of his supper till he had eaten it.

Hast. (*Aside.*) All upon the high rope! His uncle a colonel! we shall soon hear of his mother being a justice of the peace. But let's hear the bill of fare.

Mar. (*Perusing.*) What's here? For the first course; for the second course; for the dessert. The mischief, sir; do you think we have brought down a whole Joiners' Company, or the corporation of Bedford, to eat up such a supper? Two or three little things, clean and comfortable will do.

Hast. But let's hear it.

Mar. (*Reading.*) For the first course, at the top, a pig and prune sauce.

Hast. Hang your pig, I say.

Mar. And hang your prune sauce, say I.

Hard. And yet, gentlemen, to men that are hungry, pig with prune sauce is very good eating.

Mar. At the bottom, a calf's tongue and brains.

Hast. Let your brains be knocked out, my good sir, I don't like them.

Mar. Or you may clap them on a plate by themselves. I do.

Hard. (*Aside.*) Their impudence confounds me. [*To them.*] Gentlemen, you are my guests, make what alterations you please. Is there anything else you wish to retrench or alter, gentlemen?

Mar. Item, a pork pie, a boiled rabbit and sausages, a Florentine, a shaking pudding, and a dish of tiff—taff—taffety cream.

Hast. Confound your made dishes; I shall be as much at a loss in this house as at a green and yellow dinner at the French ambassador's table. I'm for plain eating.

Hard. I'm sorry, gentlemen, that I have nothing you like, but if there be anything you have a particular fancy to—

Mar. Why, really sir, your bill of fare is so exquisite, that any one part of it is full as good as another. Send us what you please. So much for supper. And now to see that our beds are aired, and properly taken care of.

Hard. I entreat you'll leave that to me. You shall not stir a step.

Mar. Leave that to you! I protest, sir, you must excuse me, I always look to these things myself.

Hard. I must insist, sir, you'll make yourself easy on that head.

Mar. You see I'm resolved on it. (*Aside.*) A very troublesome fellow this, as I ever met with.

Hard. Well, sir, I'm resolved at least to attend you. (*Aside.*) This may be modern modesty, but I never saw anything look so like old-fashioned impudence.

[*Exeunt* MARLOW *and* HARDCASTLE.

Hast. (*Alone.*) So, I find this fellow's civilities begin to grow troublesome. But who can be angry at those assiduities which are meant to please him? Ha! what do I see? Miss Neville, by all that's happy!

Enter MISS NEVILLE.

Miss Nev. My dear Hastings! To what unexpected good fortune, to what accident, am I to ascribe this happy meeting?

Hast. Rather let me ask the same question, as I could never have hoped to meet my dearest Constance at an inn.

Miss Nev. An inn! sure you mistake: my aunt, my guardian, lives here. What could induce you to think this house an inn?

Hast. My friend, Mr. Marlow, with whom I came down, and I, have been sent here as to an inn, I assure you. A young fellow, whom we accidentally met at a house hard by, directed us hither.

Miss Nev. Certainly it must be one of my hopeful cousin's tricks, of whom you have heard me talk so often; ha! ha! ha!

Hast. He whom your aunt intends for you? he of whom I have such just apprehensions?

Miss Nev. You have nothing to fear from him, I assure you. You'd adore him, if you knew how heartily he despises me. My aunt knows it too, and has undertaken to court me for him, and actually begins to think she has made a conquest.

Hast. Thou dear dissembler! You must know, my Constance, I have just seized this happy opportunity of my friend's visit here to get admittance into the family. The horses that carried us down are now fatigued with their journey, but they'll soon be refreshed; and then, if my dearest

girl will trust in her faithful Hastings, we shall
soon be landed in France, where even among
slaves the laws of marriage are respected.

Miss Nev. I have often told you, that though
ready to obey you, I yet should leave my little
fortune behind with reluctance. The greatest
part of it was left me by my uncle, the India
director, and chiefly consists in jewels. I have
been for some time persuading my aunt to let me
wear them. I fancy I'm very near succeeding.
The instant they are put into my possession, you
shall find me ready to make them and myself
yours.

Hast. Perish the baubles! Your person is all
I desire. In the meantime, my friend Marlow
must not be let into his mistake. I know the
strange reserve of his temper is such, that if
abruptly informed of it, he would instantly quit
the house before our plan was ripe for execution.

Miss Nev. But how shall we keep him in the deception? Miss Hardcastle is just returned from
walking; what if we still continue to deceive him?
—This, this way—

[They confer.

Enter MARLOW.

Mar. The assiduities of these good people teaze
me beyond bearing. My host seems to think it ill
manners to leave me alone, and so he claps not
only himself, but his old-fashioned wife, on my
back. They talk of coming to sup with us too;
and then, I suppose, we are to run the gauntlet

through all the rest of the family.—What have we got here?

Hast. My dear Charles! Let me congratulate you!—The most fortunate accident!—Who do you think is just alighted?

Mar. Cannot guess.

Hast. Our mistresses, boy, Miss Hardcastle and Miss Neville. Give me leave to introduce Miss Constance Neville to your acquaintance. Happening to dine in the neighbourhood, they called on their return to take fresh horses here. Miss Hardcastle has just stept into the next room, and will be back in an instant. Wasn't it lucky? eh!

Mar. (*Aside.*) I have been mortified enough of all conscience, and here comes something to complete my embarrassment.

Hast. Well, but wasn't it the most fortunate thing in the world?

Mar. Oh! yes. Very fortunate—a most joyful encounter—But our dresses, George, you know, are in disorder—What if we should postpone the happiness till to-morrow?—To-morrow at her own house—It will be every bit as convenient—and rather more respectful—To-morrow let it be.

[*Offering to go.*

Miss Nev. By no means, sir. Your ceremony will displease her. The disorder of your dress will show the ardour of your impatience. Besides, she knows you are in the house, and will permit you to see her.

Mar. O! how shall I support it? Hem! hem! Hastings, you must not go. You are to assist me, you know. I shall be confoundedly ridiculous. Yet, hang it! I'll take courage. Hem!

Hast. Pshaw, man! it's but the first plunge, and all's over. She's but a woman, you know.

Mar. And, of all women, she that I dread most to encounter.

Enter MISS HARDCASTLE, *as returned from walking, a bonnet, &c.*

Hast. (*Introducing them.*) Miss Hardcastle, Mr. Marlow. I'm proud of bringing two persons of such merit together, that only want to know, to esteem each other.

Miss Hard. (*Aside.*) Now for meeting my modest gentleman with a demure face, and quite in his own manner. (*After a pause, in which he appears very uneasy and disconcerted.*) I'm glad of your safe arrival, sir. I'm told you had some accidents by the way.

Mar. Only a few, madam. Yes, we had some. Yes, madam, a good many accidents, but should be sorry—madam—or rather glad of any accidents—that are so agreeably concluded. Hem!

Hast. (*To him.*) You never spoke better in your whole life. Keep it up, and I'll insure you the victory.

Miss Hard. I'm afraid you flatter, sir. You that have seen so much of the finest company, can find little entertainment in an obscure corner of the country.

Mar. (*Gathering courage.*) I have lived, indeed, in the world, madam; but I have kept very little

92*

company. I have been but an observer upon life, madam, while others were enjoying it.

Miss Nev. But that, I am told, is the way to enjoy it at last.

Hast. (*To him.*) Cicero never spoke better. Once more, and you are confirmed in assurance for ever.

Mar. (*To him.*) Hem! Stand by me, then, and when I'm down, throw in a word or two, to set me up again.

Miss Hard. An observer, like you, upon life were, I fear, disagreeably employed, since you must have had much more to censure than to approve.

Mar. Pardon me, madam. I was always willing to be amused. The folly of most people is rather an object of mirth than uneasiness.

Hast. (*To him.*) Bravo, bravo. Never spoke so well in your whole life. Well, Miss Hardcastle, I see that you and Mr. Marlow are going to be very good company. I believe our being here will but embarrass the interview.

Mar. Not in the least, Mr. Hastings. We like your company of all things. (*To him.*) What! George, sure you won't go? how can you leave us?

Hast. Our presence will but spoil conversation, so we'll retire to the next room. (*To him.*) You don't consider, man, that we are to manage a little *tête-à-tête* of our own.

[*Exeunt.*

Miss Hard. (*After a pause.*) But you have not

been wholly an observer, I presume, sir; the ladies, I should hope, have employed some part of your addresses.

Mar. (*Relapsing into timidity.*) Pardon me, madam, I—I—I—as yet have studied—only—to —deserve them.

Miss Hard. And that, some say, is the very worst way to obtain them.

Mar. Perhaps so, madam. But I love to converse only with the more grave and sensible part of the sex. But I'm afraid I grow tiresome.

Miss Hard. Not at all, sir; there is nothing I like so much as grave conversation myself; I could hear it for ever. Indeed, I have often been surprised how a man of sentiment could ever admire those light airy pleasures, where nothing reaches the heart.

Mar. It's—a disease—of the mind, madam. In the variety of tastes there must be some who, wanting a relish—for—um—a—um.

Miss Hard. I understand you, sir. There must be some who, wanting a relish for refined pleasures, pretend to despise what they are incapable of tasting.

Mar. My meaning, madam, but infinitely better expressed. And I can't help observing—a—

Miss Hard. (*Aside.*) Who could ever suppose this fellow impudent upon some occasions? (*To him.*) You were going to observe, sir—

Mar. I was observing, madam—I protest, madam, I forget what I was going to observe.

Miss Hard. (*Aside.*) I vow and so do I. (*To*

him.) You were observing, sir, that in this age of hypocrisy—something about hypocrisy, sir.

Mar. Yes, madam, in this age of hypocrisy there are few who upon strict inquiry do not—a—a—a—

Miss Hard. I understand you perfectly, sir.

Mar. (*Aside.*) Faith! and that's more than I do myself.

Miss Hard. You mean that in this hypocritical age there are few that do not condemn in public what they practise in private, and think they pay every debt to virtue when they praise it.

Mar. True, madam; those who have most virtue in their mouths, have least of it in their bosoms. But I'm sure I tire you, madam.

Miss Hard. Not in the least, sir; there's something so agreeable and spirited in your manner, such life and force—pray, sir, go on.

Mar. Yes, madam. I was saying—that there are some occasions, when a total want of courage, madam, destroys all the—and puts us—upon a—a—a—

Miss Hard. I agree with you entirely; a want of courage upon some occasions assumes the appearance of ignorance, and betrays us when we most want to excel. I beg you'll proceed.

Mar. Yes, madam. Morally speaking, madam —But I see Miss Neville expecting us in the next room. I would not intrude for the world.

Miss Hard. I protest, sir, I never was more agreeably entertained in all my life. Pray go on.

Mar. Yes, madam, I was—But she beckons us to join her. Madam, shall I do myself the honour to attend you!

Miss Hard. Well, then, I'll follow.

Mar. (*Aside.*) This pretty smooth dialogue has done for me.   [*Exit.*

Miss Hard. (*Alone.*) Ha! ha! ha! Was there ever such a sober, sentimental interview? I'm certain he scarce looked in my face the whole time. Yet the fellow, but for his unaccountable bashfulness, is pretty well too. He has good sense, but then so buried in his fears, that it fatigues one more than ignorance. If I could teach him a little confidence, it would be doing somebody that I know of a piece of service. But who is that somebody?—That, faith, is a question I can scarce answer.

[*Exit.*

Enter TONY *and* MISS NEVILLE, *followed by* MRS. HARDCASTLE *and* HASTINGS.

Tony. What do you follow me for, cousin Con? I wonder you're not ashamed to be so very engaging.

Miss Nev. I hope, cousin, one may speak to one's own relations and not be to blame.

Tony. Ay, but I know what sort of relation you want to make me, though; but it won't do. I tell you, cousin Con, it won't do; so I beg you'll keep your distance, I want no nearer relationship.

[*She follows, coquetting him to the back scene.*

Mrs. Hard. Well! I vow, Mr. Hastings, you are very entertaining. There's nothing in the world I love to talk of so much as London, and the fashions, though I was never there myself.

Hast. Never there! You amaze me. From your air and manner, I concluded you had been bred all your life either at Ranelagh, St. James's, or Tower Wharf.

Mrs. Hard. O! Sir, you're only pleased to say so. We country persons can have no manner at all. I'm in love with the town, and that serves to raise me above some of our neighbouring rustics; but who can have a manner, that has never seen the Pantheon, the Grotto Gardens, the Borough, and such places where the nobility chiefly resort? All I can do is to enjoy London at second-hand. I take care to know every *tête-à-tête* from the Scandalous Magazine, and have all the fashions, as they come out, in a letter from the two Miss Rickets of Crooked Lane. Pray how do you like this head, Mr. Hastings?

Hast. Extremely elegant and *dégagée,* upon my word, madam. Your friseur is a Frenchman, I suppose?

Mrs. Hard. I protest, I dressed it myself from a print in the Ladies' Memorandum-book for the last year.

Hast. Indeed! Such a head in a side-box at the playhouse would draw as many gazers as my Lady Mayoress at a City Ball.

Mrs. Hard. I vow, since inoculation began, there is no such thing to be seen as a plain woman; so one must dress a little particular, or one may escape in the crowd.

Hast. But that can never be your case, madam, in any dress. (*Bowing.*)

Mrs. Hard. Yet, what signifies my dressing when I have such a piece of antiquity by my side as Mr. Hardcastle: all I can say will never argue down a single button from his clothes. I have often wanted him to throw off his great flaxen wig, and where he was bald, to plaster it over, like my Lord Pately, with powder.

Hast. You are right, madam; for, as among the ladies there are none ugly, so among the men there are none old.

Mrs. Hard. But what do you think his answer was? Why, with his usual Gothic vivacity, he said I only wanted him to throw off his wig, to convert it into a *tête* for my own wearing.

Hast. Intolerable! At your age you may wear what you please, and it must become you.

Mrs. Hard. Pray, Mr. Hastings, what do you take to be the most fashionable age about town?

Hast. Some time ago, forty was all the mode; but I'm told the ladies intend to bring up fifty for the ensuing winter.

Mrs. Hard. Seriously. Then I shall be too young for the fashion.

Hast. No lady begins now to put on jewels till she's past forty. For instance, Miss there, in a polite circle, would be considered as a child, as a mere maker of samplers.

Mrs. Hard. And yet Mrs. Niece thinks herself as much a woman, and is as fond of jewels, as the oldest of us all.

Hast. Your niece, is she? And that young gentleman, a brother of yours, I should presume?

Mrs. Hard. My son, sir. They are contracted to each other. Observe their little sports. They fall in and out ten times a day, as if they were man and wife already. (*To them.*) Well, Tony, child, what soft things are you saying to your cousin Constance this evening?

Tony. I have been saying no soft things; but that it's very hard to be followed about so. I've not a place in the house now that's left to myself, but the stable.

Mrs. Hard. Never mind him, Con, my dear. He's in another story behind your back.

Miss Nev. There's something generous in my cousin's manner. He falls out before faces to be forgiven in private.

Tony. That's a confounded—crack.

Mrs. Hard. Ah! he's a sly one. Don't you think they are like each other about the mouth, Mr. Hastings? The Blenkinsop mouth to a T. They're of a size too. Back to back, my pretties, that Mr. Hastings may see you. Come, Tony.

Tony. You had as good not make me, I tell you. (*Measuring.*)

Miss Nev. O dear! he has almost cracked my head.

Mrs. Hard. O, the monster ! For shame, Tony.
You a man, and behave so !

Tony. If I'm a man, let me have my fortin.
I'll not be made a fool of no longer.

Mrs. Hard. Is this, ungrateful boy, all that
I'm to get for the pains I have taken in your
education ? I that have rocked you in your cradle,
and fed that pretty mouth with a spoon ! Did not
I work that waistcoat to make you genteel ? Did
not I prescribe for you every day, and weep
while the receipt was operating ?

Tony. You had reason to weep, for you have
been dosing me ever since I was born. I have
gone through every receipt in the Complete Hus-
wife ten times over ; and you have thoughts of
coursing me through Quincy next spring. But,
I tell you, I'll not be made a fool of no
longer.

Mrs. Hard. Wasn't it all for your good,
viper ? Wasn't it all for your good ?

Tony. I wish you'd let me and my good alone,
then. Snubbing this way when I'm in spirits.
If I'm to have any good, let it come of itself ; not
to keep dinging it, dinging it into one so.

Mrs. Hard. That's false ; I never see you when
you're in spirits. No, Tony, you then go to the
alehouse or kennel. I'm never to be delighted
with your agreeable wild notes, unfeeling
monster !

Tony. Mamma, your own notes are the wildest
of the two.

Mrs. Hard. Was ever the like ? But I see he

wants to break my heart, I see he does.

Hast. Dear madam, permit me to lecture the young gentleman a little. I'm certain I can persuade him to his duty.

Mrs. Hard. Well, I must retire. Come, Constance, my love. You see, Mr. Hastings, the wretchedness of my situation: was ever poor woman so plagued with a dear, sweet, pretty, provoking, undutiful boy?

[*Exeunt* MRS. HARDCASTLE *and* MISS NEVILLE.

Tony. (*Singing.*) "There was a young man riding by, and fain would have his will. Rang do didlo dee."—Don't mind her. Let her cry. It's the comfort of her heart. I have seen her and sister cry over a book for an hour together; and they said they liked the book the better the more it made them cry.

Hast. Then you're no friend to the ladies, I find, my pretty young gentleman.

Tony. That's as I find 'um.

Hast. Not to her of your mother's choosing, I dare answer? And yet she appears to me a pretty well-tempered girl.

Tony. That's because you don't know her as well as I. I know every inch about her; and there's not a more bitter cantankerous toad in all Christendom.

Hast. (*Aside.*) Pretty encouragement this for a lover!

Tony. I have seen her since the height of that. She has as many tricks as a hare in a thicket, or a colt the first day's breaking.

Hast. To me she appears sensible and silent.

Tony. Ay, before company. But when she's with her playmate, she's as loud as a hog in a gate.

Hast. But there is a meek modesty about her that charms me.

Tony. Yes, but curb her never so little, she kicks up, and you're flung in a ditch.

Hast. Well, but you must allow her a little beauty.—Yes, you must allow her some beauty.

Tony. Bandbox! She's all a made-up thing, mun. Ah! could you but see Bet Bouncer of these parts, you might then talk of beauty. Faith, she has two eyes as black as sloes, and cheeks as broad and red as a pulpit cushion. She'd make two of she.

Hast. Well, what say you to a friend that would take this bitter bargain off your hands?

Tony. Anon.

Hast. Would you thank him that would take Miss Neville, and leave you to happiness and your dear Betsy?

Tony. Ay; but where is there such a friend, for who would take her?

Hast. I am he. If you but assist me, I'll engage to whip her off to France, and you shall never hear more of her.

Tony. Assist you! I will, to the last drop of my blood. I'll clap a pair of horses to your chaise that shall trundle you off in a twinkling, and may be get you a part of her fortin beside, in jewels, that you little dream of.

Hast. My dear 'squire, this looks like a lad of spirit.

Tony. Come along, then, and you shall see more of my spirit before you have done with me. (*Singing.*)

> "We are the boys
> That fear no noise
> Where the thundering cannons roar."

[*Exeunt.*

ACT THE THIRD

SCENE.—*The same.*

Enter HARDCASTLE, *alone.*

Hard. What could my old friend Sir Charles mean by recommending his son as the modestest young man in town? To me he appears the most impudent piece of brass that ever spoke with a tongue. He has taken possession of the easy-chair by the fireside already. He took off his boots in the parlour, and desired me to see them taken care of. I'm desirous to know how his impudence affects my daughter. She will certainly be shocked at it.

Enter MISS HARDCASTLE, *plainly dressed.*

Hard. Well, my Kate, I see you have changed your dress, as I bade you; and yet, I believe, there was no great occasion.

Miss Hard. I find such a pleasure, sir, in obeying your commands, that I take care to observe them without ever debating their propriety.

Hard. And yet, Kate, I sometimes give you some cause, particularly when I recommended my modest gentleman to you as a lover to-day.

Miss Hard. You taught me to expect something extraordinary, and I find the original exceeds the description.

Hard. I was never so surprised in my life ! He has quite confounded all my faculties.

Miss Hard. I never saw anything like it: and a man of the world too !

Hard. Ay, he learned it all abroad—what a fool was I, to think a young man could learn modesty by travelling. He might as soon learn wit at a masquerade.

Miss Hard. It seems all natural to him.

Hard. A good deal assisted by bad company and a French dancing-master.

Miss Hard. Sure you mistake, papa ! A French dancing-master could never have taught him that timid look—that awkward address—that bashful manner—

Hard. Whose look ? whose manner, child ?

Miss Hard. Mr. Marlow's: his *mauvaise honte,* his timidity, struck me at the first sight.

Hard. Then your first sight deceived you ; for I think him one of the most brazen first sights that ever astonished my senses.

Miss Hard. Sure, sir, you rally ! I never saw any one so modest.

Hard. And can you be serious ? I never saw such a bouncing, swaggering puppy since I was born. Bully Dawson was but a fool to him.

Miss Hard. Surprising ! He met me with a respectful bow, a stammering voice, and a look fixed on the ground.

Hard. He met me with a loud voice, a lordly air, and a familiarity that made my blood freeze again.

Miss Hard. He treated me with diffidence and respect; censured the manners of the age; admired the prudence of girls that never laughed; tired me with apologies for being tiresome; then left the room with a bow, and " Madam, I would not for the world detain you."

Hard. He spoke to me as if he knew me all his life before; asked twenty questions, and never waited for an answer; interrupted my best remarks with some silly pun; and when I was in my best story of the Duke of Marlborough and Prince Eugene, he asked if I had not a good hand at making punch. Yes, Kate, he asked your father if he was a maker of punch!

Miss Hard. One of us must certainly be mistaken.

Hard. If he be what he has shown himself, I'm determined he shall never have my consent.

Miss Hard. And if he be the sullen thing I take him, he shall never have mine.

Hard. In one thing then we are agreed—to reject him.

Miss Hard. Yes; but upon conditions. For if you should find him less impudent, and I more presuming—if you find him more respectful, and I more importunate—I don't know—the fellow is well enough for a man—Certainly, we don't meet many such at a horse-race in the country.

Hard. If we should find him so—But that's impossible. The first appearance has done my business. I'm seldom deceived in that.

Miss Hard. And yet there may be many good qualities under that first appearance.

Hard. Ay, when a girl finds a fellow's outside to her taste, she then sets about guessing the rest of his furniture. With her, a smooth face stands for good sense, and a genteel figure for every virtue.

Miss Hard. I hope, sir, a conversation begun with a compliment to my good sense, won't end with a sneer at my understanding?

Hard. Pardon me, Kate. But if young Mr. Brazen can find the art of reconciling contradictions, he may please us both, perhaps.

Miss Hard. And as one of us must be mistaken, what if we go to make further discoveries?

Hard. Agreed. But depend on't I'm in the right.

Miss Hard. And depend on't I'm not much in the wrong.

[*Exeunt.*

Enter TONY *running in with a casket.*

Tony. Well, I have got them. Here they are. My cousin Con's necklaces, bobs and all. My mother sha'n't cheat the poor souls out of their fortin neither. O! my genus, is that you?

Enter HASTINGS.

Hast. My dear friend, how have you managed with your mother? I hope you have amused her with pretending love for your cousin, and thát

you are willing to be reconciled at last? Our
horses will be refreshed in a short time, and we
shall soon be ready to set off.

Tony. And here's something to bear your
charges by the way (*giving the casket*); your
sweetheart's jewels. Keep them; and hang those,
I say, that would rob you of one of them.

Hast. But how have you procured them from
your mother?

Tony. Ask me no questions, and I'll tell you
no fibs. I procured them by the rule of thumb.
If I had not a key to every drawer in mother's
bureau, how could I go to the alehouse so often
as I do? An honest man may rob himself of his
own at any time.

Hast. Thousands do it every day. But to be
plain with you; Miss Neville is endeavouring to
procure them from her aunt this very instant. If
she succeeds, it will be the most delicate way at
least of obtaining them.

Tony. Well, keep them till you know how it
will be. But I know how it will be well enough;
she'd as soon part with the only sound tooth in
her head.

Hast. But I dread the effects of her resentment,
when she finds she has lost them.

Tony. Never you mind her resentment, leave *me*
to manage that. I don't value her resentment the
bounce of a cracker. Why, here they are. Morrice!
Prance!

[*Exit* HASTINGS.

Enter MRS. HARDCASTLE *and* MISS NEVILLE.

Mrs. Hard. Indeed, Constance, you amaze me.
Such a girl as you want jewels! It will be time
enough for jewels, my dear, twenty years hence,
when your beauty begins to want repairs.

Miss Nev. But what will repair beauty at
forty, will certainly improve it at twenty,
madam.

Mrs. Hard. Yours, my dear, can admit of
none. That natural blush is beyond a thousand
ornaments. Besides, child, jewels are quite out at
present. Don't you see half the ladies of our
acquaintance, my Lady Kill-daylight, and Mrs.
Crumb, and the rest of them, carry their jewels
to town, and bring nothing but paste and mar-
casites back.

Miss Nev. But who knows, madam, but somebody that shall be nameless would like me best
with all my little finery about me?

Mrs. Hard. Consult your glass, my dear, and
then see if, with such a pair of eyes, you want
any better sparklers. What do you think, Tony,
my dear? Does your cousin Con want any jewels
in your eyes to set off her beauty?

Tony. That's as thereafter may be.

Miss Nev. My dear aunt, if you knew how it
would oblige me.

Mrs. Hard. A parcel of old-fashioned rose and
table-cut things. They would make you look like
the court of King Solomon at a puppet-show.
Besides, I believe I can't readily come at them.

They may be missing, for aught I know to the contrary.

Tony. (*Apart to* MRS. HARDCASTLE.) Then why don't you tell her so at once, as she's so longing for them? Tell her they're lost. It's the only way to quiet her. Say they're lost, and call me to bear witness.

Mrs. Hard. (*Apart to* TONY.) You know, my dear, I'm only keeping them for you. So if I say they're gone, you'll bear me witness, will you? He! he! he!

Tony. Never fear me. Why! I'll say I saw them taken out with my own eyes.

Miss Nev. I desire them but for a day, madam. Just to be permitted to show them as relics, and then they may be locked up again.

Mrs. Hard. To be plain with you, my dear Constance, if I could find them you should have them. They're missing, I assure you. Lost, for aught I know; but we must have patience where-ever they are.

Miss Nev. I'll not believe it! this is but a shallow pretence to deny me. I know they are too valuable to be so slightly kept, and as you are to answer for the loss—

Mrs. Hard. Don't be alarmed, Constance. If they be lost, I must restore an equivalent. But my son knows they are missing, and not to be found.

Tony. That I can bear witness to. They are missing; and not to be found; I'll take my oath on't.

Mrs. Hard. You must learn resignation, my dear; for though we lose our fortune, yet we should not lose our patience. See me, how calm I am.

Miss Nev. Ay, people are generally calm at the misfortunes of others.

Mrs. Hard. Now I wonder a girl of your good sense should waste a thought upon such trumpery. We shall soon find them; and in the mean time you shall make use of my garnets till your jewels be found.

Miss Nev. I detest garnets.

Mrs. Hard. The most becoming things in the world to set off a clear complexion. You have often seen how well they look upon me. You *shall* have them.

[*Exit.*

Miss Nev. I dislike them of all things. You sha'n't stir.—Was ever anything so provoking, to mislay my own jewels, and force me to wear her trumpery.

Tony. Don't be a fool. If she gives you the garnets, take what you can get. The jewels are your own already. I have stolen them out of her bureau, and she does not know it. Fly to your spark, he'll tell you more of the matter. Leave me to manage her.

Miss Nev. My dear cousin!

Tony. Vanish. She's here, and has missed them already. [*Exit* Miss Neville.] See! how she fidgets and spits about like a Catherine wheel.

Enter MRS. HARDCASTLE.

Mrs. Hard. Confusion! thieves! robbers! we are cheated, plundered, broke open, undone.

Tony. What's the matter, what's the matter, mamma? I hope nothing has happened to any of the good family!

Mrs. Hard. We are robbed. My bureau has been broken open, the jewels taken out, and I'm undone.

Tony. Oh! is that all? Ha! ha! ha! By the laws, I never saw it acted better in my life. Why, I thought you was ruined in earnest, ha! ha! ha!

Mrs. Hard. Why, boy, I *am* ruined in earnest. My bureau has been broken open, and all taken away.

Tony. Stick to that: ha! ha! ha! stick to that. I'll bear witness, you know; call me to bear witness.

Mrs. Hard. I tell you, Tony, by all that's precious, the jewels are gone, and I shall be ruined for ever.

Tony. Sure I know they are gone, and I'm to say so.

Mrs. Hard. My dearest Tony, but hear me. They're gone, I say.

Tony. By the laws, mamma, you make me for to laugh, ha! ha! I know who took them well enough, ha! ha! ha!

Mrs. Hard. Was there ever such a blockhead, that can't tell the difference between jest and earnest? I tell you I'm not in jest, booby.

Tony. That's right, that's right; you must be in a bitter passion, and then nobody will suspect either of us. I'll bear witness that they are gone.

Mrs. Hard. Was there ever such a cross-grained brute, that won't hear me? Can you bear witness that you're no better than a fool? Was ever poor woman so beset with fools on one hand, and thieves on the other?

Tony. I can bear witness to that.

Mrs. Hard. Bear witness again, you blockhead you, and I'll turn you out of the room directly. My poor niece, what will become of her? Do you laugh, you unfeeling brute, as if you enjoyed my distress?

Tony. I can bear witness to that.

Mrs. Hard. Do you insult me, monster? I'll teach you to vex your mother, I will.

Tony. I can bear witness to that.

[*He runs off, she follows him.*

Enter MISS HARDCASTLE *and* Maid.

Miss Hard. What an unaccountable creature is that brother of mine, to send them to the house as an inn! ha! ha! I don't wonder at his impudence.

Maid. But what is more, madam, the young gentleman, as you passed by in your present dress, asked me if you were the barmaid? He mistook you for the barmaid, madam.

Miss Hard. Did he? Then as I live, I'm resolved to keep up the delusion. Tell me, Pimple, how do

you like my present dress? Don't you think
I look something like Cherry in the Beaux'
Stratagem?

Maid. It's the dress, madam, that every lady
wears in the country, but when she visits or
receives company.

Miss Hard. And are you sure he does not remember my face or person?

Maid. Certain of it.

Miss Hard. I vow, I thought so; for, though
we spoke for some time together, yet his fears
were such, that he never once looked up during
the interview. Indeed, if he had, my bonnet
would have kept him from seeing me.

Maid. But what do you hope from keeping
him in his mistake.

Miss Hard. In the first place I shall be seen,
and that is no small advantage to a girl who
brings her face to market. Then I shall perhaps
make an acquaintance, and that's no small victory gained over one who never addresses any
but the wildest of her sex. But my chief aim is,
to take my gentleman off his guard, and, like an
invisible champion of romance, examine the
giant's force before I offer to combat.

Maid. But are you sure you can act your part,
and disguise your voice so that he may mistake that, as he has already mistaken your
person?

Miss Hard. Never fear me. I think I have got
the true bar cant—Did your honour call?—
Attend the Lion there—Pipes and tobacco for

the angel.—The Lamb has been outrageous this
half-hour.

Maid. It will do, madam. But he's here.

[*Exit* Maid.

Enter MARLOW.

Mar. What a bawling in every part of the
house ! I have scarce a moment's repose. If I go
to the best room, there I find my host and his
story: if I fly to the gallery, there we have my
hostess with her curtsey down to the ground. I
have at last got a moment to myself, and now
for recollection.

[*Walks and muses*.

Miss Hard. Did you call, sir ? Did your honour
call ?

Mar. (*Musing*.) As for Miss Hardcastle, she's
too grave and sentimental for me.

Miss Hard. Did your honour call ? (*She still
places herself before him, he turning away*.)

Mar. No, child. (*Musing*.) Besides, from the
glimpse I had of her, I think she squints.

Miss Hard. I'm sure, sir, I heard the bell ring.

Mar. No, no. (*Musing*.) I have pleased my
father, however, by coming down, and I'll to-
morrow please myself by returning.

[*Taking out his tablets and perusing*.

Miss Hard. Perhaps the other gentleman called,
sir ?

Mar. I tell you, no.

Miss Hard. I should be glad to know, sir. We
have such a parcel of servants !

Mar. No, no, I tell you. (*Looks full in her face.*) Yes, child, I think I did call. I wanted—I wanted—I vow, child, you are vastly handsome.

Miss Hard. O la, sir, you'll make one ashamed.

Mar. Never saw a more sprightly malicious eye. Yes, yes, my dear, I did call. Have you got any of your—a—what d'ye call it, in the house?

Miss Hard. No, sir, we have been out of that these ten days.

Mar. One may call in this house, I find, to very little purpose. Suppose I should call for a taste, just by way of a trial, of the nectar of your lips; perhaps I might be disappointed in that too.

Miss Hard. Nectar! nectar! That's a liquor there's no call for in these parts. French, I suppose. We sell no French wines here, sir.

Mar. Of true English growth, I assure you.

Miss Hard. Then it's odd I should not know it. We brew all sort of wines in this house, and I have lived here these eighteen years.

Mar. Eighteen years! Why, one would think, child, you kept the bar before you were born. How old are you?

Miss Hard. O! sir, I must not tell my age. They say women and music should never be dated.

Mar. To guess at this distance, you can't be much above forty (*approaching*). Yet, nearer, I don't think so much (*approaching*). By coming close to some women they look younger still; but when we come very close indeed—(*attempting to kiss her*).

Miss Hard. Pray, sir, keep your distance. One

93

would think you wanted to know one's age, as
they do horses, by mark of mouth.

Mar. I protest, child, you use me extremely
ill. If you keep me at this distance, how is it possible you and I can ever be acquainted?

Miss Hard. And who wants to be acquainted
with you? I want no such acquaintance, not I.
I'm sure you did not treat Miss Hardcastle, that
was here awhile ago, in this obstropalous manner.
I'll warrant me, before her you looked dashed,
and kept bowing to the ground, and talked, for
all the world, as if you was before a justice of
peace.

Mar. (*Aside.*) She has hit it, sure enough! (*To
her.*) In awe of her, child? Ha! ha! ha! A mere
awkward squinting thing; no, no. I find you
don't know me. I laughed and rallied her a little;
but I was unwilling to be too severe. No, I could
not be too severe.

Miss Hard. O! then, sir, you are a favourite,
I find, among the ladies?

Mar. Yes, my dear, a great favourite. And yet
hang me, I don't see what they find in me to follow. At the Ladies' Club in town I'm called their
agreeable Rattle. Rattle, child, is not my real
name, but one I'm known by. My name is Solomons; Mr. Solomons, my dear, at your service.
(*Offering to salute her.*)

Miss Hard. Hold, sir; you are introducing me
to your club, not to yourself. And you're so great
a favourite there, you say?

Mar. Yes, my dear. There's Mrs. Mantrap,

Lady Betty Blackleg, the Countess of Sligo, Mrs. Langhorns, old Miss Biddy Buckskin, and your humble servant, keep up the spirit of the place.

Miss Hard. Then it's a very merry place, I suppose?

Mar. Yes, as merry as cards, supper, wine, and old women can make us.

Miss Hard. And their agreeable Rattle, ha! ha! ha!

Mar. (*Aside.*) I don't quite like this chit. She looks knowing, methinks. You laugh, child?

Miss Hard. I can't but laugh, to think what time they all have for minding their work or their family.

Mar. (*Aside.*) All's well; she don't laugh at me. (*To her.*) Do you ever work, child?

Miss Hard. Ay, sure. There's not a screen or quilt in the whole house but what can bear witness to that.

Mar. Indeed! then you must show me your embroidery. I embroider and draw patterns myself a little. If you want a judge of your work you must apply to me. (*Seizing her hand.*)

Miss Hard. Ay, but the colours do not look well by candlelight. You shall see all in the morning. (*Struggling.*)

Mar. And why not now, my angel? Such beauty fires beyond the power of resistance.— Pshaw! the father here! My old luck: I never nicked seven that I did not throw ames ace three times following.

[*Exit* MARLOW.

Enter Hardcastle, *who stands in surprise.*

Hard. So, madam. So, I find *this* is your *modest* lover. This is your humble admirer, that kept his eyes fixed on the ground, and only adored at humble distance. Kate, Kate, art thou not ashamed to deceive your father so?

Miss Hard. Never trust me, dear papa, but he's still the modest man I first took him for; you'll be convinced of it as well as I.

Hard. By the hand of my body, I believe his impudence is infectious! Didn't I see him seize your hand? Didn't I see him haul you about like a milkmaid? And now you talk of his respect and his modesty, forsooth!

Miss Hard. But if I shortly convince you of his modesty, that he has only the faults that will pass off with time, and the virtues that will improve with age, I hope you'll forgive him.

Hard. The girl would actually make one run mad! I tell you, I'll not be convinced. I am convinced. He has scarce been three hours in the house, and he has already encroached on all my prerogatives. You may like his impudence, and call it modesty; but my son-in-law, madam, must have very different qualifications.

Miss Hard. Sir, I ask but this night to convince you.

Hard. You shall not have half the time, for I have thoughts of turning him out this very hour.

Miss Hard. Give me that hour then, and I hope to satisfy you.

Hard. Well, an hour let it be then. But I'll have no trifling with your father. All fair and open, do you mind me.

Miss Hard. I hope, sir, you have ever found that I considered your commands as my pride; for your kindness is such, that my duty as yet has been inclination.

[*Exeunt.*

ACT THE FOURTH

SCENE—*The Same.*

Enter HASTINGS *and* MISS NEVILLE.

Hast. You surprise me ; Sir Charles Marlow expected here this night ! Where have you had your information ?

Miss Nev. You may depend upon it. I just saw his letter to Mr. Hardcastle, in which he tells him he intends setting out a few hours after his son.

Hast. Then, my Constance, all must be completed before he arrives. He knows me ; and should he find me here, would discover my name, and perhaps my designs, to the rest of the family.

Miss Nev. The jewels, I hope, are safe ?

Hast. Yes, yes, I have sent them to Marlow, who keeps the keys of our baggage. In the meantime, I'll go to prepare matters for our elopement. I have had the 'squire's promise of a fresh pair of horses ; and if I should not see him again, will write him further directions.

[*Exit.*

Miss Nev. Well ! success attend you. In the meantime I'll go and amuse my aunt with the old pretence of a violent passion for my cousin.

[*Exit.*

Enter MARLOW, *followed by a* Servant.

Mar. I wonder what Hastings could mean by

sending me so valuable a thing as a casket to keep for him, when he knows the only place I have is the seat of a post-coach at an inn-door. Have you deposited the casket with the landlady, as I ordered you? Have you put it into her own hands?

Ser. Yes, your honour.

Mar. She said she'd keep it safe, did she?

Ser. Yes, she said she'd keep it safe enough; she asked me how I came by it; and she said she had a great mind to make me give an account of myself.

[*Exit* Servant.

Mar. Ha! ha! ha! They're safe, however. What an unaccountable set of beings have we got amongst! This little bar-maid though runs in my head most strangely, and drives out the absurdities of all the rest of the family. She's mine, she must be mine, or I'm greatly mistaken.

Enter HASTINGS.

Hast. Bless me! I quite forgot to tell her that I intended to prepare at the bottom of the garden. Marlow here, and in spirits too!

Mar. Give me joy, George. Crown me, shadow me with laurels! Well, George, after all, we modest fellows don't want for success among the women.

Hast. Some women, you mean. But what success has your honour's modesty been crowned with now, that it grows so insolent upon us?

Mar. Didn't you see the tempting, brisk, lovely

little thing, that runs about the house with a bunch of keys to its girdle?

Hast. Well, and what then?

Mar. She's mine, you rogue you. Such fire, such motion, such eyes, such lips; but 'faith! she would not let me kiss them though.

Hast. But are you so sure, so very sure of her?

Mar. Why, man, she talked of showing me her work above stairs, and I am to improve the pattern.

Hast. But how can you, Charles, go about to pay meaningless attentions to a woman?

Mar. Pshaw! pshaw! We all know the ways of the barmaid of an inn. I don't intend to go too far with her, take my word for it.

Hast. I believe the girl has virtue.

Mar. And if she has, I should be the last man in the world that would attempt to corrupt it.

Hast. You have taken care, I hope, of the casket I sent you to lock up? Is it in safety?

Mar. Yes, yes. It's safe enough. I have taken care of it. But how could you think the seat of a post-coach at an inn-door a place of safety? Ah! numskull! I have taken better precautions for you than you did for yourself—I have—

Hast. What?

Mar. I have sent it to the landlady to keep for you.

Hast. To the landlady!

Mar. The landlady.

Hast. You did?

93*

Mar. I did. She's to be answerable for its forth-coming, you know.

Hast. Yes, she'll bring it forth with a witness.

Mar. Wasn't I right? I believe you'll allow that I acted prudently upon this occasion.

Hast. (*Aside.*) He must not see my uneasiness.

Mar. You seem a little disconcerted though, methinks. Sure nothing has happened?

Hast. No, nothing. Never was in better spirits in all my life. And so you left it with the landlady, who, no doubt, very readily undertook the charge.

Mar. Rather too readily. For she has not only kept the casket, but, through her great precaution, was going to keep the messenger too. Ha! ha! ha!

Hast. He! he! he! They're safe, however.

Mar. As a guinea in a miser's purse.

Hast. (*Aside.*) So now all hopes of fortune are at an end, and we must set off without it. (*To him.*) Well, Charles, I'll leave you to your meditations on the pretty barmaid, and, he! he! he! may you be as successful for yourself, as you have been for me!

[*Exit.*

Mar. Thank ye, George: I ask no more. Ha! ha! ha!

Enter HARDCASTLE.

Hard. I no longer know my own house. It's turned all topsy-turvy. His servants have got drunk already. I'll bear it no longer; and yet, from my respect for his father, I'll be calm. (*To him.*) Mr. Marlow, your servant. I'm your very humble servant. (*Bowing low.*)

Mar. Sir, your humble servant. (*Aside.*) What's to be the wonder now?

Hard. I believe, sir, you must be sensible, sir, that no man alive ought to be more welcome than your father's son, sir. I hope you think so?

Mar. I do from my soul, sir. I don't want much entreaty. I generally make my father's son welcome wherever he goes.

Hard. I believe you do, from my soul, sir. But though I say nothing to your own conduct, that of your servants is insufferable. Their manner of drinking is setting a very bad example in this house, I assure you.

Mar. I protest, my very good sir, that is no fault of mine. If they don't drink as they ought, they are to blame. I ordered them not to spare the cellar. I did, I assure you. (*To the side scene.*) Here, let one of my servants come up. (*To him.*) My positive directions were, that as I did not drink myself, they should make up for my deficiencies below.

Hard. Then they had your orders for what they do? I'm satisfied!

Mar. They had, I assure you. You shall hear from one of themselves.

Enter Servant, *drunk.*

Mar. You, Jeremy! Come forward, sirrah! What were my orders? Were you not told to drink freely, and call for what you thought fit, for the good of the house?

Hard. (*Aside*.) I begin to lose my patience.

Jer. Please your honour, liberty and Fleet Street for ever! Though I'm but a servant, I'm as good as another man. I'll drink for no man before supper, sir, hang me! Good liquor will sit upon a good supper, but a good supper will not sit upon—hiccup—on my conscience, sir.

Mar. You see, my old friend, the fellow is as drunk as he can possibly be. I don't know what you'd have more unless you'd have the poor wretch soused in a beer-barrel.

Hard. He'll drive me distracted, if I contain myself any longer. Mr. Marlow—Sir; I have submitted to your insolence for more than four hours, and I see no likelihood of its coming to an end. I'm now resolved to be master here, sir; and I desire that you and your drunken pack may leave my house directly.

Mar. Leave your house!—Sure you jest, my good friend! What? when I'm doing what I can to please you.

Hard. I tell you, sir, you don't please me; so I desire you'll leave my house.

Mar. Sure you cannot be serious? At this time o' night, and such a night? You only mean to banter me.

Hard. I tell you, sir, I'm serious! and now that my passions are roused, I say this house is mine, sir; this house is mine, and I command you to leave it directly.

Mar. Ha! ha! ha! A puddle in a storm. I

sha'n't stir a step, I assure you. (*In a serious tone*.) This your house, fellow! It's my house. This is my house. Mine, while I choose to stay. What right have you to bid me leave this house, sir? I never met with such impudence, confound me; never in my whole life before.

Hard. Nor I, confound me if ever I did. To come to my house, to call for what he likes, to turn me out of my own chair, to insult the family, to order his servants to get drunk, and then to tell me, "This house is mine, sir." By all that's impudent, it makes me laugh. Ha! ha! ha! Pray, sir (*bantering*), as you take the house, what think you of taking the rest of the furniture? There's a pair of silver candlesticks, and there's a fire-screen, and here's a pair of brazen-nosed bellows; perhaps you may take a fancy to them?

Mar. Bring me your bill, sir; bring me your bill, and let's make no more words about it.

Hard. There are a set of prints, too. What think you of the Rake's Progress, for your own apartment?

Mar. Bring me your bill, I say; and I'll leave you and your infernal house directly.

Hard. Then there's a mahogany table that you may see your own face in.

Mar. My bill, I say.

Hard. I had forgot the great chair for your own particular slumbers, after a hearty meal.

Mar. Bring me my bill, I say, and let's hear no more on't.

Hard. Young man, young man, from your

father's letter to me, I was taught to expect a
well-bred modest man as a visitor here, but now
I find him no better than a coxcomb and a bully ;
but he will be down here presently, and shall hear
more of it.

[*Exit.*

Mar. How's this ? Sure I have not mistaken
the house. Everything looks like an inn. The
servants cry, coming ; the attendance is awkward ;
the barmaid, too, to attend us. But she's here,
and will further inform me. Whither so fast,
child ? A word with you.

Enter MISS HARDCASTLE.

Miss Hard. Let it be short, then. I'm in a
hurry. (*Aside.*) I believe he begins to find out his
mistake. But it's too soon quite to undeceive him.

Mar. Pray, child, answer me one question.
What are you, and what may your business in
this house be ?

Miss Hard. A relation of the family, sir.

Mar. What, a poor relation ?

Miss Hard. Yes, sir. A poor relation, appointed
to keep the keys, and to see that the guests want
nothing in my power to give them.

Mar. That is, you act as the barmaid of this
inn.

Miss Hard. Inn ! O law—what brought that in
your head ? One of the best families in the
country keep an inn—Ha ! ha ! ha ! old Mr. Hardcastle's house an inn !

Mar. Mr. Hardcastle's house! Is this Mr.

Hardcastle's house, child?

Miss Hard. Ay, sure! Whose else should it be?

Mar. So then, all's out, and I have been finely imposed on. O, confound my stupid head, I shall be laughed at over the whole town. I shall be stuck up in caricatura in all the print-shops. The *Dullissimo Maccaroni*. To mistake this house of all others for an inn, and my father's old friend for an innkeeper! What a swaggering puppy must he take me for! What a silly puppy do I find myself! There again, may I be hanged, my dear, but I mistook you for the barmaid.

Miss Hard. Dear me! dear me! I'm sure there's nothing in my *behaviour* to put me on a level with one of that stamp.

Mar. Nothing, my dear, nothing. But I was in for a list of blunders, and could not help making you a subscriber. My stupidity saw everything the wrong way. I mistook your assiduity for assurance, and your simplicity for allurement. But it's over. This house I no more show *my* face in.

Miss Hard. I hope, sir, I have done nothing to disoblige you. I'm sure I should be sorry to affront any gentleman who has been so polite, and said so many civil things to me. I'm sure I should be sorry (*pretending to cry*) if he left the family upon my account. I'm sure I should be sorry if people said anything amiss, since I have no fortune but my character.

Mar. (*Aside*.) By heaven! she weeps. This is the first mark of tenderness I ever had from a

modest woman, and it touches me. (*To her.*)
Excuse me, my lovely girl; you are the only
part of the family I leave with reluctance. But to
be plain with you, the difference of our birth,
fortune, and education, makes an honourable
connection impossible; and I can never harbour
a thought of abusing simplicity that trusted in my
honour, of bringing grief upon one whose only
fault was being too lovely.

Miss Hard. (*Aside.*) Generous man! I now
begin to admire him. (*To him.*) But I am sure
my family is as good as Miss Hardcastle's; and
though I'm poor, that's no great misfortune to
a contented mind; and, until this moment, I
never thought that it was bad to want a fortune.

Mar. And why now, my pretty simplicity?

Miss Hard. Because it puts me at a distance
from one that, if I had a thousand pounds, I
would give it all to.

Mar. (*Aside.*) This simplicity bewitches me, so
that if I say, I'm undone. I must make one bold
effort and leave her. (*To her.*) Your partiality in
my favour, my dear, touches me most sensibly:
and were I to live for myself alone, I could easily
fix my choice. But I owe too much to the
opinion of the world, too much to the authority of
a father; so that—I can scarcely speak it—it
affects me. Farewell.

[*Exit.*

Miss Hard. I never knew half his merit till
now. He shall not go, if I have power or art to
detain him. I'll still preserve the character in

which I *stooped to conquer*; but will undeceive my papa, who perhaps may laugh him out of his resolution.

[Exit.

Enter TONY *and* MISS NEVILLE.

Tony. Ay, you may steal for yourselves the next time. I have done my duty. She has got the jewels again, that's a sure thing; but she believes it was all a mistake of the servants.

Miss Nev. But, my dear cousin, sure you won't forsake us in this distress? If she in the least suspects that I am going off, I shall certainly be locked up, or sent to my aunt Pedigree's, which is ten times worse.

Tony. To be sure, aunts of all kinds are very bad things. But what can I do? I have got you a pair of horses that will fly like Whistle-jacket; and I'm sure you can't say but I have courted you nicely before her face. Here she comes, we must court a bit or two more, for fear she should suspect us.

[They retire and seem to fondle.

Enter MRS. HARDCASTLE.

Mrs. Hard. Well, I was greatly fluttered, to be sure. But my son tells me it was all a mistake of the servants. I sha'n't be easy, however, till they are fairly married, and then let her keep her own fortune. But what do I see? fondling together, as I'm alive. I never saw Tony so sprightly before. Ah! have I caught you, my pretty doves? What, billing, exchanging stolen glances and broken murmurs? Ah!

Tony. As for murmurs, mother, we grumble a little now and then, to be sure. But there's no love lost between us.

Mrs. Hard. A mere sprinkling, Tony, upon the flame, only to make it burn brighter.

Miss Nev. Cousin Tony promises to give us more of his company at home. Indeed, he sha'n't leave us any more. It won't leave us, cousin Tony, will it?

Tony. O! it's a pretty creature. No, I'd sooner leave my horse in a pound, than leave you when you smile upon one so. Your laugh makes you so becoming.

Miss Nev. Agreeable cousin! Who can help admiring that natural humour, that pleasant, broad, red, thoughtless (*patting his cheek*)—ah! it's a bold face.

Mrs. Hard. Pretty innocence!

Tony. I'm sure I always loved cousin Con's hazel eyes, and her pretty long fingers, that she twists this way and that over the haspicholls, like a parcel of bobbins.

Mrs. Hard. Ah! he would charm the bird from the tree. I was never so happy before. My boy takes after his father, poor Mr. Lumpkin, exactly. The jewels, my dear Con, shall be yours incontinently. You shall have them. Isn't he a sweet boy, my dear? You shall be married to-morrow, and we'll put off the rest of his education, like Dr. Drowsy's sermons, to a fitter opportunity.

Enter DIGGORY.

Dig. Where's the 'squire! I have got a letter for your worship.

Tony. Give it to my mamma. She reads all my letters first.

Dig. I had orders to deliver it into your own hands.

Tony. Who does it come from?

Dig. Your worship mun ask that o' the letter itself.

Tony. I could wish to know though (*turning the letter, and gazing on it*).

Miss Nev. (*Aside.*) Undone! undone! A letter to him from Hastings. I know the hand. If my aunt sees it, we are ruined for ever. I'll keep her employed a little if I can. (*To* MRS. HARDCASTLE.) But I have not told you, madam, of my cousin's smart answer just now to Mr. Marlow. We so laughed.—You must know, madam.—This way a little, for he must not hear us.

[*They confer.*

Tony. (*Still gazing.*) A confounded cramp piece of penmanship, as ever I saw in my life. I can read your print hand very well. But here are such handles, and shanks, and dashes, that one can scarce tell the head from the tail.—"To Anthony Lumpkin, Esquire." It's very odd, I can read the outside of my letters, where my own name is, well enough; but when I come to open it, it's all—buzz. That's hard, very hard; for the inside of the letter is always the cream of the correspondence.

Mrs. Hard. Ha ! ha ! ha ! Very well, very well. And so my son was too hard for the philosopher.

Miss Nev. Yes, madam ; but you must hear the rest, madam. A little more this way, or he may hear us. You'll hear how he puzzled him again.

Mrs. Hard. He seems strangely puzzled now himself, methinks.

Tony. (*Still gazing.*) A confounded up-and-down hand, as if it was disguised in liquor.— (*Reading.*) Dear sir,—ay, that's that. Then there's an M, and a T, and an S, but whether the next be an izzard, or an R, confound me, I cannot tell.

Mrs. Hard. What's that, my dear ? Can I give you any assistance ?

Miss Nev. Pray, aunt, let me read it. Nobody reads a cramp hand better than I. (*Twitching the letter from him.*) Do you know who it is from ?

Tony. Can't tell, except from Dick Ginger, the feeder.

Miss Nev. Ay, so it is. (*Pretending to read.*) Dear 'Squire, hoping that you're in health, as I am at this present. The gentlemen of the Shakebag club has cut the gentlemen of Goose-green quite out of feather. The odds—um—odd battle —um—long fighting—um—here, here it's all about cocks and fighting ; it's of no consequence ; here, put it up, put it up. (*Thrusting the crumpled letter upon him.*)

Tony. But I tell you, miss, it's of all the consequence in the world. I would not lose the rest of it for a guinea. Here, mother, do you make it out. Of no consequence! (*Giving* MRS. HARDCASTLE *the letter.*)

Mrs. Hard. How's this?—(*Reads.*) "Dear 'Squire, I'm now waiting for Miss Neville, with a post-chaise and pair, at the bottom of the garden, but I find my horses yet unable to perform the journey. I expect you'll assist us with a pair of fresh horses, as you promised. Dispatch is necessary, as the *hag* (ay, the hag), your mother, will otherwise suspect us! Yours, Hastings." Grant me patience. I shall run distracted! My rage chokes me.

Miss Nev. I hope, madam, you'll suspend your resentment for a few moments, and not impute to me any impertinence, or sinister design, that belongs to another.

Mrs. Hard. (*Curtseying very low.*) Fine spoken, madam, you are most miraculously polite and engaging, and quite the very pink of courtesy and circumspection, madam. (*Changing her tone.*) And you, you great ill-fashioned oaf, with scarce sense enough to keep your mouth shut: were you, too, joined against me? But I'll defeat all your plots in a moment. As for you, madam, since you have got a pair of fresh horses ready, it would be cruel to disappoint them. So, if you please, instead of running away with your spark, prepare, this very moment, to run off with *me*. Your old aunt Pedigree will keep you secure, I'll warrant

me. You, too, sir, may mount your horse, and
guard us upon the way. Here, Thomas, Roger,
Diggory! I'll show you that I wish you better
than you do yourselves.

[*Exit.*

Miss Nev. So now I'm completely ruined.

Tony. Ay, that's a sure thing.

Miss Nev. What better could be expected from
being connected with such a stupid fool,—and
after all the nods and signs I made him?

Tony. By the laws, miss, it was your own
cleverness, and not my stupidity, that did your
business. You were so nice and so busy with
your Shake-bags and Goose-greens, that I thought
you could never be making believe.

Enter HASTINGS.

Hast. So, sir, I find by my servant, that you
have shown my letter, and betrayed us. Was this
well done, young gentleman?

Tony. Here's another. Ask miss there, who
betrayed you. It was her doing, not mine.

Enter MARLOW.

Mar. So I have been finely used here among
you. Rendered contemptible, driven into ill
manners, despised, insulted, laughed at.

Tony. Here's another. We shall have old Bed-
lam broke loose presently.

Miss Nev. And there, sir, is the gentleman to
whom we all owe every obligation.

Mar. What can I say to him, a mere boy, an

idiot, whose ignorance and age are a protection?

Hast. A poor contemptible booby, that would but disgrace correction.

Miss Nev. Yet with cunning and malice enough to make himself merry with all our embarrassments.

Hast. An insensible cub.

Mar. Replete with tricks and mischief.

Tony. Baw! I'll fight you both, one after the other—with baskets.

Mar. As for him, he's below resentment. But your conduct, Mr. Hastings, requires an explanation. You knew of my mistakes, yet would not undeceive me.

Hast. Tortured as I am with my own disappointments, is this a time for explanations? It is not friendly, Mr. Marlow.

Mar. But, sir—

Miss Nev. Mr. Marlow, we never kept on your mistake till it was too late to undeceive you.

Enter Servant.

Ser. My mistress desires you'll get ready immediately, madam. The horses are putting to. Your hat and things are in the next room. We are to go thirty miles before morning.

[*Exit* Servant.

Miss Nev. Well, well: I'll come presently.

Mar. (*To* HASTINGS.) Was it well done, sir, to assist in rendering me ridiculous? To hang me out for the scorn of all my acquaintance? Depend upon it, sir, I shall expect an explanation.

Hast. Was it well done, sir, if you're upon that subject, to deliver what I intrusted to yourself, to the care of another, sir?

Miss Nev. Mr. Hastings! Mr. Marlow! Why will you increase my distress by this groundless dispute? I implore, I entreat you—

Enter Servant.

Ser. Your cloak, madam. My mistress is impatient.

[*Exit* Servant.

Miss Nev. I come. Pray be pacified. If I leave you thus, I shall die with apprehension.

Enter Servant.

Ser. Your fan, muff, and gloves, madam. The horses are waiting.

Miss Nev. O, Mr. Marlow! if you knew what a scene of constraint and ill-nature lies before me, I'm sure it would convert your resentment into pity.

Mar. I'm so distracted with a variety of passions, that I don't know what I do. Forgive me, madam. George, forgive me. You know my hasty temper, and should not exasperate it.

Hast. The torture of my situation is my only excuse.

Miss. Nev. Well, my dear Hastings, if you have that esteem for me that I think, that I am sure you have, your constancy for three years will but increase the happiness of our future connection. If—

Mrs. Hard. (*Within.*) Miss Neville. Constance, why Constance, I say.

Miss Nev. I'm coming. Well, constancy, remember, constancy is the word.

[*Exit.*

Hast. My heart! how can I support this? To be so near happiness, and such happiness!

Mar. (*To* TONY.) You see now, young gentleman, the effects of your folly. What might be amusement to you, is here disappointment, and even distress.

Tony. (*From a reverie.*) Stop, I have hit it. It's here. Your hands. Yours and yours, my poor Sulky!—My boots there, ho!—Meet me two hours hence at the bottom of the garden; and if you don't find Tony Lumpkin a more good-natured fellow than you thought for, I'll give you leave to take my best horse, and Bet Bouncer into the bargain. Come along. My boots, ho!

[*Exeunt.*

ACT THE FIFTH

Scene I.—*The same.*

Enter Hastings *and* Servant.

Hast. You saw the old lady and Miss Neville drive off, you say?

Ser. Yes, your honour. They went off in a post-coach, and the young 'squire went on horseback. They're thirty miles off by this time.

Hast. Then all my hopes are over.

Ser. Yes, sir. Old Sir Charles has arrived. He and the old gentleman of the house have been laughing at Mr. Marlow's mistake this half hour. They are coming this way.

Hast. Then I must not be seen. So now to my fruitless appointment at the bottom of the garden. This is about the time.

[*Exit.*

Enter Sir Charles *and* Hardcastle.

Hard. Ha! ha! ha! The peremptory tone in which he sent forth his sublime commands!

Sir Cha. And the reserve with which I suppose he treated all your advances.

Hard. And yet he might have seen something in me above a common innkeeper, too.

Sir Cha. Yes, Dick, but he mistook you for

411

an uncommon innkeeper, ha ! ha ! ha !

Hard. Well, I'm in too good spirits to think of anything but joy. Yes, my dear friend, this union of our families will make our personal friendships hereditary ; and though my daughter's fortune is but small—

Sir Cha. Why, Dick, will you talk of fortune to *me* ? My son is possessed of more than a competence already, and can want nothing but a good and virtuous girl to share his happiness and increase it. If they like each other, as you say they do—

Hard. If, man ! I tell you they *do* like each other. My daughter as good as told me so.

Sir Cha. But girls are apt to flatter themselves, you know.

Hard. I saw him grasp her hand in the warmest manner myself : and here he comes to put you out of your *ifs,* I warrant him.

Enter MARLOW.

Mar. I come, sir, once more, to ask pardon for my strange conduct. I can scarce reflect on my insolence without confusion.

Hard. Tut, boy, a trifle ! You take it too gravely. An hour or two's laughing with my daughter will set all to rights again. She'll never like you the worse for it.

Mar. Sir, I shall be always proud of her approbation.

Hard. Approbation is but a cold word, Mr. Marlow ; if I am not deceived, you have something more than approbation thereabouts. You take me?

Mar. Really, sir, I have not that happiness.

Hard. Come, boy, I'm an old fellow, and know what's what as well as you that are younger. I know what has passed between you; but mum.

Mar. Sure, sir, nothing has passed between us but the most profound respect on my side, and the most distant reserve on hers. You don't think, sir, that my impudence has been passed upon all the rest of the family.

Hard. Impudence! No, I don't say that—not quite impudence—though girls like to be played with, and rumpled a little too, sometimes. But she has told no tales, I assure you.

Mar. I never gave her the slightest cause.

Hard. Well, well, I like her modesty in its place well enough. But this is over-acting, young gentleman. You may be open. Your father and I will like you all the better for it.

Mar. May I die, sir, if I ever—

Hard. I tell you, she don't dislike you; and as I'm sure you like her—

Mar. Dear sir—I protest, sir—

Hard. I see no reason why you should not be joined as fast as the parson can tie you.

Mar. But hear me, sir—

Hard. Your father approves the match, I admire it; every moment's delay will be doing mischief. So—

Mar. But why won't you hear me? By all that's just and true, I never gave Miss Hardcastle the slightest mark of my attachment, or even the most distant hint to suspect me of affection. We had but one interview, and that was formal, modest, and uninteresting.

Hard. (*Aside.*) This fellow's formal modest impudence is beyond bearing.

Sir Cha. And you never grasped her hand, or made any protestations?

Mar. As Heaven is my witness, I came down in obedience to your commands. I saw the lady without emotion, and parted without reluctance. I hope you'll exact no further proofs of my duty, nor prevent me from leaving a house in which I suffer so many mortifications.

[*Exit.*

Sir Cha. I'm astonished at the air of sincerity with which he parted.

Hard. And I'm astonished at the deliberate intrepidity of his assurance.

Sir Cha. I dare pledge my life and honour upon his truth.

Hard. Here comes my daughter, and I would stake my happiness upon her veracity.

Enter MISS HARDCASTLE.

Hard. Kate, come hither, child. Answer us sincerely and without reserve; has Mr. Marlow made you any professions of love and affection?

Miss Hard. The question is very abrupt, sir. But since you require unreserved sincerity, I think he has.

Hard. (*To* SIR CHARLES.) You see.

Sir Cha. And pray, madam, have you and my son had more than one interview?

Miss Hard. Yes, sir, several.

Hard. (*To* SIR CHARLES.) You see.

Sir Cha. But did he profess any attachment?

Miss Hard. A lasting one.

Sir Cha. Did he talk of love?

Miss Hard. Much, sir.

Sir Cha. Amazing! And all this formally.

Miss Hard. Formally.

Hard. Now, my friend, I hope you are satisfied.

Sir Cha. And how did he behave, madam?

Miss Hard. As most profest admirers do: said some civil things of my face, talked much of his want of merit, and the greatness of mine; mentioned his heart, gave a short tragedy speech, and ended with pretended rapture.

Sir Cha. Now I'm perfectly convinced, indeed. I know his conversation among women to be modest and submissive: this forward canting ranting manner by no means describes him; and, I am confident, he never sat for the picture.

Miss Hard. Then, what, sir, if I should convince you to your face of my sincerity? If you and my papa, in about half an hour, will place yourselves behind that screen, you shall hear him declare his passion to me in person.

Sir Cha. Agreed. And if I find him what you describe, all my happiness in him must have an end.

[*Exit*.

Miss Hard. And if you don't find him what I describe—I fear my happiness must never have a beginning.

[*Exeunt.*

Scene II.—*The back of the Garden.*

Enter Hastings.

Hast. What an idiot am I, to wait here for a fellow who probably takes a delight in mortifying me. He never intended to be punctual, and I'll wait no longer. What do I see? It is he! and perhaps with news of my Constance.

Enter Tony, *booted and spattered.*

Hast. My honest 'squire! I now find you a man of your word. This looks like friendship.

Tony. Ay, I'm your friend, and the best friend you have in the world, if you knew but all. This riding by night, by the bye, is cursedly tiresome. It has shook me worse than the basket of a stage-coach.

Hast. But how? where did you leave your fellow-travellers? Are they in safety? Are they housed?

Tony. Five and twenty miles in two hours and a half is no such bad driving. The poor beasts have smoked for it: rabbit me, but I'd rather ride forty miles after a fox than ten with such varment.

Hast. Well, but where have you left the ladies? I die with impatience.

Tony. Left them ! Why, where should I leave them but where I found them ?

Hast. This is a riddle.

Tony. Riddle me this then. What's that goes round the house, and round the house, and never touches the house ?

Hast. I'm still astray.

Tony. Why, that's it, mon. I have led them astray. By jingo, there's not a pond or a slough within five miles of the place but they can tell the taste of.

Hast. Ha ! ha ! ha ! I understand : you took them in a round, while they supposed themselves going forward, and so you have at last brought them home again.

Tony. You shall hear. I first took them down Feather-bed Lane, where we stuck fast in the mud. I then rattled them crack over the stones of Up-and-down Hill. I then introduced them to the gibbet on Heavy-tree Heath ; and from that, with a circumbendibus, I fairly lodged them in the horse-pond at the bottom of the garden.

Hast. But no accident, I hope ?

Tony. No, no. Only mother is confoundedly frightened. She thinks herself forty miles off. She's sick of the journey ; and the cattle can scarce crawl. So if your own horses be ready, you may whip off with cousin, and I'll be bound that no soul here can budge a foot to follow you.

Hast. My dear friend, how can I be grateful ?

Tony. Ay, now it's dear friend, noble 'squire. Just now, it was all idiot, cub, and run me

94

through the guts. Hang *your* way of fighting, I say. After we take a knock in this part of the country, we kiss and be friends. But if you had run me through the guts, then I should be dead, and you might go kiss the hangman.

Hast. The rebuke is just. But I must hasten to relieve Miss Neville: if you keep the old lady employed, I promise to take care of the young one.

[*Exit* HASTINGS.

Tony. Never fear me. Here she comes. Vanish. She's got from the pond, and draggled up to the waist like a mermaid.

Enter MRS. HARDCASTLE.

Mrs. Hard. Oh, Tony, I'm killed! Shook! Battered to death. I shall never survive it. That last jolt, that laid us against the quickset hedge, has done my business.

Tony. Alack, mamma, it was all your own fault. You would be for running away by night, without knowing one inch of the way.

Mrs. Hard. I wish we were at home again. I never met so many accidents in so short a journey. Drenched in the mud, overturned in a ditch, stuck fast in a slough, jolted to a jelly, and at last to lose our way. Whereabouts do you think we are, Tony?

Tony. By my guess we should come upon Crackskull common, about forty miles from home.

Mrs. Hard. O dear! O dear! The most notorious spot in all the country. We only want a

robbery to make a complete night on't.

Tony. Don't be afraid, mamma, don't be afraid. Two of the five that kept here are hanged, and the other three may not find us. Don't be afraid. Two of the five that kept here are hanged, us? No! it's only a tree.—Don't be afraid.

Mrs. Hard. The fright will certainly kill me.

Tony. Do you see anything like a black hat moving behind the thicket?

Mrs. Hard. Oh, death!

Tony. No; it's only a cow. Don't be afraid, mamma; don't be afraid.

Mrs. Hard. As I'm alive, Tony, I see a man coming towards us. Ah! I'm sure on't. If he perceives us, we are undone.

Tony. (*Aside.*) Father-in-law, by all that's unlucky, come to take one of his night walks. (*To her.*) Ah! it's a highwayman with pistols as long as my arm. A most ill-looking fellow.

Mrs. Hard. Good Heaven defend us! He approaches.

Tony. Do you hide yourself in that thicket, and leave me to manage him. If there be any danger, I'll cough, and cry hem. When I cough, be sure to keep close. (MRS. HARDCASTLE *hides behind a tree in the back scene.*)

Enter HARDCASTLE.

Hard. I'm mistaken, or I heard voices of people in want of help. Oh, Tony! is that you? I did not expect you so soon back. Are your mother and her charge in safety?

Tony. Very safe, sir, at my aunt Pedigree's. Hem!

Mrs. Hard. (*From behind.*) Ah, death! I find there's danger.

Hard. Forty miles in three hours; sure that's too much, my youngster.

Tony. Stout horses and willing minds make short journeys, as they say. Hem!

Mrs. Hard. (*From behind.*) Sure he'll do the dear boy no harm.

Hard. But I heard a voice here; I should be glad to know from whence it came.

Tony. It was I, sir, talking to myself, sir. I was saying that forty miles in four hours was very good going. Hem! As to be sure it was. Hem! I have got a sort of cold by being out in the air. We'll go in, if you please. Hem!

Hard. But if you talked to yourself you did not answer yourself. I'm certain I heard two voices, and am resolved (*raising his voice*) to find the other out.

Mrs. Hard. (*From behind.*) Oh! he's coming to find me out. Oh!

Tony. What need you go, sir, if I tell you? Hem! I'll lay down my life for the truth—hem!—I'll tell you all, sir.

[*Detaining him.*

Hard. I tell you I will not be detained. I insist on seeing. It's in vain to expect I'll believe you.

Mrs. Hard. (*Running forward from behind.*) O dear! he'll murder my poor boy, my darling! Here, good gentleman, whet your rage upon me.

Take my money, my life, but spare that young gentleman; spare my child, if you have any mercy.

Hard. My wife, as I'm a Christian. From whence can she come? or what does she mean?

Mrs. Hard. (*Kneeling.*) Take compassion on us, good Mr. Highwayman. Take our money, our watches, all we have, but spare our lives. We will never bring you to justice; indeed we won't, good Mr. Highwayman.

Hard. I believe the woman's out of her senses. What, Dorothy, don't you know *me*?

Mrs. Hard. Mr. Hardcastle, as I'm alive. My fears blinded me. But who, my dear, could have expected to meet you here, in this frightful place, so far from home? What has brought you to follow us?

Hard. Sure, Dorothy, you have not lost your wits? So far from home, when you are within forty yards of your own door! (*To him.*) This is one of your old tricks, you graceless rogue, you. (*To her.*) Don't you know the gate, and the mulberry-tree; and don't you remember the horse-pond, my dear?

Mrs. Hard. Yes, I shall remember the horse-pond as long as I live; I have caught my death in it. (*To* TONY.) And is it to you, you graceless varlet, I owe all this? I'll teach you to abuse your mother, I will.

Tony. Well, mother, all the parish says you have spoiled me, and so you may take the fruits on't.

Mrs. Hard. I'll spoil you, I will.
                    [*Follows him off the stage. Exit.*
Hard. There's morality, however, in his reply.
                                        [*Exit.*

Enter HASTINGS *and* MISS NEVILLE.

Hast. My dear Constance, why will you deliberate thus? If we delay a moment, all is lost for ever. Pluck up a little resolution, and we shall soon be out of the reach of her malignity.

Miss Nev. I find it impossible. My spirits are so sunk with the agitations I have suffered, that I am unable to face any new danger. Two or three years' patience will at last crown us with happiness.

Hast. Such a tedious delay is worse than inconstancy. Let us fly, my charmer. Let us date our happiness from this very moment. Perish fortune! Love and content will increase what we possess beyond a monarch's revenue. Let me prevail!

Miss Nev. No, Mr. Hastings, no. Prudence once more comes to my relief, and I will obey its dictates. In the moment of passion fortune may be despised, but it ever produces a lasting repentance. I'm resolved to apply to Mr. Hardcastle's compassion and justice for redress.

Hast. But though he had the will, he has not the power to relieve you.

Miss Nev. But he has influence, and upon that I am resolved to rely.

Hast. I have no hopes. But since you persist, I must reluctantly obey you.

[*Exeunt.*

SCENE III, *as in Scene I.*

Enter SIR CHARLES *and* MISS HARDCASTLE.

Sir Cha. What a situation am I in! If what you say appears, I shall then find a guilty son. If what he says be true, I shall then lose one that, of all others, I most wished for a daughter.

Miss Hard. I am proud of your approbation, and to show I merit it, if you place yourselves as I directed, you shall hear his explicit declaration. But he comes.

Sir Cha. I'll to your father, and keep him to the appointment.

[*Exit* SIR CHARLES.

Enter MARLOW.

Mar. Though prepared for setting out, I come once more to take leave; nor did I, till this moment, know the pain I feel in the separation.

Miss Hard. (*In her own natural manner.*) I believe these sufferings cannot be very great, sir, which you can so easily remove. A day or two longer, perhaps, might lessen your uneasiness, by showing the little value of what you now think proper to regret.

Mar. (*Aside.*) This girl every moment improves upon me. (*To her.*) It must not be, madam. I have already trifled too long with my heart. My very pride begins to submit to my passion. The disparity of education and fortune, the anger of a parent, and the contempt of my equals, begin to lose their weight; and nothing can restore me to myself but this painful effort of resolution.

Miss Hard. Then go, sir: I'll urge nothing more to detain you. Though my family be as good as hers you came down to visit, and my education, I hope, not inferior, what are these advantages without equal affluence? I must remain contented with the slight approbation of imputed merit; I must have only the mockery of your addresses, while all your serious aims are fixed on fortune.

Enter HARDCASTLE *and* SIR CHARLES *from behind.*

Sir Cha. Here, behind this screen.

Hard. Ay, ay, make no noise. I'll engage my Kate covers him with confusion at last.

Mar. By heavens, madam! fortune was ever my smallest consideration. Your beauty at first caught my eye; for who could see that without emotion? But every moment that I converse with you steals in some new grace, heightens the picture, and gives it stronger expression. What at first seemed rustic plainness, now appears refined simplicity. What seemed forward assurance, now strikes me as the result of courageous innocence and conscious virtue.

Sir Cha. What can it mean? He amazes me!
Hard. I told you how it would be. Hush!
Mar. I am now determined to stay, madam;

and I have too good an opinion of my father's discernment, when he sees you, to doubt his approbation.

Miss Hard. No, Mr. Marlow, I will not, cannot detain you. Do you think I could suffer a connection in which there is the smallest room for repentance? Do you think I would take the mean advantage of a transient passion, to load you with confusion? Do you think I could ever relish that happiness which was acquired by lessening yours?

Mar. By all that's good, I can have no happiness but what's in your power to grant me! Nor shall I ever feel repentance but in not having seen your merits before. I will stay even contrary to your wishes; and though you should persist to shun me, I will make my respectful assiduities atone for the levity of my past conduct.

Miss Hard. Sir, I must entreat you'll desist. As our acquaintance began, so let it end, in indifference. I might have given an hour or two to levity; but seriously, Mr. Marlow, do you think I could ever submit to a connection where I must appear mercenary, and you imprudent? Do you think I could ever catch at the confident addresses of a secure admirer?

Mar. (*Kneeling.*) Does this look like security? Does this look like confidence? No, madam, every moment that shows me your merit, only serves to increase my diffidence and confusion. Here let me continue—

Sir Cha. I can hold it no longer. Charles,

Charles, how hast thou deceived me! Is this your indifference, your uninteresting conversation?

Hard. Your cold contempt; your formal interview! What have you to say now?

Mar. That I'm all amazement! What can it mean?

Hard. It means that you can say and unsay things at pleasure: that you can address a lady in private, and deny it in public: that you have one story for us, and another for my daughter.

Mar. Daughter—this lady your daughter?

Hard. Yes, sir, my only daughter; my Kate; whose else should she be?

Mar. Oh, the mischief!

Miss Hard. Yes, sir, that very identical tall squinting lady you were pleased to take me for (*courtseying*); she that you addressed as the mild, modest, sentimental man of gravity, and the bold, forward agreeable Rattle of the Ladies' Club. Ha! ha! ha!

Mar. What! there's no bearing this; it's worse than death!

Miss Hard. In which of your characters, sir, will you give us leave to address you? As the faltering gentleman, with looks on the ground, that speaks just to be heard, and hates hypocrisy; or the loud confident creature, that keeps it up with Mrs. Mantrap, and old Miss Biddy Buckskin, till three in the morning? Ha! ha! ha!

Mar. O, curse on my noisy head. I never attempted to be impudent yet, that I was not taken down. I must be gone.

Hard. By the hand of my body, but you shall not. I see it was all a mistake, and I am rejoiced to find it. You shall not, sir, I tell you. I know she'll forgive you. Won't you forgive him, Kate? We'll all forgive you. Take courage, man. (*They retire, she tormenting him, to the back scene.*)

Enter MRS. HARDCASTLE *and* TONY.

Mrs. Hard. So, so, they're gone off. Let them go, I care not.

Hard. Who gone?

Mrs. Hard. My dutiful niece and her gentleman, Mr. Hastings, from town. He who came down with our modest visitor here.

Sir Cha. Who, my honest George Hastings? As worthy a fellow as lives, and the girl could not have made a more prudent choice.

Hard. Then, by the hand of my body, I'm proud of the connection.

Mrs. Hard. Well, if he has taken away the lady, he has not taken her fortune; that remains in the family to console us for her loss.

Hard. Sure, Dorothy, you would not be so mercenary?

Mrs. Hard. Ay, that's my affair, not yours.

Hard. But you know if your son, when of age, refuses to marry his cousin, her whole fortune is then at her own disposal.

Mrs. Hard. Ay, but he's not of age, and she has not thought proper to wait for his refusal.

Enter HASTINGS *and* MISS NEVILLE.

Mrs. Hard. (*Aside.*) What, returned so soon! I begin not to like it.

Hast. (*To* HARDCASTLE.) For my late attempt to fly off with your niece let my present confusion be my punishment. We are now come back, to appeal from your justice to your humanity. By her father's consent I first paid her my addresses, and our passions were first founded in duty.

Miss Nev. Since his death, I have been obliged to stoop to dissimulation to avoid oppression. In an hour of levity I was ready to give up my fortune to secure my choice. But I am now recovered from the delusion, and hope from your tenderness what is denied me from a nearer connection.

Mrs. Hard. Pshaw, pshaw! this is all but the whining end of a modern novel.

Hard. Be it what it will, I'm glad they're come back to reclaim their due. Come hither, Tony, boy. Do you refuse this lady's hand whom I now offer you?

Tony. What signifies my refusing? You know I can't refuse her till I'm of age, father.

Hard. While I thought concealing your age, boy, was likely to conduce to your improvement, I concurred with your mother's desire to keep it secret. But since I find she turns it to a wrong use, I must now declare you have been of age these three months.

Tony. Of age! Am I of age, father?

Hard. Above three months.

Tony. Then you'll see the first use I'll make of my liberty. (*Taking* MISS NEVILL's *hand.*) Witness all men by these presents, that I, Anthony Lumpkin, Esquire, of BLANK place, refuse you, Constantia Neville, spinster, of no place at all, for my true and lawful wife. So Constance Neville may marry whom she pleases, and Tony Lumpkin is his own man again.

Sir Cha. O brave 'squire.

Hast. My worthy friend!

Mrs. Hard. My undutiful offspring!

Mar. Joy, my dear George! I give you joy sincerely. And could I prevail upon my little tyrant here to be less arbitrary, I should be the happiest man alive, if you would return me the favour.

Hast. (*To* MISS HARDCASTLE.) Come, madam, you are now driven to the very last scene of all your contrivances. I know you like him, I'm sure he loves you, and you must and shall have him.

Hard. (*Joining their hands.*) And I say so too. And, Mr. Marlow, if she makes as good a wife as she has a daughter, I don't believe you'll ever repent your bargain. So now to supper. To-morrow we shall gather all the poor of the parish about us, and the mistakes of the night shall be crowned with a merry morning. So, boy, take her; and as you have been mistaken in the mistress, my wish is, that you may never be mistaken in the wife.

[*Exeunt Omnes.*

EPILOGUE

Well, having stoop'd to conquer with success,
And gain'd a husband without aid from dress:
Still as a barmaid, I could wish it too
As I have conquered him to conquer you:
And let me say, for all your resolution,
That pretty barmaids have done execution.
Our life is all a play, compos'd to please,
"We have our exits and our entrances."
The first act shows the simple country maid,
Harmless and young, of everything afraid;
Blushes when hir'd, and with unmeaning action,
"I hope as how to give you satisfaction."
Her second act displays a livelier scene—
Th' unblushing barmaid of a country-inn,
Who whisks about the house, at market caters,
Talks loud, coquets the guests, and scolds the
          waiters.
Next the scene shifts to town, and there she soars,
The chop-house toast of ogling *connoisseurs*.
On squires and cits she there displays her arts,
And on the gridiron broils her lovers' hearts—
And as she smiles, her triumphs to complete,
E'en common-councilmen forget to eat.
The fourth act shows her wedded to the squire,
And madam now begins to hold it higher;

Pretends to taste, at operas cries caro,
And quits her Nancy Dawson for Che Faro:
Doats upon dancing, and in all her pride
Swims round the room, the Heinel of Cheapside.
Ogles and leers with artificial skill,
Till having lost in age the power to kill,
She sits all night at cards, and ogles at spadille.
Such, through our lives the eventful history—
The fifth and last act remains for me.
The barmaid now for your protection prays,
Turns female Barrister, and pleads for Bays.

Made and Printed in Great Britain by
Hazell, Watson & Viney Ltd., London and Aylesbury